ALREADY SEEN

(A Laura Frost Suspense Thriller —Book Two)

BLAKE PIERCE

Blake Pierce

Blake Pierce is the USA Today bestselling author of the RILEY PAGE mystery series, which includes seventeen books. Blake Pierce is also the author of the MACKENZIE WHITE mystery series, comprising fourteen books; of the AVERY BLACK mystery series, comprising six books; of the KERI LOCKE mystery series, comprising five books; of the MAKING OF RILEY PAIGE mystery series, comprising six books; of the KATE WISE mystery series, comprising seven books; of the CHLOE FINE psychological suspense mystery, comprising six books; of the JESSIE HUNT psychological suspense thriller series, comprising nineteen books; of the AU PAIR psychological suspense thriller series, comprising three books; of the ZOE PRIME mystery series, comprising six books; of the ADELE SHARP mystery series, comprising thirteen books; of the EUROPEAN VOYAGE cozy mystery series, comprising six books (and counting); of the new LAURA FROST FBI suspense thriller, comprising four books (and counting); of the new ELLA DARK FBI suspense thriller, comprising six books (and counting); of the A YEAR IN EUROPE cozy mystery series, comprising nine books (and counting); of the AVA GOLD mystery series, comprising three books (and counting); and of the RACHEL GIFT mystery series, comprising three books (and counting).

An avid reader and lifelong fan of the mystery and thriller genres, Blake loves to hear from you, so please feel free to visit www.blakepierceauthor.com to learn more and stay in touch.

BOOKS BY BLAKE PIERCE

RACHEL GIFT MYSTERY SERIES
HER LAST WISH (Book #1)
HER LAST CHANCE (Book #2)
HER LAST HOPE (Book #3)

AVA GOLD MYSTERY SERIES
CITY OF PREY (Book #1)
CITY OF FEAR (Book #2)
CITY OF BONES (Book #3)

A YEAR IN EUROPE
A MURDER IN PARIS (Book #1)
DEATH IN FLORENCE (Book #2)
VENGEANCE IN VIENNA (Book #3)
A FATALITY IN SPAIN (Book #4)
SCANDAL IN LONDON (Book #5)
AN IMPOSTOR IN DUBLIN (Book #6)
SEDUCTION IN BORDEAUX (Book #7)
JEALOUSY IN SWITZERLAND (Book #8)
A DEBACLE IN PRAGUE (Book #9)

ELLA DARK FBI SUSPENSE THRILLER
GIRL, ALONE (Book #1)
GIRL, TAKEN (Book #2)
GIRL, HUNTED (Book #3)
GIRL, SILENCED (Book #4)
GIRL, VANISHED (Book 5)
GIRL ERASED (Book #6)

LAURA FROST FBI SUSPENSE THRILLER
ALREADY GONE (Book #1)
ALREADY SEEN (Book #2)
ALREADY TRAPPED (Book #3)
ALREADY MISSING (Book #4)

EUROPEAN VOYAGE COZY MYSTERY SERIES
MURDER (AND BAKLAVA) (Book #1)

DEATH (AND APPLE STRUDEL) (Book #2)
CRIME (AND LAGER) (Book #3)
MISFORTUNE (AND GOUDA) (Book #4)
CALAMITY (AND A DANISH) (Book #5)
MAYHEM (AND HERRING) (Book #6)

ADELE SHARP MYSTERY SERIES
LEFT TO DIE (Book #1)
LEFT TO RUN (Book #2)
LEFT TO HIDE (Book #3)
LEFT TO KILL (Book #4)
LEFT TO MURDER (Book #5)
LEFT TO ENVY (Book #6)
LEFT TO LAPSE (Book #7)
LEFT TO VANISH (Book #8)
LEFT TO HUNT (Book #9)
LEFT TO FEAR (Book #10)
LEFT TO PREY (Book #11)
LEFT TO LURE (Book #12)
LEFT TO CRAVE (Book #13)

THE AU PAIR SERIES
ALMOST GONE (Book#1)
ALMOST LOST (Book #2)
ALMOST DEAD (Book #3)

ZOE PRIME MYSTERY SERIES
FACE OF DEATH (Book#1)
FACE OF MURDER (Book #2)
FACE OF FEAR (Book #3)
FACE OF MADNESS (Book #4)
FACE OF FURY (Book #5)
FACE OF DARKNESS (Book #6)

A JESSIE HUNT PSYCHOLOGICAL SUSPENSE SERIES
THE PERFECT WIFE (Book #1)
THE PERFECT BLOCK (Book #2)
THE PERFECT HOUSE (Book #3)
THE PERFECT SMILE (Book #4)
THE PERFECT LIE (Book #5)
THE PERFECT LOOK (Book #6)

CHAPTER ONE

Special Agent Laura Frost glanced into her rearview mirror, not at the road, but at the back seat. At the six-year-old girl who was sitting there, strapped in and looking both brave and terrified at once. The light of the sun flashing through the window played over tearstains on her cheeks, but her eyes were wide open now and she sat silently, her own arms wrapped tightly around herself.

Laura bit her lip, concentrating again on the road ahead. She'd made a big mistake.

But then again, there was nothing else to do. She'd had to rush in there and grab six-year-old Amy Fallow right out of her own home, because no one else was going to stop her father from beating her. Of course, the only evidence Laura had that this was taking place was Amy herself.

The only reason she'd known about it was because she'd seen it in a psychic vision – and those didn't tend to hold up well in court.

Laura hadn't had any choice but going in to rescue Amy. But now she had a huge problem. You didn't just kidnap a young girl without consequences – and when that young girl's father was State Governor John Fallow, the consequences would have to be big.

"Alright," Laura said out loud, just to hear the sound of her own voice and to maybe, just maybe, reassure Amy as well as herself. "We're going to go see someone who can help us out."

"Who is it?" Amy asked, the first thing she'd said since getting in the car. Her voice had less of a hitch to it now that she was no longer sobbing, but she still sounded so young and small that it made Laura's heart squeeze painfully in her chest.

"My boss," Laura said, glancing in her mirrors as she switched lanes. "He's a good man, and he's going to know exactly what to do."

In fact, she hadn't known where she was going until just now. She'd only thought about getting Amy out of a dangerous situation before anything worse could happen. The vision she had seen had been heartbreaking, and she knew that it probably wasn't the first time Fallow had laid into his daughter. His wife, too, cowered in front of him. Laura knew how to recognize the classic signs of abuse. Not that it

1

had made her any more sympathetic towards a woman who could allow her own daughter to endure horrific treatment like this.

Just like she'd had no choice about rescuing Amy, she now had no choice but to go to the FBI headquarters and Division Chief Chuck Rondelle. The Governor would call in the kidnapping of his daughter – the second in as many months – and send the whole state's worth of law enforcement after her. She had threatened him to not do so, but she was under no illusions. A man like that wouldn't just let his daughter escape his clutches with no consequences. The only way this didn't end with Laura in prison and Amy right back where she started was if Laura tried to get ahead of it, relying on her Chief's sense of justice and the goodwill she'd garnered by solving difficult cases.

If he couldn't help her, then it was all over.

Laura drove as fast as she dared, with a six-year-old in the back seat. Her unconscious thoughts must have already been taking her to the squat, ugly FBI headquarters building, because they were already so close that they reached it after taking one more exit. The gray concrete echoed her mood as she pulled up into the parking lot and got out of the car, opening Amy's door for her. She'd thought Amy would want to walk up there on her own – most children at that age were starting to feel like they wanted to be more grown-up, more independent – but Amy was shaking so badly that Laura ended up lifting her into her arms. She realized for the first time that Amy was clutching a faded, threadbare stuffed rabbit – it must have been a favorite toy that Amy had grabbed on the way out of her bedroom.

She knew they cut an odd figure together. The FBI agent in her early thirties, blonde and blue-eyed herself, dressed in a sharp suit and power boots that were good for walking, running, and holding authority over the people they had to interview or order around. Cradled in her arms, a girl who could have been her daughter but wasn't, dressed in pajamas, the signs of distress faded but still visible on her cheeks. Both of them striding through the hallways of the FBI building, entering the elevator and going right up to the floor on which the Division Chief kept his office, ignoring the stares and curious looks they got.

"Will he make me go back?" Amy whispered in Laura's ear, in the privacy of the elevator. Her tiny arms were locked around Laura's neck. Laura shifted slightly to look at the girl, who was keeping her gaze on the floor. Six years old, and she'd already learned to stay quiet and not make eye contact for fear of making someone angry. Laura's blood boiled, the clench in her chest coming again, and more powerfully.

"I won't let him, sweetie," Laura said, even though she really had no idea whether she was telling the truth.

The elevator pinged to announce their arrival on the correct floor, and Laura took a breath before the doors slid open. Then she marched to Rondelle's door, reaching out and knocking on it before she could allow herself to lose her nerve.

"Come."

The command was simple and terse, and the voice was distracted. Laura had the feeling she was about to walk in on her boss doing paperwork, as he often was, and she hoped it wasn't going to put him in a bad mood before they even got anywhere. She pushed the door open, stepping through with Amy still in her arms and closing it firmly behind them before she stepped in front of his desk.

At first, Rondelle didn't look up. Then he did glance, and when he glanced, he froze; his pen dropped onto the table, and he fixed Laura with a raised eyebrow. "Agent Frost. And who's this? ... Not little Amy Fallow?"

Of course, he would recognize the girl. She had been part of one of the state's highest-profile kidnappings in decades. Rondelle had personally congratulated Laura on her work in finding Amy. He wasn't going to mistake the child now.

"Yes," Amy said shyly, and Laura found herself clutching the girl tighter before she realized what she was doing. Then she forced herself to relax, looking around for a chair to sit Amy on. There was one pushed up against the wall, and she carefully settled Amy down there.

"Now, Amy, I'm glad to see you," Rondelle said. He was transforming in front of Laura's eyes: from a small, wiry, and sharply inquisitive career agent into a grandfatherly figure, fitting for the gray hair that was sprouting through the black on his head. He opened a drawer in his desk and pulled out a ball of rubber bands, and a couple of small, empty pots. "I've been needing some help with something. I think you might be just the girl for the job. Do you think you can help me out?"

"What is it?" Amy asked, all wide-eyed innocence.

Rondelle laughed as he got up, walking over to kneel in front of her. "Good girl – always ask before you agree to something. Well, you see, someone's put all of these rubber bands into a ball. That was silly of them, wasn't it?"

3

Amy giggled, nodding. The flash of a smile was short-lived, but it gave Laura hope. She wasn't completely destroyed, yet, by what her father had done.

"Now, how about you help me separate all these bands? You see how some of them are brown, and some of them are blue? Will you take them off the ball and put them into these pots for me, so we can keep the colors separate?"

Amy nodded eagerly, reaching her hands out for the ball and pots. She placed them on her knee and bent her head over them, quickly starting to work out how to stretch the bands and take them off the ball.

"Alright, Frost," Rondelle said, moving back behind his desk. Laura followed him to the opposite end of the room, where they could talk quietly without Amy hearing every word if they were careful. Rondelle kept his voice light and cheerful, but his face told a different story as he looked at her. It was all sharp angles, and Laura knew she was in trouble if she couldn't make him understand. "Why don't you tell me why you're here today?"

"I had noticed certain signs after..." Laura glanced at Amy, who seemed to be concentrating on her task, and lowered her voice all the same. "After the kidnapping. I attempted to follow up and speak with Mrs. Fallow, the Governor, and Amy herself on a number of occasions, but I'd become increasingly worried that something wasn't right in the household." It was true enough, even if she was leaving out the biggest part. The fact that she had seen the truth in a vision, not in any real sign of abuse. For all she knew, the violence had only spilled over after Amy was returned home.

"Signs of what, exactly?" Rondelle asked, his eagle-sharp eyes drifting over to Amy with an assessing look.

"An anger problem," Laura said. "I went around to the house today and, while I was at the door, I overheard shouting. I used my right as an agent, on hearing what I thought to be sounds of distress, to go inside and take a look. I found Governor Fallow with his belt in his hand."

Rondelle was silent for a moment. Laura followed his gaze, tried to see Amy as he did. There were bruises on the girl's tiny arms, and she was thin for her age, even taking into account her kidnapping. Where she leaned over, a small part of her back was visible from her pajama top riding up; there, too, another bruise stood out against her pale skin.

Laura bit her lip in the silence. This could go one of two ways. Either she was going to be protected, because she had done the right

4

thing and was – technically – theoretically – within the bounds of the law.

Or, her flimsy story was going to be ripped to shreds, she was going to be accused of stalking, harassment, and kidnapping, and the FBI would bend to the political power of the Governor to protect him instead.

"I'm going to call in a few people," Rondelle said, his voice a low, gruff rumble. "We need to proceed very carefully here. Laura, go out down the hall and find another Agent to look after Amy for a short while as we talk."

Laura swallowed hard, glanced at Amy to be sure she was comfortable, and nodded. She stepped out, rushing down the corridor.

She had to find someone who she could trust. Someone who was good with children. Someone who would make Amy feel safe, and not say a word.

Laura knew exactly who she needed to find.

CHAPTER TWO

Suzanna looked down as she walked out of the community center, rooting around inside her purse for her car keys. She knew they were in here somewhere. There was always too much stuff hanging around in her purse – lipstick, old receipts, tissues, notebooks. She knocked them all aside until she managed to find the keys jangling alone at the very bottom and fished them out, looking up across the parking lot.

She crossed the lot to her car, wrapping a cardigan slightly tighter around herself. The weather in Seattle was variable at this time of year, the temperature dropping as it moved firmly from summer into fall. She hadn't realized it would be so cool after leaving her acting class. She was going to have to start bringing a jacket.

Suzanna felt a little uneasy as she reached her car, pausing rather than unlocking it right away. She had this strange feeling like someone was nearby, watching her – like she wasn't alone... There was a chill running down her spine as she glanced around. She fumbled with the keys, thinking she'd better get inside quick in case there was someone -

"Suzanna!"

Suzanna's head flew around, her hand going to her chest over her fluttering heart as she recognized the woman who had called her name. "Oh, Christ, Leilah! I almost had a heart attack!"

"Sorry!" Leilah said, putting her own hand over her mouth for a moment. "Sorry, I thought you'd seen me!"

Suzanna leaned against her car to try and get her breath back, shaking her head. "I didn't. It's a bit creepy here after everyone's gone home, isn't it?"

Leilah laughed. "Yes, you're not wrong there. I'm glad I saw you. I knew your class finished not long ago, and I wanted to chat with you, but I didn't catch you inside before you left."

Suzanna nodded, feeling more composed now. "Yes, I was just filing my paperwork so I could get going. What was it you wanted?"

"Oh, it's about the paperwork, actually," Leilah said with a smile. She'd only started teaching at the community center a few weeks ago, and Suzanna had been going a lot longer than that. "I was just wondering if you knew what code to put down in the lesson type box?"

"There's a guide in the teachers' break room," Suzanna said. Now that she had calmed down, she didn't feel quite so annoyed about the interruption. It was nice, having Leilah come to her for help. "It's hung up on the wall next to the noticeboard – a little laminated booklet, have you seen it?"

"Oh!" Leilah exclaimed, nodding and putting a hand to her forehead with a grin. "You know what? I'm such an idiot. They showed me that on my first day. I'd just totally forgotten about it."

"Not to worry," Suzanna said, smiling back. "You'll get the hang of things. I know it's a lot to take in, at first."

"Thanks, Suzanna," Leilah said. She shifted her yoga mat on her shoulder, gesturing to a car just a couple of rows away. "I'd better get going, too. I'll see you next week, right?"

"Yes, I think we're permanently scheduled around the same time now," Suzanna said. "I'll see you then!"

"Bye!" Leilah called over her shoulder. "And thanks again!"

Suzanna chuckled, shaking her head at the young teacher's enthusiasm. Suzanna had felt the same way when she first started. Not that she hated her job now – she loved it. Teaching others how to act, using all her experience – and more importantly, for an actress in her thirties who hadn't managed to get a big break, being employed. There was a lot to like about this gig.

She turned and unlocked her car, checking her phone quickly before she got inside. There were a few messages – mostly social media notifications, nothing particularly important. The sound of Leilah's engine starting up roused her, and Suzanna got inside the car, slinging her purse onto the passenger seat.

She looked up; that was strange. Her rearview mirror wasn't quite pointing in the right direction. Had she knocked it earlier, when she was getting out of the car? Suzanna shrugged to herself, reaching up to adjust it. She was staring right into it as she changed the angle, accidentally putting it too far down and giving herself a clear view of the back seat.

A view that made her blood run cold.

"What are you - " she began, before he cut her off, lunging forward with the knife in his hand.

CHAPTER THREE

Laura rubbed her mouth with one hand, anxiously glancing around the bullpen. This wasn't what she had expected.

But she hadn't been thinking straight. Today was a day off for her, because of the case they had only just finished. And that meant it was a day off for her partner, Nate Lavoie, too. He wasn't here. She couldn't call on him for his help.

"Are you alright, Laura?"

Laura turned from her survey of the empty desks where she normally worked alongside Nate to see a fellow agent, Jones, watching her with his hands on his hips. The small, but determined, agent was a little older than her, and very much a family man. He was constantly asking after her daughter, Lacey, and talking about his own son, even though he knew full well Laura didn't have custody. Or even visitation rights.

It was possible to suggest that Laura cared so much about saving Amy because the little blonde and blue-eyed girl reminded her of Lacey, but that would have been cruel. Laura didn't wish abuse on anyone, and it was not only her moral duty but also her duty as an FBI agent to prevent it if she could. That was all this was, she told herself. She was doing her job.

And doing it well, because Agent Jones was an even better candidate than Nate for looking after a scared little girl.

"Come with me," she told him, turning and not waiting to find out if he would agree. He didn't have a choice, as far as she was concerned. As she called the elevator, she was gratified to see him pitching up beside her, wearing a puzzled expression.

"I need to you to watch someone for me," Laura said. "A little girl."

Jones' face brightened at the idea, but then darkened again immediately. "A victim?"

Laura nodded, glad he was keeping up. "Amy Fallow. Her father has been beating her. I took her out of the situation, but – well, now there's an incident brewing."

Jones nodded sharply. "You got her safe. Now you're up in front of the firing squad?"

"Something like that," Laura said. She wanted to smile ruefully, but the situation was so serious she couldn't get her facial muscles to comply. "I need to explain everything to them, and Amy can't sit there and listen. But I can't leave her alone, either. She's too delicate right now."

"I've got this," Jones said. He drew himself up and put on a fatherly expression, a gentle smile. "You've come to the right guy."

"I appreciate that," Laura said, feeling their ride bump to a halt. She only hoped Amy would get on with Jones as well as he did with other children.

The doors of the elevator opened on the right floor, and Laura led Jones on a rapid dash down the hall to Rondelle's office. The door was already open, and as Laura stepped inside, she almost quailed: Rondelle hadn't just called anyone in to consult on this. The room was full of the most senior members of the FBI administration, including the Director himself.

"Amy," Laura called out, swallowing down her nerves. The little girl, still seated on the chair but now looking considerably more nervous, looked up immediately. "Come here, sweetie!"

Amy scrambled down from the chair and raced across the room, nearly bumping right into one of the other chiefs in her hurry. He stepped back with a noise of surprise, and Amy was free to run right to Laura, throwing her arms around Laura's legs.

"It's okay, sweetie," Laura said. "Don't worry about all those men, they just want to help out. I want you to meet my friend, okay?"

"Who's your friend?" Amy asked, looking up with wide eyes, her voice trembling a little but still strong.

"This is Agent Jones," Laura said, turning to her colleague.

Jones hitched his trousers at the knees and got down to Amy's leave, a gentle smile on his face. "You can call me Freddie," he said. "You know what?"

"What?" Amy asked curiously.

"I've got a son about your age, and he really loves playing this game with me. You want to try it?"

Amy giggled. "Yeah," she said.

"Alright, then," Jones said, standing up but leaning down to offer Amy his hand. "Let's go next door and wait for Laura to talk to those men while we play a game, okay?"

Amy glanced at Laura uncertainly.

"That sounds like so much fun," Laura said, smiling encouragingly.

"Okay," Amy said decisively, allowing Jones to lead her by the hand into the next room. Laura watched them go to be sure Amy wouldn't get scared or turn back, and then finally walked into Rondelle's office.

It felt like walking into a den of lions. All five of the men in the room were higher ranking than her, and Laura knew she had caused trouble by bringing Amy here. She could only hope that she hadn't caused so much trouble they would decide not to help her.

"This has already gone out of control," one of them was saying. He wasn't in Laura's chain of command, but she recognized him; of course, she did. He was the Attorney General. "I've been informed there's an APB out with the state police for Agent Frost."

"Has Governor Fallow made an accusation of kidnapping at this stage?" Rondelle asked, furrowing his brow. Despite all of the important high-ranking officials in the room, he remained behind his desk, and ostensibly in charge of the discussion.

"Not at this time," the Attorney General replied. "He wants everything kept under wraps, I should imagine. This won't poll well. Having a daughter kidnapped once is going to garner sympathy – twice makes him look like a man who can't guarantee the safety of the people in this state."

"Then we currently have that advantage," Rondelle mused. "We have a little more time before the allegations get serious enough that we need to hand her over."

Laura's heart leapt in her chest. They were talking about her like she wasn't even in the room – like she was some stranger, not one of their own. Being 'handed over', like she was a thing and not a person, rankled. Laura herself was being talked about, not to, as if she didn't exist. And besides, it made her pulse race with fear. Would they really just abandon Amy to Governor Fallow?

"What about the abuse?" she said, speaking up. She felt she had to. It was now or never, and if she didn't stand up for herself, she couldn't count on anyone else to do the same. "If we share our own allegations with the press to counteract Fallow's, and bring charges against him, then me taking a child into federal custody is absolutely justified."

There was what felt like a very long moment of silence in the room, everyone else looking at Laura. She glanced around quickly, unable to help noticing so many different badges of insignia on so many different jackets. "Sirs," she added quickly, as an afterthought.

"Do you have any evidence of all of this?" One of the men, who she recognized as being in charge of one of the other divisions, asked her. "Any proof?"

Laura swallowed hard. "No," she admitted. "But there are witnesses. Governor Fallow's wife and his employees."

"People who are never going to testify against him," the Division Chief snapped. "You should know better than to abduct a child without proof – Rondelle, what kind of agents are you training these days?"

Chief Rondelle opened his mouth to protest, but he was cut off easily by the most powerful man in the room.

"Well, gentlemen, she still brings up a good point regarding the abuse," said Director Grenfell. His height as well as his rank made him tower over the others in the room. He had aquiline features and a superior bearing that even outmatched those in the small office who'd had military backgrounds; and though he spoke quietly, no one interrupted. "I wonder if you'd all let us get on with this, and give us the room? Chuck, Agent Frost, you can stay."

There wasn't a word of complaint as the other various officials filed out of the room, but once they hit the corridor, they seemed to have no problem in finding their voices. Laura heard some of them murmuring that she should be handed over immediately, even though it might risk the girl if the agent was right, because the system was in place for a reason. Another replied that they had to intervene to prevent further abuse, and then the door closed behind them, and Laura couldn't hear the rest.

"Alright," the Director said, steepling his hands in front of himself deliberately and slowly. He looked Laura over with a sharp gaze, his blond head seeming to fix her in place like a bird of prey would with a mouse. "Now, I've heard things about Governor Fallow which leads me to suspect you are telling the truth."

"Thank you, sir," Laura said, with a rush of relief. He wasn't going to hand Amy back somewhere like that. He believed her. It was going to be alright.

"But," he said, and Laura's heart sank as though he'd tolled a bell. "If we do not have solid proof that abuse is taking place, then there's nothing we can do. The state police have a right to their own investigation, and we can't be accused of bias or cover-up. Bruises aren't enough. Children can be clumsy, they can play rough – bruises can be explained away."

11

Laura looked over at Division Chief Rondelle. His face was flaming with fury, an emotion she seconded. But he wasn't moving to intervene or saying anything.

Feeling her heart sink into her boots, Laura realized he didn't disagree.

Then again, how could he? The Director was his boss, too. An order was an order.

Laura had to try again. She had to persuade him to change his mind. Not for her own sake, but for Amy's. "Sir," she began – but she never got the chance to finish.

The door burst open with a slam against the opposite wall, and all three of the people in the room turned with lightning-fast reflexes to face the incoming threat. Training had Laura reaching for her gun, but she wasn't carrying one today. Knowing she had been going to see Amy, she hadn't wanted it on her hip.

And even if she was carrying, she wouldn't have been able to use it. Because standing framed in the doorway were several uniformed members of the state police, staring at her with heavy frowns and their hands on their own weapons.

"Laura Frost?" one of them barked.

There wasn't much point in lying. Not in front of her own boss and the head of her entire organization, given that she worked in a profession where honesty was part of the job description. "Yes," she said, her voice cracking and failing her as she admitted it.

"We are placing you under -"

"No," Division Chief Rondelle said, stepping out from behind his desk with his hands raised. "No, just hang on a minute. Come inside."

The policemen exchanged a glance with one another, but the one who had been speaking – evidently the superior officer – nodded. They stepped over the threshold of the room and closed the door behind them. The office was once again cramped with people, and once again Laura knew her head could be on the chopping block.

Division Chief Rondelle – and the amount of sway he had over Director Grenford – was now her only hope.

"We've been directed to arrest Agent Frost, on the orders of Governor Fallow," the officer heading up the team from the state police said. "We've heard some very serious allegations to do with harassment and trespassing, and a potential threat to the Governor's security."

"We're aware of the allegations," Director Grenford said smoothly. Glancing at him, Laura was glad she wasn't on the other side. He had

12

turned to ice, like a carved sculpture. Laura had the distinct impression that anyone who tried to cross him would end up finding him sharp enough to cut. "At this time, we are also gathering intelligence relating to allegations against the Governor himself."

"Be that as it may, we have to deal with the offense which has been presented to us now," the leader of the state police replied, his tone just as frosty and evenly matched in formality. "We are not prepared to leave without significant evidence that paints Agent Frost in an innocent light."

There was a pause; Laura looked between the two groups uneasily. What evidence could she even provide? She'd done what the Governor had said she had done. The fact that there were mitigating circumstances was beside the point. The arrest came first, the excuses later.

"Sir," Rondelle said, turning his back on the state police and speaking urgently to Director Grenford. "We can't allow this to happen. I trust Agent Frost implicitly. If she says the situation is dangerous for the child to return to, then it's dangerous. We can't allow her to go back." Laura felt a flare of both hope and gratitude in her chest at the words, recognizing that Rondelle was putting his own reputation – and maybe even his job – on the line to stand up for her.

Director Grenford took this plea in, quietly, seeming to digest it before his eyes shot towards Laura. He seemed to be responding to Rondelle's words, but it was Laura he spoke to. "I'm afraid we can't have it both ways. I can try to de-escalate the situation by speaking with the Governor, but if I am to prevent you from being arrested, we need to let the girl go. There's nothing we can do without solid proof at this stage."

"So, you'll just send her back to be beaten?" Laura asked. She could hardly believe she was bold enough to question Director Grenford, particularly given the icy-cold front he was putting up now. She could easily see how he had risen to the top of the FBI; he was formidable.

But this mattered so much more. Laura couldn't let herself be intimidated out of making a stand. She had to protect Amy.

Director Grenford's mouth moved slightly, a wavering line that resolved flat. "I'm sorry," he said, and despite his stiffness Laura found she actually believed him. "But without evidence, she simply has to go home. We can launch a formal investigation from there and see about assessing her home environment."

"That could take months," Laura said, her voice almost failing her.

Months of being beaten. Months of psychological trauma that could never be undone. Months for a six-year-old girl, stuck at home with a bully who wielded a belt and no one who was brave enough to stop him. Amy had no chance.

And the Governor would probably be furious about this – about Laura confronting him and taking Amy. Would he take that anger out on his daughter? Laura didn't doubt it.

Amy had left her toy rabbit on the chair. Laura moved forward to pick it up. If anyone was going to tell Amy she was going home, Laura would take that burden herself – and maybe it would give her the chance to play for time, to think of something else.

But as her fingers made contact with the rabbit, she felt a familiar stab of pain in her temple. A headache.

The same kind of headache that always preceded a vision.

Laura felt herself pulled down into it with horror, praying as she went that she would not be forced to see Amy beaten and broken at the end of her young life.

CHAPTER FOUR

The vision sucked Laura under like a whirlpool of darkness, dragging her away from the present and into the future. Even though her physical body remained still, and everything happened in only the blink of an eye, reality inside the vision was different. She never knew how long the vision would last, or where it would take her.

Only one thing was certain: the amount of pain she felt before and after the vision was a clue to how far into the future the vision took place. And with this one, she could work out that it had to be at least a couple of years away. The pain wasn't bad enough for it to be current – so why was she seeing it now?

She found herself in a courtroom, hovering over the assembled onlookers and the jury like an eagle. The edges of the room were nebulous, floating off into darkness, but the center of the vision was strong. Below her, Laura could see a prosecutor and a defense team, lawyers in sharp, expensive suits who had to be from one of the top law firms in the state. Governor Fallow was sitting between them.

He was balding a little; Laura could see from up here. His frame seemed to have thinned out a little, his shoulders sloping more than she remembered. He was focused ahead, as everyone was; Laura felt her gaze being sucked in that direction, powerless to resist.

At the front of the courtroom, a television had been wheeled into place. There was something playing on the screen. A recording. Laura's heart leapt into her throat. It was Amy on there, Amy as she was now, small and delicate and fragile. And the Governor was standing over her with his belt in his hand, and he brought it down –

Laura forced her eyes closed, fighting against the vision as hard as she could. She didn't want to see this, but she heard it, and she heard the gasps of shock from the jury. She knew what this was: a trial of John Fallow, surely not still Governor at this point. The trial for his abuse of his daughter.

Laura opened her eyes and looked around, away from the video, but there was no sign of Amy in the courtroom. At least, not that Laura could see. Maybe she was giving evidence remotely. Perhaps she hadn't been called yet.

But, wait – the video. Laura focused on it again. It was… yes, it was filmed sometime recently. Amy looked just the same as she had only a few minutes ago when Laura had left her with Agent Jones. And the footage was distorted somewhat, part of the screen covered by something. Something fluffy and white and…

The toy rabbit. Laura would bet on it. It was the toy rabbit Amy was carrying around with her, leaning slightly in front of the screen. She needed to study it for more clues – to see what else she could figure out – how she could get this footage before Amy had to go back -

Laura surfaced from the vision like she was shooting up out of water and gasping for air. Cold ice drenched down the back of her spine. What the vision told her was that, right now, they were on the right path – that they might end up in court, if they carried on how they were.

But that courtroom had been far into the future. And that footage might have been the first of many. And even if Laura was seeing it now, that didn't mean that it was guaranteed to happen – anything could take place between now and then to push the future she had seen off-course. She couldn't tell whether the video had been taken already or would be taken in the future. And if it still had yet to be taken, that meant Amy would be beaten again.

She couldn't let that happen.

So, why had she seen it now? Just because she was touching the rabbit? Laura looked down at the stuffed toy in her hands, her mind racing. If she could figure out if that footage existed yet…

"Agent Frost?" Director Grenford prompted, making her realize she had been staring at the toy in silence. "I'll come along with you to meet the Governor, to see if we can't come to an agreement. Yes?"

Laura could barely concentrate on what he was saying. It didn't matter. What mattered was this. The toy rabbit had been in the footage. It had been central to the footage. That was why it had triggered the vision, right?

But for a stuffed toy, why was it… so heavy…?

Laura prodded the rabbit's plush stomach and felt something hard inside. Turning it over, she realized it wasn't a toy – at least, not just a toy. It had a zip up the back, concealed beneath a strip of fur folded over. It was probably supposed to contain a heated pad for comfort, but that wasn't the only thing that was in there now.

It was a cell phone.

16

"Wait a second," Laura said frantically, needing to delay everything, to make everyone stop until she could figure this out. She dug the phone out and turned it over, tapping the screen. To her relief, it woke up – and there was no password protection, no fingerprint needed.

It was an old model, and a simplified one from what she could see on the screen. The wallpaper was a photograph of Amy with her mother, both of them smiling – though Laura could see the ghost of tension around Mrs. Fallow's eyes. The apps were all brightly colored cartoon logos, looking like the kid-friendly locked version of the phone. This was Amy's. She must have put it inside the rabbit so that she could keep her two dearest possessions close at hand at all times.

A six-year-old having her own phone seemed ridiculous to Laura, but then, Amy's father was rich enough to provide her with whatever he wanted. And it wasn't as though Laura was up to date on parenting, exactly. It had been a long time since she'd even been able to see her own daughter, with the ongoing custody struggle – *no, don't think about that now, focus, save Amy...*

Laura opened up the gallery app, scrolling through the photos and videos. There were a few recent ones, and her heart almost stopped when she saw a frame she recognized. The phone half-covered by the rabbit's ear.

Laura's heart continued to thud loudly in her ears as she pressed the thumbnail, bringing the whole video up. It played from the start: the phone propped up properly, showing Amy standing at the other side of her bedroom. She was walking back quickly until she reached what she clearly thought was the appropriate distance and struck a pose, her hands on her hips like a little diva. It almost brought Laura to tears, the thought of this little girl being normal and playing happily. All of that would be taken away from her forever if this wasn't the video she needed.

"Okay," Amy said on the video, her voice obviously a childish imitation of something she had seen on television or on social media. "Today we're going to show you how to dance!" She threw her arms up on this word, pronounced in her young tones slightly wrong, probably an attempt at a copy of an accent she had heard. She started to jump around then, performing in her own way. Laura found herself smiling, even though she was so tense and afraid. She couldn't not. The girl was adorable.

How could anyone hurt someone this innocent?

Then Laura heard something else on the recording: a male voice, bellowing Amy's name from further away. She didn't have to guess that it would be the Governor's voice. She had heard him shouting before, in a vision. There was a bang as the door of the room slammed open, hitting the wall, and the phone toppled over from its hiding place.

Laura knew what was going to happen next. She couldn't watch. She couldn't bring herself to do it. She turned and lifted the phone wordlessly, handing it to Director Grenford. Let him have the nightmares. Laura already had enough of her own.

She heard it again, though. They all did. The head of the state police cohort took an involuntary step back, and Laura looked up to see Rondelle's face drained of color.

"Proof," Laura said, her throat dry and her eyes aching to release tears. "You wanted it, you got it."

Director Grenford put the phone down on the side of Rondelle's desk, his expression grim. He had evidently seen enough, shutting off the audio and the video before it played out. Laura wondered if Amy even realized she'd filmed what had happened. The Governor certainly hadn't. With the phone falling down from its propped-up position, he probably hadn't even seen it behind the rabbit.

"Excuse me a moment," Grenford said, his voice harsh and tight. It left no illusion that his polite words were a request. They were an order, and not one to be ignored.

The atmosphere in the room was tense as he stepped outside, leaving Laura, Rondelle, and the three state police standing around. Rondelle moved to sit behind his desk, taking his chair heavily. Even though he was a fit and healthy man still, he was twenty or perhaps thirty years older than Laura. She wasn't surprised he needed to sit down.

She sank down into the chair that Amy had once occupied herself, realizing even in the moment that she wasn't as stable as she had thought.

There was silence in the room, the five people inside it all studiously avoiding looking at one another. The state police shifted restlessly, and Laura couldn't help but tense up again. If Grenford couldn't figure this out – if he ended up throwing her to the wolves anyway – she had no doubt they would gleefully march her out of here in handcuffs. Getting one up on the FBI would make them heroes among their colleagues.

18

Grenford swept back into the room without warning, making them all collectively jump. He was putting a cell phone down from his ear, and he swept an imperious eye towards the state police.

"You've been called off," he said, sharply. "You can expect a call from your superior. Now, get out of my building."

"But…" the leader began, obviously unsure if he should just trust the word of a rival law enforcement agency. But then a cell phone began to ring in his own pocket, and with a glance at the name flashing up on the screen, he beckoned his backup out of the room with him by a toss of the head. They all walked out past Grenford's outstretched arm, and he closed the door after them smartly. Laura felt her heart hammering in her chest. Until the relief washed over her, she hadn't realized how afraid she had been of the idea of being arrested.

It would have affected everything. Her job. Her life. Getting Lacey back. There would have been no hope of getting shared custody if she had been arrested.

"What now?" Laura asked, making to get out of her chair. Was she going to be free to take Amy to the Child and Family Services Agency? Could she get her into the care of someone who was actually going to look after her, a temporary place to stay until all of this was sorted out, somewhere she would be safe?

"You stay put," Director Grenford said. Despite the fact she had proven her point, he didn't look particularly pleased with her – or anyone else. "The Governor is on his way. We're going to hash this out and get it settled. Going after him in public would make too much of a mess. If he comes here under pretense of talking, we can arrest him without alerting the press too early."

Laura's heart dropped from her throat into her stomach.

Governor John Fallow was coming – and she was going to be expected just to talk with him? After everything she had seen?

Laura didn't know if she would be able to hold herself back – or if she was going to get out of this unscathed, once the powerful Governor had his way. It was in the hands of the Director, and from the way he was staring coldly at her, Laura didn't know if that meant she was safe…

Or if she was still going to be put behind bars and left unable to do anything for Amy.

CHAPTER FIVE

Laura watched as Governor Fallow strode into the room alone, his tall frame encased in a powerful deep blue suit that seemed to defy anyone to question him. His face was marred by a glower, red-hot rage clearly billowing right beneath the surface. As soon as he saw Laura, his eyes narrowed in on her like he wanted to destroy her with just a look.

They had moved into a more comfortable conference room, with a vast, dark table surrounded by chairs. Seated at one side of it already with Division Chief Rondelle, Laura was glad to have an ocean of wood between herself and Fallow. He looked as though he would smash the table in half just to get his hands around her neck.

"No retinue with you today, Governor?" Director Grenford asked, showing him to a chair opposite Laura and Rondelle. Grenford himself finally sat at a position directly between the two parties, halfway around the curve. A neutral position. Laura only hoped that it was just for show.

"There's no sense in involving others in this," Fallow grunted, his words hitting the air like slaps. He clearly didn't want the rumors to spread any further about why his daughter had been taken this time. "It seems like you may be wasting my time as it is. Why are you insisting on this meeting, and not allowing your Agent to be arrested?"

"We thought we might do you a courtesy, Governor," Grenford said. His tone was deceptively calm and cool, as though they were discussing no more than the weather. Laura was constantly reminded of the fact that he had risen to the rank as a former Attorney General. He must have been a formidable foe in the courtroom in his time. "You should see the evidence that we have recently collected."

In the intervening time, the footage had been uploaded to a laptop; it was more secure than playing it on Amy's phone, given that such a small device could easily be taken or broken. Grenford pressed a button, and the video began playing on a projector screen – thankfully, one that was above Laura's head. She didn't want to see, as she hadn't wanted to the first or the second time.

20

She had seen enough of Amy's suffering to last her a lifetime already.

Instead, she watched John Fallow. She watched as he looked up with a frown, wondering why on Earth they were playing some video of his daughter playing around. She watched as his face contorted with anger at the intrusion, then the way the shock registered in his eyes as he heard his own voice and remembered what had happened next.

Laura watched him see himself hit his daughter, all without flinching. He didn't look away or close his eyes. He watched to the end, and even though his face paled, he didn't waver. Looking at him, Laura thought he had no remorse. No shame. The only reason he looked so pale was because he'd been caught on camera, not because he accepted that what he had done was wrong.

Laura's hands curled into fists on the table. If she thought it would solve anything, she could have leapt across the wood then, trying to fit her hands around his neck.

But it wouldn't make a difference.

"Now, Governor Fallow," Grenford said, in the same dangerously calm tone. "You see why it was necessary for us to meet in person on this matter."

"Is this a threat?" Fallow sneered immediately, turning towards him with an angry gesture at the screen. "You think you can intimidate me?"

"It's not a threat," Grenford replied evenly. "It's what we have against you. We're putting our cards on the table. The thing is, Governor, I don't want to start a war between the FBI and the state. I don't even want to drag your name through the mud. What I'm interested in, as I'm sure you are, is avoiding a public scandal."

That took some of the wind out of Fallow's sails. Laura saw it in his face. He had come in expecting a fight, and now he was being told there wasn't one on offer. But he didn't cool down completely. His face was still that light purple-red tone she had seen when she confronted him at the house. Anger, bubbling inside him so strongly that he couldn't hide it on his face.

"Then what are you proposing?" Fallow asked. Laura could see that he resented having to ask. It put all the power in Grenford's court. Grenford, being extremely skilled at debate and negotiation, obviously knew that.

"I want you to drop the charges against Agent Frost," Grenford said. "As well as not pursuing any further charges related to your daughter. She will remain free to do her job, and we don't have to report to the media why she felt the need to step in."

"And she's happy with that, is she?" Fallow scoffed.

Laura knew why he was skeptical. She was the one who had given him the big speech about how he was going to pay, how if he even tried to get Amy back that she would bring down the rains of Hell on him. Now, it looked as though she was backing down, giving up.

But she wasn't. There was no way she was just going to let him get away with this. There was no way she was putting Amy back into his hands. She knew Director Grenford was doing his best, trying to make sure that there would never be any blowback on her. But that wasn't good enough.

"No," Laura said. "She isn't."

She felt Director Grenford staring at her. She wasn't supposed to go against the word of a superior agent – and he was the most superior of all. She was risking her career by even speaking up. On the other side, Division Chief Rondelle shifted uncomfortably. He, too, had risked his reputation with Grenford by standing up for her.

But Laura couldn't – wouldn't – back down. Not only Amy's face, but her own daughter's surfaced in her mind. She couldn't let them down. And to let Amy down now would be as bad as letting Lacey down again.

"I agree with the other terms," she said. "No arrest, no scandal. But only on one further condition. Amy goes into foster care and gets the help she needs."

Governor Fallow scoffed, shaking his head vehemently. "Don't be ridiculous," he said. "Amy is my daughter. She's coming home with me, where she belongs. And how would I even explain to the public that my daughter has been taken into care? Preposterous!"

"I -" Laura began, but Director Grenford lifted a hand and cut her off.

"That will do for now, Agent Frost," he said, his tone full of warning. "Governor, we can't stop you from taking your daughter at this phase."

Laura turned and gaped at him. How could he say that, after everything he had seen? It wasn't safe! They had enough evidence with the video – they could have him taken into custody himself right now – this wasn't right!

"I thought as much," Governor Fallow said smugly, though there was enough of a trace of doubt left on his quickly smoothed expression

22

that Laura thought he must have been almost as surprised as she was. He hadn't expected that to work.

And it shouldn't have.

Fallow stood, buttoning his jacket. Laura opened her mouth to protest again, but Director Grenford gave her such a sharp glance that she closed her mouth. What was happening here? She was getting a direct and unignorable signal to stay quiet, but why? Just because the Director was scared of what the Governor could do in a political sense if they stopped him, or for another reason?

Did he have a plan?

CHAPTER SIX

Laura's heart was in her throat, along with all the words she wanted to scream at Governor Fallow, as he swept out of the room. All she could do was trail behind him, behind Director Grenford and Division Chief Rondelle, feeling like a forgotten piece of the puzzle. She was supposed to be stopping this from happening. She was supposed to be keeping Amy safe.

With horror, Laura realized that Director Grenford was leading Governor Fallow right to the room where Amy was sequestered with Agent Jones. Right to the very place where he could do the most harm. Laura tried to step forward again, to protest, but she found her way barred. Without even looking around at her, Director Grenford put out a hand and placed it on her shoulder, preventing her from moving forward any further. Despite the fact that he was several decades older than her, he held her in place with just one hand easily.

"Amy," Governor Fallow said, his voice booming out as he entered the room. "It's time to go home."

As he passed through the door into the room, Laura was able to see past him. She could see Amy, sitting on the floor and seemingly engaged in a game of something with Agent Jones. The smile on the little girl's face dropped away completely as she looked up and saw her father, and Laura saw the exact moment that happiness changed into fear.

Anyone in the room would have seen it. There was no mistaking it. Amy was terrified, and no matter how much bluster he brought to the table, Governor Fallow was never going to be able to deny that.

Amy looked up at her father, and then behind him to where Laura was standing in the corridor, watching. She shook her head rapidly, shuffling away across the carpet. "She said I didn't need to go home ever again. She said I could go somewhere safe instead," she said, her voice coming out as a pleading whine to the room in general. When she looked up at her father's face again, she froze in fear, seeing something there that paralyzed her.

Laura could only see the back of Governor Fallow's neck. But that was enough. She saw it turning redder, deepening in color, as his anger rose. "Amy, don't be so ridiculous," he said, his voice coming out sharp and loud. "Come with me this instant. We're going home. This silliness has to stop."

Amy shook her head again, shuffling back further. She backed into Agent Jones, who had been sitting on the floor with her. The fatherly agent instinctively put out a hand to steady her, supporting her shoulder. "Don't make me go," she whined, tears spilling quickly down her cheeks. She looked up at Laura, and Laura felt her heart breaking. This little girl had trusted her. This little girl had heard her say that everything was going to be alright, and now here was her father ready to take her away again.

"This is ludicrous," Governor Fallow said, turning around and snapping fire at Laura. "It's this woman's fault. This woman right here! She has poisoned my own daughter against me!"

"Governor Fallow," Director Grenford said quietly, his voice even and subtle. "If your daughter does not want to go with you, perhaps we should make a different arrangement."

"What arrangement?" Fallow asked, his tone derisive.

"Protective custody," Grenford replied. "Unofficial, for the time being. I'm sure you don't want all of the media attention that would come with an official ruling."

At first, Fallow opened his mouth to argue. Laura saw it, saw how the thoughts flashed across his face in quick succession. First, that this man was being insufferably impertinent. That he, Fallow, should simply take his daughter and be done with it, and not let any man tell him what he could or could not do. Straight after that, right on the heels, was the realization that all of this was making him look terrible. Laura could almost see poll numbers flashing up before his eyes. She saw the way that anger made him grit his teeth, his eyes flashing. She saw the moment he came to his decision.

He turned on his heel, striding down the corridor past them all as if they were nothing more than an inconvenience to him. "Fine," he threw over his shoulder. "Have it your way. I agree to your terms, insulting as they are. But this isn't over."

Laura could only gape at his back, watching him disappear down the hall. He had come alone, and he left alone, no one making any attempt to follow him. Director Grenford waited until he was gone and then turned to Laura with an expression that she could only describe as smugly satisfied.

"Well, Agent Frost," he said. "Are you satisfied now?"

25

Laura weighed her reply. She couldn't say that justice had been done. Not completely. Governor Fallow should have been rotting away in a police cell, awaiting trial, but at least Amy was safe now. She was out of his hands.

For now.

"Do you think he will keep up his end of the agreement?" she asked, looking into Director Grenford's eyes. She wanted to know what he really thought. She didn't want to miss the truth, if he ever allowed such a thing to show on his face.

"Leave it to us now," he said, instead of answering the question. "There are specialists who can look after Amy, make sure that she gets somewhere safe. We will keep her out of her father's hands. A little paperwork is all that is needed to follow up on this, and then we can be sure that he won't be able to get his hands on her again. Not without going through all of us."

So, Laura thought to herself privately, the answer was no. He didn't believe that it was over. He didn't believe that Governor Fallow would keep his promise. But what mattered now was making sure that Amy was far enough away so he couldn't get his hands on her even if he tried – and that she would be safe in the meantime. Safe, happy, and healthy.

"Promise me that she'll go somewhere good," Laura said. "Somewhere where she's really looked after, not a crappy foster home. She deserves that."

"I give you my word," Director Grenford said, nodding solemnly. "I can see how much this means to you. I assure you; I'm taking it as seriously as you are. Amy will be looked after."

"Alright," Laura said, the word hanging heavy in her ears. She knew that, in some kind of way, everyone was waiting on her agreement. They didn't want her to kick up a fuss and upset the apple cart again. Her approval of the plan meant that it was going to go ahead, out of her hands and without her further involvement.

But if that was what it took to make sure that Amy was safe, that was what she needed to do.

"Alright, Amy," Director Grenford said, putting on a falsely bright voice for the little girl. In any other circumstance, Laura would have had to stifle a laugh. The cold, powerful, manipulative Director of the FBI, brought to lightness and cheer to impress a child. It was the first time she'd ever had a glimpse of what she realized must be the family man he was at home. "It's time for you to see your new home now.

26

We're going to go and talk to a wonderful lady that I know in Child and Family Services, and she's going to make sure you're happy and safe tonight. How does that sound?"

Amy looked up at Laura with doubt and confusion. "Aren't I going home with you?" she asked.

Laura's heart clenched so hard in her chest it almost stopped. She bit her own lip, hard, curling her fingernails into her palm to keep herself from crying. "No, sweetie, it's better if you go somewhere else," she said. "I'm not at home all the time – remember, we talked about how my job is to save lots of little girls and boys? And big ones, too?"

"But I want to stay with you," Amy said, tears spilling down her cheeks again for the second time in as many minutes. She got up and ran headlong towards Laura, wrapping her tiny arms around her legs, holding her in place. Laura felt her sobbing, heard it like a wrench that just kept tearing at her heart over and over again.

"I'm so sorry, sweetie," she said, hugging Amy back as best she could. In spite of herself, tears began to fall down her own face, and she didn't want to let go for long enough to wipe them away. "It's just not allowed."

"But why?" Amy whined, her mouth open and upturned, her eyes half-shut with crying as she tilted her head to look up at Laura. "I'll be really, really good!"

Laura closed her eyes tight, holding Amy as close as she could. This was the last time, she knew. She had to make it count. She had to put as much love into this one hug as Amy would need to get her through the next weeks and months before she began to settle again.

She thought of Lacey, her own daughter, who had also gone for months without feeling her mother's embrace. Lacey, who probably no longer even knew whether her mother loved her or not. It had been so long. Everything poured out of Laura, a dark wave of misery: was she ever going to get the chance to really be there for these little girls who needed her?

But no, she realized, as she squeezed Amy one last time and then tried to pry her off. No, the darkness wasn't misery.

It was a feeling. Not quite a vision, not yet. Whatever she was seeing was too vague now, maybe too far in the future, to trigger a vision of something concrete. It was just a feeling that something was off.

That something in Amy's future was destined to be dark.

Reluctantly, Laura let Amy go. If she could, she would intervene again, stop anything bad from ever happening to her. But the truth was, if Amy was kept away from Laura, there wasn't much she would be able to do. Her visions only came with physical contact, be that with the person in the center of the vision or something related to them. Just like she had only been able to see Amy's future by touching the rabbit, she had no idea if she was ever going to be able to get close enough to Amy again to trigger something else. She didn't know if she would even be aware that Amy was in danger ever again, so how could she prevent it?

For a moment, as Amy followed Director Grenford with sobs still wracking her body, Laura saw a flash of something else. She saw herself, raising Amy at her own home. The two of them sitting together for a tea party, doing the kind of things that six-year-old girls were supposed to be doing. She imagined, too, Lacey joining them. One day, Laura might be able to get her own daughter back, and one day she might be able to make Amy safe. Both of them felt like far off dreams at the moment.

What she had seen was not a vision, not in the normal sense. It was a dream, a fantasy of what might one day be. But that didn't mean that it couldn't come true.

It didn't mean that Laura had to keep letting people down, over and over again. First Lacey, and now Amy. Both of them must think she didn't care for them at all.

But that wasn't true. She would do everything she could behind the scenes to make sure that Amy had the best life possible. Just as she would do as much as she could in all of her power to make her ex, Marcus, trust her again so that she might get access to Lacey.

She'd come so far already. She'd stayed off the alcohol for longer than she had before, with Lacey's image inside her mind's eye keeping her sober. She could go further. All she needed to do was to make Marcus listen to her, to see that she was serious about sobriety now. To prove that she was never, ever, going to let alcohol come between her and her daughter ever again.

Which was why, as she left the FBI building with a heavy heart, it was odd that Laura's next intended destination was a bar.

CHAPTER SEVEN

He walked after her, unseen, studying her every move. Worshipping her.

His muse. His inspiration. The only perfect being in the world.

He watched how she moved through patches of dappled sunlight between buildings, the way she didn't flinch at the touch of the sun but instead gloried in it. It brought her to life, from the highlights in her hair to the tan of her skin.

She was perfect, in every way. He studied her from a distance away, watching the gestures she made. They were so casual, so easy, as if she didn't even have to think about what she was doing. But every single move was just right, like a perfectly choreographed dance. This was what it was like, he thought, to observe the pinnacle of life in action. This was the peak of existence. Floating on the currents of the world, attuned to them exactly, everything around you moving in time.

He studied her movements, from the way that she walked to the most subtle gestures. Her body language told so much without saying a single word. He could read emotions in every line, from the way her finger extended through her arm to the way her foot landed on the floor. When he was sure that no one was watching him, every now and then, he would attempt one of these moves himself, committing them to the memory of his muscles. Trying them out, how they felt on his own frame. Learning.

She spoke to people on the sidewalk, exchanging a quick word before moving on. He heard the light-hearted peal of laughter, so free and fine. So happy. It was like a recording of a laugh, like the archetype of a laugh. Something that could be recorded to film and used again and again. Almost too good to be the real thing, but it was real. She was real.

She was real, and she was perfect. Every single move, every word, every expression that passed over her face. He saw it all, and it was perfect.

He didn't know how he had missed it before. The last one, he had been so sure that she was the one. He had believed that she was perfection, the muse he was waiting for. But time had passed, and as he had observed her, he had noticed more and more. Seeing the mistakes. Seeing how she did not move in time with the current of the world, but instead tried to fight against it.

Over time, he had come to know that he was wrong. He had come to realize that what he had thought was a muse was nothing more than a human being, just a person. Nothing special. In many ways, a liar. The realization had been so hurtful, so disappointing.

And the one before that, too. She had been even more of a liar. It had all begun back then, when he was so angry with her that he couldn't take it. He couldn't be lied to like that. He couldn't allow someone to trick him into worshipping a false muse, a fake idol.

But that was over now. He finally had found his muse. This time, he was sure that she was the one. She danced through the sunlight on the sidewalk like no one else. She floated like a butterfly on the breeze, bringing life and light to everyone that she passed by. He could even see it in the faces of those she passed. It would be in his own face, if he turned to catch the reflection in a window.

When you found the one true thing in the world, there was no mistaking it. He had found her now. It had been a long and difficult journey to get here, but he was happy at last. His heart felt light. Everything that had gone before, all the anger and disappointment, all the blood, it had been worth it.

Because now he could walk along the street behind his muse, watching her, learning from her. Worshipping every single thing that she did. And he would continue to watch her until he had learned it all, because that was what a muse was for. Inspiration that could last a lifetime. He wasn't going to waste this chance.

CHAPTER EIGHT

Laura rushed in through the doors of the bar, feeling scattered and frantic. She would have liked to think this wasn't normal for her, but the sad truth is that it was. Alcohol had been a strong force in her life for years, the only thing she had been able to turn to that could numb the pain of the visions she had. Disorganization, lateness, the constant capacity to let people down. These had become hallmarks of Laura's life.

But she was turning a corner now, trying not to do these kind of things anymore. Trying not to let people down. That was why she felt so flustered, because not only had she failed to get Governor Fallow put behind bars where he belonged, but she was also running horrendously late for an appointment that she herself had made.

She had been looking forward to this meeting for a while. While she and her partner Nate were out of town during the last case they worked on, she'd had a hit on one of the forums she frequented looking for other people like her. She had organized to meet him, even though she wasn't totally convinced that he was the real deal. But he seemed more convincing than anyone she had come across lately.

And now she was late, which was exactly the sort of first impression she had been hoping to avoid.

Laura pitched up beside the dark marble bar and looked around, trying to spot someone who might seem familiar or as though they were waiting for someone. The whole place was decked out like a tropical island bar with wooden carvings, surfboards on the walls, and Tiki-shaped glasses for the drinks. Laura glanced past the décor and at the people standing around, all of them dressed in variations of short dresses and relaxed suits.

There were a couple of women, looking nervously at watches or phones and evidently waiting for dates, but Laura knew that she was waiting for a man. She took a breath, trying to calm her racing mind. One thing at a time, she told herself. Right now, she needed to focus on this, because it could help her get to the bottom of all of the issues that threatened to overwhelm her life on a daily basis.

31

If she could get to the bottom of those issues, she would be a better and more present mother for Lacey. If she could be a better mother, then she might get shared custody, or at least better visitation rights. And if she was being more of a mother to Lacey, then maybe she could convince the state to let her take care of Amy. Everything had to trickle onwards from this one first point.

And, if it didn't work out, she reminded herself, it couldn't be the end of the world. She couldn't get drunk to forget her sorrows. She needed to carry on, find another way to get through.

"I'll take a virgin colada," she said, catching the attention of the bartender. He nodded and began to mix her up a fruit-based drink, making no comment at all on her choice to stay teetotal. There were so many reasons why someone would not drink alcohol at a bar. Designated driver, an early start in the morning, or simply for safety. But still, whenever she ordered a soft drink somewhere like this, Laura couldn't help but feel like she had a neon sign pointing to her head with the word alcoholic above it.

These environments were not the best ones for her to hang around in, especially while she was alone. She hadn't told the man she was meeting that she was an alcoholic, and he had picked the meeting place. At the very least, she thought, he certainly wasn't able to just conjure up facts about people from speaking to them online, or he would have known that.

Still, it wasn't like her ability worked that way. She just wished he would get here soon, so she could stop paying attention to the other drinks the bartender was making and how good they looked.

"Hello?" Laura started, turning around at the sound of a voice just over her shoulder. "You must be AnnaSmith8932."

Laura found herself smiling, a reaction to calm her racing heart more than anything else. Had he known that, right then, she was wishing he would appear? "Yes. You must be VirginiaMan383."

She took him in, a welcome distraction from the busy bar and the people drinking what amounted to liquid temptation all around her. He was younger than she had expected, probably close to her own age. He had red hair, styled up over his forehead just so, and he was dressed in a sharp, stylish blazer over a V-neck white shirt that made him look as though he'd just come off a plane from some exotic location. He was not what she had pictured in her mind at all.

"Please, call me Nolan," he said, chuckling. "It's Nolan Perry."

"Laura," she replied, holding back just in time before she gave him her full name. Given that she was an FBI agent, perhaps it would be a better idea to wait until she knew she could trust him before she gave her away her full identity. After all, even Division Chief Rondelle wouldn't be able to do much to help her if a rumor got out that she was a believer in the kind of idiotic psychic stuff that the FBI usually scoffed at. Never mind that she knew it was true.

"Shall we get a table?" Nolan asked, gesturing towards the side. it was the kind of gesture that actually meant the idea was a statement, not a question, and she was meant to follow. She wondered if he was used to taking charge at work.

She stopped herself forcibly, walking after him towards one of the free tables in the bar and trying to focus just on the moment. She didn't need to analyze every single person she met or try to detect every single thing about them. He wasn't a suspect. He would tell her, if he wanted her to know. Besides, the more important question was how he had managed to pick her out. Had he simply looked around and found her by coincidence, picking her out from the other women at the bar? But how had he managed to do that? Could it be that he was the real thing, that he had seen her in a vision already and knew who to expect?

They sat down together, Nolan waving over one of the roving waitresses to order a drink. Laura noted that he'd gone for a whiskey-based cocktail, a manly kind of drink and definitely full-on with the alcohol. She didn't say a thing. Maybe that could be one more test, like everything else about herself. If he could tell her any facts without being told them, it might mean something. Laura resolved to hold back as much as she possibly could about her real life and circumstances.

"So, I wasn't expecting to get a response to my post on the forum so quickly," Laura said.

Nolan chuckled, running a hand up over his hair. Or, at least, lightly brushing it. Laura noticed, looking closely, that he hadn't upset a single strand. It seemed it was more for the look of the gesture, and he was too vain to risk upsetting his carefully styled hair. "I just happened to see it," he said. "I guess I was drawn to it, somehow. Something made me want to log in right at the time when you were posting it, and when I saw it, I couldn't believe my luck."

Laura took a sip of her drink, more to hide her emotions than anything else. A vague idea making him turn on his computer and look at a post on a forum - that didn't sound like the kind of psychic ability she had been hoping to hear about. It was nothing like her own, for example. But that didn't mean anything, she reminded herself. It was still possible that he was the real deal, just in a different way from how she was. Just because every so-called psychic she had ever met until now had been a fraud, she still had to hope that someone out there wasn't.

"Well, I'm glad you reached out," she said at last. "I've been wanting to meet someone who could do things like I can."

"Me, too," Nolan said, flashing her a smile. "Don't tell me. You grew up thinking you were the only one like you in the world."

"That's right," Laura nodded, then shrugged with a half-smile. "Well, after I realized that what I could do wasn't normal, anyway."

Nolan laughed at that. "I know exactly what you mean," he said. "So, you're in law enforcement?"

Laura looked at him sharply. She hadn't given anything away, had she? She hadn't said anything about it. So, how had he known that she was in that line of work? Could it be…?

"I am," she said, trying to hide or dampen down her surprise a little. "What about you? What do you do?"

It didn't occur to her until just then that maybe she should have been trying to impress him, as well. She knew she had the ability that she had told him about online. Whether he did or not was what was of interest to her. She thought he could decide for himself whether he trusted her or not. And if they needed some kind of proof to settle things, she could always touch his hand later and see if a vision would come about his future.

"I'm in sales," Nolan said, shrugging self-effacingly. "It's no big deal. I just have this kind of gift for helping people to find the thing that they're looking for. All part of the power, I suppose. When I look at someone, I know exactly what they want."

"Really?" Laura asked. "Every single time?"

Nolan accepted his drink from the returning waitress, thanking her quickly before turning to answer her question. "Almost," he said. "Of course, there are days when the power just doesn't quite seem to be as strong. But most of the time, I get a good hit. Employee of the month for several years in a row, you know what I mean?"

Laura nodded, trying to pretend that she was impressed by this information while she processed it internally. She wasn't getting anywhere from just trying to guess things on her own. She needed to just get over it and ask him questions, find out what his power actually entailed. That was the only way she was going to figure out if they had anything in common or not.

"So, how does it work for you?" She asked. Her voice was tentative, her words hesitant. She'd never spoken to anyone quite so openly about this before. Not since she was a child, when, as she suggested a moment ago, she had realized that she was different. That was the last time she had been open with anyone about this kind of conversation topic – when they had laughed at her, and when the laughter had turned to looks of horror and distrust. "How do you your visions come? Or do they manifest as visions at all?"

Nolan shrugged casually. "It can be different from time to time," he said. "Sometimes I get these dreams that end up coming true. Of course, it's a bit of work to interpret them. You never quite know what they mean until it happens. Anyway, sometimes it's just a feeling. How about you? Do you get the same thing?"

Laura took another swallow of her drink. That didn't sound right to her at all. Actually, it sounded like what people who didn't have psychic abilities at all, but were just superstitious and gullible, would think. She didn't say that, though. Maybe he was telling the truth. Maybe he really did get a sense of things. Maybe it was like the sense of death or foreboding that she got sometimes when the vision wasn't strong enough, and it was just that Nolan had never learned how to make the visions come on stronger.

Not that she knew exactly how to do it, either. It just happened. It wasn't something that she was in control of.

"It's a bit different for me," she said, at last. Again, she wondered how much she should give away. "I suppose it's a bit like the dreams, but I'm usually awake."

"Oh, like a premonition?" Nolan said, nodding as if this made total sense to him. "Yes, I've heard of that. forgive me for asking something so personal, but you're divorced, aren't you?"

Laura again felt startled. She definitely hadn't mentioned anything about Lacey or Marcus. How had he managed to work that one out?

"Yes, I am," she said. "It was a few years ago now. We're still trying to get things back to an amicable level."

"Because you have a child together?" Nolan asked.

Laura could barely hold herself back from gaping at him. That was something she definitely hadn't given away, not in her forum profile, not in their messages to meet, not anywhere. He was the real thing. He had to be. How else would he have figured it out?

Laura's phone rang in her pocket, distracting her momentarily.

"Sorry," she said. "Just give me a minute, I need to answer this…"

She looked down at the screen and felt her heart hit the back of her throat. It was Chief Rondelle calling.

There had to be something wrong with Amy.

Laura got up and fled the bar, needing to get to a quiet spot where she could hear what he had to say.

CHAPTER NINE

"Laura Frost," Laura said, gasping out her own name by way of answering the phone. She gripped onto a windowsill in the wall outside the bar to steady herself. She didn't want to hear the news if it was bad – but she needed to know.

"Agent Frost," Rondelle said, his voice calm and measured. How could he be calm and measured when calling her about something like this?

"What is it? What's happened to her?" Laura asked, feeling her breath seize in her throat.

"Who?" Rondelle asked, seeming puzzled. "Oh – no, no, Agent Frost, I'm calling you about a new assignment."

Laura breathed again finally, leaning on the wall for support. "Oh, thank God."

But a moment later, it hit her: a new assignment? They'd only just come back from the last case. Normally they would be allowed more time, the chance to catch up on paperwork and debriefs.

"We've got a couple of murders in Seattle that I'd like you and Agent Lavoie to look into," Rondelle said. "I won't tell you too much now – it's late. You'll get the full briefing on the plane – I'm putting you on the earliest possible flight tomorrow morning, so you'll want to get some rest now."

"Understood," Laura said, then hesitated. "But... why so soon?"

Rondelle made a noise in his throat. "Because I need to know that you're somewhere working on a case, not here harassing Governor Fallow – no matter how much he may deserve it," he admitted. "Laura, go do your job. Get stuck into this case, let it clear your mind. Things aren't going to move fast with getting Amy to a new foster family, and I can't let you go and visit her. I know you're going to be good on the ground in Seattle, so don't see this as a punishment. I want my best agents on this one. Local PD have hit a dead end, and with two similar killings happening in two days, we have reason to believe there is a serious danger of a third."

"Alright," Laura sighed. Privately, she didn't believe a word of it. She knew he just wanted her out of the way so that she wouldn't cause a scandal – or get herself arrested for real. Nate was going to suffer for it, too. But there wasn't anything she could do about it now. If Rondelle wanted them on the case, they were on the case.

Laura hesitated before heading back inside. She looked through the window that she had leaned against, spotting Nolan sitting at their table. He was talking to the waitress now, and she seemed to be enjoying it a lot. She was smiling and laughing, her hand going to her hip to accentuate how small her waist was. Nolan said something to her, and the waitress giggled and put a hand to her mouth, her eyes wide in surprise.

Almost as if he had predicted something about her that she had not told him. Laura narrowed her eyes, watching closely.

She saw Nolan's eyes flick up and down the waitress's body, before he made another statement that seemed to surprise her all the more.

Laura paused, switching her attention to her own reflection in the glass. He had asked if she was in law enforcement, but he had not been any more specific than that. He hadn't said FBI. Looking at herself, Laura tried to see what a stranger would see. Her straight posture, the fact that she was used to being formal around other people. He probably would have noticed that she glanced around at everyone in the bar, assessing them. She had even tried to assess him. Could he have worked it out from her behavior, rather than getting some kind of psychic hint?

Almost unwillingly, Laura glanced down at her right hand. It had been a few years since she and Marcus had broken up, but the damage had all been on his side. He had been the one to walk out, taking Lacey with him. He had been the one to file for divorce. She had only agreed because she wanted to try and work out a way that they could both parent Lacey without it being acrimonious.

She had worn her wedding ring for longer than he had. Looking at her finger now, it was still possible to see a faint distortion in the outline of her finger. When you wore a ring every day for years, that was what happened. They hadn't exactly had a long and healthy marriage, but it had been long enough to leave an imprint. It was rapidly fading now, and soon enough her finger would look as though a ring had never sat on it, but today it was still visible.

Nolan was not psychic at all. He had simply done a cold read on her, like every fraud before him in the history of all psychics.

Laura sighed to herself and headed inside, her heart sinking even lower than it had already. Another bust. Another hope raised for nothing. Still, she at least owed him the courtesy of telling him that she was leaving, instead of just walking out.

"Hi," she said, sitting down. She'd interrupted the conversation, and the waitress shot daggers at her before scurrying off to serve someone else. "Sorry about that. It was work."

"Big case?" Nolan asked, sipping on his drink casually. Now she knew what he was doing, Laura could see that it wasn't exactly a huge assumption. She had had a call in the middle of the evening from work, and it had been more than a brief conversation. From that, it was easy to guess that something big was happening.

"Yes," Laura said. "Actually, I'm going to have to go. It was nice to meet you, but I'm afraid my job takes precedence. They need me."

"Oh," Nolan said looking as though she had slapped him in the face. His eyes widened, his mouth dropped open, and for a moment he looked much younger than he had previously. It was like she was seeing him stripped down, all of the vanity and arrogance taken down a notch. "You have to go right now? We were just getting started."

"Sorry," Laura said again, though she didn't exactly feel it. She was fairly sure, too, but it wouldn't take a psychic to know that she actually didn't care so much at all whether she continued this conversation or not. She just didn't have the time to be nice to this fraud. "Hazard of the job, I suppose."

"Wait a second," Nolan said, his tone more desperate now. He set down his drink, obviously getting more serious – but it was too little, too late. Laura had already seen enough. "Just – please? I wanted to prove what I can do. Will you just let me demonstrate for you?"

Laura shook her head, standing up and gathering herself to leave. "I'm sorry, Nolan," she said. He was desperate, she could see that, but she had a job to do. A job that was more important than the feelings of a stranger. She'd had the feeling he was just another poser like the rest of them, and if he was, he didn't deserve her sympathy. Still, she didn't want to shut him down completely – the small voice in the back of her mind still wondered whether there was a chance that he was telling the truth. "Have a nice evening. You looked like you were making a new friend – don't let me stop you."

She turned and left, not giving him a backwards glance. She had a flight to prepare for, and a few hours' sleep to snatch – before she had to face Nate again and all of the questions she had been avoiding since they got back from their last case.

CHAPTER TEN

Laura looked up as Nate's familiar figure approached. She didn't need to have a vision of his presence to sense him. They had worked together for enough years now that she had a feeling for when he was in the room, a familiarity that felt comfortable and warm. He cut across the crowd of anonymous travelers easily, standing out head and shoulders above most of them.

Quite literally so, because at six-two and with a well-built frame, Nathaniel Lavoie was not someone you could miss. His dark skin also made him stand out in the lounge, which was mostly full of white businessmen in their fifties getting ready for a commute. Washington, D.C., to Seattle, Washington, was apparently quite a popular route.

"You awake yet?" he said, by way of greeting.

Laura looked sideways, out of the wide windows that gave a view of the runway. The sky was a very pale, thin blue, almost white. The sun had only just risen, and everything seemed far too bright and far too bleary inside the airport.

"Not completely," she said. "You?"

Nate grinned. "Not at all," he said, sitting down beside her. He had a small travel case which he laid down between his legs, shifting his ankles to keep a grip on it. Laura's own bag was already positioned similarly, a deliberately cautious placement to prevent their things from being tampered with. "I've got the briefing documents."

"Thank you," Laura said, infusing it with true gratefulness. She hadn't relished the idea of heading over to the J. Edgar Hoover Building early this morning to pick them up before going to the airport, so when Nate had volunteered over text last night, she'd been only too happy to accept.

"I hear you had a busy day yesterday, anyway," Nate said. His tone was casual, but Laura could tell he wanted to know everything. She couldn't blame him. It was probably big news around the whole building, not just with her partner.

But it was still far too early to talk about that, and still far too raw. Even the comfort of Nate's familiar presence was not enough, could not be enough, to ease her worries about Amy and the anger she still felt towards Governor Fallow.

"I've had a busy week," Laura replied. "We both have. Did you even manage to rest, since the last case?"

Nate shook his head. "Not really," he said. "But that's the job, I guess. Murderers don't stop murdering just because we're tired."

Another wave of gratitude swept through Laura. Nate must have known, or at least suspected, that their deployment so soon was as a direct result of her actions. A way to get them out of the state – way across the other side of the country – and out of trouble. But still, he didn't complain or blame her.

"No, they don't," Laura sighed. "Speaking of..."

"Right," Nate said. He glanced around the small lounge; everyone around them was busy with their own things, and most of them were typing on laptops. Even so, he made sure that no one was in a position to see the files. With their backs against a wall and no one sitting to either side of them, it seemed safe enough, and he nodded at Laura before pulling out the familiar brown folder and opening it to the first page. "Do the honors?"

Laura smiled and nodded in agreement. She did what he had done, glancing around to check that no one would be listening in, either, before starting to read the files' information in a low voice. "We're dealing with two murders, so far."

"Don't say 'so far'," Nate grimaced. "It makes it sound like there are going to be more."

Laura suppressed a smile. "Both victims are female, and both are acting coaches. It's believed that there could be a link between them, which seems obvious – both being in the same profession."

"Acting coaches," Nate mused. "You ever thought about acting?"

Laura laughed. "No, never. What about you?" she said. She tried to imagine what that would be like for someone like her: seeing visions of bad reviews before they happened, learning one of her fellow actors was going to die right in the middle of a scene when she needed to remember her lines. The thought made her shift subtly away from Nate.

She hadn't felt it, yet: the darkness that surrounded him. She'd been careful to avoid contact with him as much as possible since she first sensed it, before the last case. It was the shadow of death, an indescribable sensation that she only knew meant his death was some way down the line. She'd had no visions yet to shed any light on it, no idea of what might cause it, no idea of how to prevent it.

Except for the fact that, when she'd thought about telling him the truth about her ability, it had seemed to fade. And when she changed her mind, it came back. It was just one more thing that Laura had to try and wrestle with during all of this. A whirlwind of a case in which her visions had come thick and fast and left her with almost crippling headaches: Amy, her own daughter, the struggle not to pick up a bottle when everything felt so hard, Nate's death. And now another case, right back in at the deep end without any time to breathe.

If she had time to breathe, maybe she could think about it. Work out what to do. How to tell him, if she was going to tell him at all. But she hadn't had the time, not really, to fully process it and everything it could mean.

And so she simply shifted away from him, so that there was no chance for them to accidentally brush up against one another and send that sickening darkness crashing over her again like a wave.

"I think I would make a great leading man!" Nate was saying, leaning back from her a little to give himself room to flex his guns as though he was posing for a photoshoot. "Don't you think?"

"Yes, Nate," Laura deadpanned, in a tone that made it very clear she was only indulging him.

He laughed and shook his head. "Alright. What do we have on them so far?"

"Looks like the M.O. is the same on both," Laura said, flipping back and forward between files. "Stab wounds to the heart, a couple of them in both. The knife was left in place, but initial analysis suggests that the killer was wearing gloves – there are no fingerprints on the handle."

"Very dramatic," Nate grunted.

"The first one was killed in an alleyway near her apartment, and the second was killed inside her own car." Laura shuddered a little, thinking of the horror of finding out you were no longer safe even inside your own vehicle. "It looks like the killer approached both of them from behind, pulled them against him or the back of the seat, and then plunged his knife down into their chests – as if stabbing himself, almost."

"How long was the knife?" Nate asked.

Laura shuffled through the pages. "It looks like it was long enough to reach the heart, but not to penetrate through the back of the body."

"So, he would have avoided getting most of the blood spatter on himself," Nate mused. "And he would have been able to restrain them

42

with the same motion that killed them – his arms going around their arms. Smart."

"Hm." Laura flicked through the pages to the end. "Looks like the local PD have established that there's no known link between the two women, except that they may have been aware of each other in a professional capacity. No circle of friends, no shared plays or short films, or anything like that."

"Attention: all passengers from the five-fifty flight to Seattle, Washington, should begin boarding now," the speaker above their heads chimed. "Please head to Gate C with your boarding pass at the ready."

Laura folded the file back together and handed it to Nate. "That's our call," she said.

Nate stuffed it quickly into his carry-on case, nodding. "After you. Let's hope it's a quick flight. I know I said I didn't want to tempt fate, but… two acting coaches in a row makes it feel like there might be a third acting coach coming soon."

Though she hadn't had any hint of a vision just yet, Laura had to agree.

**

Laura settled into her seat, trying to get comfortable. The flight was long enough that she could try to catch a bit more sleep. She'd had an early awakening in order to get to the airport in time for the flight, and Nate must have been even more tired with his diversion.

"Laura," Nate said, and there was a funny tone to his voice that made Laura stiffen up. It didn't sound good. It sounded awkward and tense, the way things were every time he brought up the fact that he thought she was hiding something. "Do you want to tell me about what happened, yesterday?"

Laura swallowed, looking out of the window. The plane had levelled out past the uncomfortable ear-popping stage, and with the cloudy weather, all she could see below was white. "I went to check up on Amy and I heard her father shouting. The housekeeper let me in – she was clearly afraid, so I rushed upstairs and saw him. He was about to beat her. I couldn't just leave her there, so I brought her to Rondelle."

"Wait, back up a little," Nate said. "Why did you go and check on Amy? You didn't say anything about this to me."

43

"I just had a… a gut feeling," Laura said.

"A gut feeling?"

Laura dared to glance at Nate. He was looking at her with a raised eyebrow, an almost contemptuous expression. Only almost, because she knew it came from a place of respect. A respect he wanted to be mutual, rather than having her lie to him and expect him to buy it.

"It was just a hunch," Laura said, looking down at her hands. "You wouldn't have picked up on it. I'm a mother. I have a feeling for when a little girl isn't saying something. I knew something was off."

Nate made an offended noise deep in his throat. "Assuming that's even true," he said. "How did you get away with just walking out of there? Jones told me the whole state police was marching into Rondelle's office to look for you, and you had to have the Director intervene."

Laura closed her eyes silently. Jones. She should have known he would gossip. "I found video footage of the abuse on Amy's cell phone," she said. "There wasn't a whole lot the Governor could say to that. Amy's being taken into foster care, and if he tries to get her back, there will be hell to pay."

"A video?" Nate repeated incredulously. "Amy told you she'd filmed it? What, on purpose?"

"No, no," Laura sighed. The idea of a six-year-old collecting evidence of a crime was, she agreed, a bit of a far-fetched story. "She filmed it by accident. The phone was on when he went for her. Neither of them knew it was even being recorded."

"Well, then…" Nate paused, as if trying to answer his own question but finding no way to do so. "How did you know it was there?"

Laura's eyes snapped to his. He was looking at her not with confusion or suspicion, but with a kind of knowing expression on his face.

He knew that she was lying, that she was covering something up. Of course, he did. They had been partners for three years, and they'd become good friends in that time. Of course, he could tell when she was just trying to fob him off.

"I just looked on her phone," Laura said, looking away from him. "It was luck, that's all. I was kind of surprised a six-year-old had a phone in the first place. Marcus won't let Lacey get one, and I think he's right, even though it would make it easier for me to call her."

Nate regarded her silently for a moment as Laura grabbed the in-flight magazine, something to look at so that she could pretend she was busy and get out of the conversation. A moment later, his hand landed on her arm, making her jump.

"You don't want to tell me. Fine," he said, his voice calm and not at all unkind. "But I have to know what's going on, sooner or later."

Laura wasn't paying much attention to his words, even though she heard them on some level.

She couldn't pay attention. Because as soon as his skin came into contact with her skin, the feeling flooded over her again: the dark shroud that came with the shadow of death. It was strong, swirling around her with an almost physical presence, pressing in on all sides. Laura could barely breathe. She felt as though if she had sucked in air, she would also have consumed some of the shadow, drawing death into herself.

Nate let go, and the sensation flooded away, leaving Laura to turn and stare out of the window so he wouldn't see the tears in her eyes.

The sense of death was still only a sense, not a vision. The shadow had not yet solidified into anything concrete. It had when she had foreseen her father's death; she had eventually begun to see images of him flashing through her head, dying in a hospital, in a cancer wing. So far, though, she had no hints of what might happen to Nate, of why the feeling of death was so strong around him.

Maybe a vision would never come, and that was what scared her. If she couldn't see what was going to happen, she wouldn't be able to save him.

Laura couldn't help but wonder. Was it really possible that her decision to tell him – or not tell him – about her ability would change things? Would it save his life?

If she had proof, if she knew for sure, then she would do it, she knew. She would tell him everything in a heartbeat to save his life, even if it meant he would turn away from her.

But if he turned away from her because of what she could do – and then he died anyway – what kind of a waste would that be? For him to die hating or fearing her, when she might otherwise have been able to save him?

Laura looked for answers through her window, but she saw only blank white space.

She closed her eyes, tucking her head against the side of the seat. She needed to sleep. When they landed in Seattle, they needed to hit the ground running – and she couldn't let a murderer get away to kill again just because she was distracted.

CHAPTER ELEVEN

It was just past ten in the morning as Laura stretched her arms over her head and blinked in the sun, scanning the front of SeaTac Airport with a squint in her eyes. Fall was in the air, but it was still warm and sunny. They had arrived to no fanfare, no escort, and no local police officer wielding a badly-spelled sign with their names on it.

"Do you think they've remembered we're here?" she asked Nate, her words coming out with a bit more of a snap than she intended. A nap seemed to have made him much more calm and malleable. It had made her touchy.

"I'd say so," Nate said, and when she looked up to catch his grin, he nodded off to the side.

Laura turned to see a harassed-looking policeman in uniform, hurrying across the tarmac towards them. He wore the insignia of a Captain, and there was another officer – a Sergeant, as far as Laura could see – trailing behind him.

"Special Agents?" he panted, clearly having clocked them from far enough away.

"Yes," Laura said. "Agent Laura Frost. This is my partner, Agent Nathaniel Lavoie."

"Nate, please," Nate said, reaching his hand out for the man to shake.

"Captain Mills," he replied, not offering a first name. He was in his late forties, Laura guessed, with close-cropped hair that was such a pale blond it would have been hard to pick out any white. He was of average height and an average build, perhaps gaining a little weight since making Captain. That was common enough, given the added paperwork and reduced legwork that came with the job. "This is Sergeant Thornton."

Laura smiled and leaned over to shake both of their hands. Sergeant Thornton was much younger – in her late twenties, Laura would have estimated. She was Black and pretty, slim and slight, with sleek hair tied into a ponytail under her hat. Laura's eyes drifted, without her permission, over to Nate. He smiled just the same way she had done, shaking Thornton's hand.

Why was it that Laura felt a spike of jealousy as she wondered whether Nate found Thornton attractive? And why was that spike followed up by a flare of worry: that somehow, this woman would lead Nate to his death?

Well, the last part wasn't exactly unusual. She was thinking that about every person and everything that came their way, lately. Which was why she also still felt extremely guilty about forcing him to come out on yet another case with her, right after the last one had wrapped up.

"We're happy to hit the ground running, if that's alright with you," Laura said. "We had a chance for a bit of rest on the plane, and we can check into whatever motel we have booked later."

"Good thinking," Captain Mills said, straightening up slightly. Laura got the idea that she'd impressed him. "We can take you directly to the latest crime scene, if that suits you. Actually, that's why we're a little late – we just came from there. We're wrapping up our forensics tests in situ, and should be able to remove the car later today."

Laura nodded and gestured for him to lead them back towards the car as they spoke. Nate's bag scraped across the sidewalk, the wheels raising a cacophony, as they walked. "This is the car in the parking lot of the community center?"

"Yes, that's right," Captain Mills nodded. He had a rapid walk, but the pace was certainly calmer than when he had been rushing to greet them. "The victim was found in the driver's seat. We don't know much about her yet – the crime was discovered last night, and we've been sending out detectives to interview the people who were at the community center yesterday throughout this morning."

Laura nodded as she listened. They reached a squad car which was parked in a temporary waiting spot, with an irate-looking taxi driver stopped right behind it and clearly waiting for the place. He said nothing, though Laura guessed he was biting his tongue hard because of the uniforms. "Have you discovered anything about the victim? All we had was the name – Suzanna Brice – and that she was a thirty-two-year-old acting coach."

"Nothing much more than that," Captain Mills confirmed. "We did as much admin work as we could overnight while any potential witnesses or interviewees were asleep, aside from her family. As far as we can tell from public records, she never acted with the first victim or taught in the same area."

Nate hefted his bag into the back of the car before taking Laura's from her hands and putting it inside as well. She wanted to protest that she was strong enough to lift her own bag, but it wasn't as though Nate had done any harm. In fact, he'd been helpful. She closed her mouth and got into the back of the car, which was always an odd feeling: an FBI agent in the back of a police car as though she'd been arrested.

Given recent events, it wasn't exactly a comfortable thought.

"What has her family told you?" Nate asked, settling himself in the seat and doing up his seatbelt.

"Not much," Captain Mills said from the front passenger seat, bending around to look at them as Thornton drove. "She was unmarried, and her parents have both passed away. She does have an older sister, however. We've spoken to her last night, but she was understandably inconsolable."

"Then we go to her next," Laura said.

"Agreed," Nate said. "We'll get onto the first victim afterwards, but I take it from the briefing notes that you don't have much to go on with her yet, either?"

"No, sadly," Mills sighed. "She did have a boyfriend, but we've spoken to him and he does have an alibi, which we've been able to check out. Her family all live in different states, but we've had liaison officers from different police forces talking to them and there doesn't seem to be much light they can shed. They didn't spend too much time together over recent years."

"Got it," Laura nodded. "Not a lot of clues to go on at all. Which is why you need us."

Captain Mills looked just a tiny bit affronted at the suggestion, but he had to nod. "We're obviously quite concerned that we're now looking at a pattern. Two female acting coaches – it could be that they just so happened to make the wrong person very angry, and now it's over. But it could be the start of something bigger, and we want to nip that in the bud."

Laura exchanged a glance with Nate. It was exactly what they had said.

They had been driving along a highway, making good speed, but now Sergeant Thornton steered them off at an exit and out into a more residential area. Laura looked around quickly, trying to get her bearings: the buildings were low and long, separated by long stretches of empty space between familiar fast-food chains, auto repair shops, and car dealerships. They were still far from central Seattle, but when the community center came into view, Laura realized they were already at their first scene.

They got out of the car without a word when Thornton pulled up; they didn't need to discuss where to go. The place where Suzanna Brice had been killed was obvious enough. White-suited forensics specialists were still swarming all over it, and the whole car park had been fenced off to preserve any potential evidence the killer might have left. Laura approved of that, at least. The worst thing, sometimes, was turning up in some rural area and finding that the local police had no idea how to deal with a crime on this scale. In Seattle, she guessed they were more used to murder.

"The body has been removed already?" Laura asked, getting a glimpse of the car between passing people.

"Yes, in the early hours of the night," Mills replied. There were temporary floodlights set up in a square around the car; Laura figured they must have been able to create enough light for a full examination before moving Suzanna. "She's with the coroner now. The cause of death was pretty obvious, though. The knife wounds to the heart were very deep – no chance she could have survived that, and the initial report was that there was enough blood on the body to suggest this was the fatal wound."

Laura stepped close enough to look inside the car and then stopped, peering forward instead of trying to get inside. Even though the forensics team was apparently almost done, she didn't want to be the one to disturb or contaminate any evidence. From the sound of things, there wasn't much of it in the first place.

The car was innocuous enough, which was somehow jarring. It was a modern model, somewhat new but not very expensive. The exterior was a bright grass green, an unusual but cheerful color. Contrasted against the dark red blood that had soaked into the driver's seat and sprayed across both the windshield and the windows in arcs following the knife, it was a grim juxtaposition.

"No hair or fibers found in the back seat?" Laura asked.

"Nothing yet," Mills replied. "We're having the seats and footwells removed and brought in for closer examination in the lab, once we can move the whole thing to the forensics garage."

Laura nodded at this. They clearly knew what they were doing. Which was almost a shame, because it was so much easier to clean up the investigation and get a result when the cops on the ground were floundering.

"Do we have any camera footage from around here?" Nate asked, from the other side of the car. Mills strolled a couple of paces in his direction to answer, and Laura took advantage of the moment to step forward.

"No, unfortunately nothing that covers the car," Mills said. "There would have been one by the entrance, but apparently it hasn't worked for a couple of years. The community center has never quite had the funds to get it fixed or replaced, so they say. I should think they consider it more of a priority now."

Only half-listening to him, Laura reached out delicately and touched just the very edge of the car door with her fingertips. She had chosen a spot that she hoped had the least potential for ruining any evidence, but she needed to make that contact. She needed to see if she could trigger a vision.

Nothing.

Laura sighed, stepping back and quickly hiding the movement of her hand. Unless anyone had been looking directly at her, they wouldn't have known she had touched it. It had been useless, anyway. All she felt here was death, and that wasn't from her psychic ability. That was just soaked into the very air, the grim mood that surrounded the car.

"We should start by looking into their students," Laura said. "Have you been able to cross-reference their class lists?"

"I'm afraid not," Mills said. "That was one of our setbacks this morning. We have a full list of students for Lucile Maddison, the first victim. But Suzanna Brice's class was not quite as formal. Students didn't have to sign up ahead of time and could simply turn up when they liked, paying on the day. The manager of the center told us this morning that they don't keep any records in the center, but that Suzanna herself might have done so."

"Then we'd better go and visit her home," Laura said. "And that sister of hers."

"You're in luck," Captain Mills said. "They're both at the same place. Suzanna lived with her sister."

"Then we'd better not waste any time," Laura said, glancing at Nate and seeing that he was also done with the crime scene. "Let's get over there now and see if she can provide us with the name of a suspect."

CHAPTER TWELVE

Laura knocked on the door and then stepped back patiently, putting herself back in line with Nate. They both faced the house with the expectant and yet sympathetic look of law enforcement officers fully aware they were about to speaking to a grieving woman.

It wasn't the sister who opened the door, however. It was a police officer, one of Mills', who nodded politely and allowed them inside. Mills and Thornton trailed behind them but hung back. As Laura followed Nate through the door into a sitting room sparsely decorated with mismatched furniture, they remained in the hall, talking in low voices together.

"Miss Brice?" Laura said, her gaze focusing on the woman who was seated on the sofa in the center of the room. She was pale faced, her eyes a contrast in red. She was holding a crushed-up tissue in one hand and staring into space, as if she was dazed.

"Oh, yes," she replied, seeming to come back to herself. "Yes. Please, call me Vicky."

"Vicky," Laura said, with a reassuring smile. "My name is Agent Laura Frost."

"I'm Agent Nate Lavoie," Nate put in, holding out a hand to gesture to an armchair. "Do you mind if we sit down and ask you some questions about your sister?"

"Please," Vicky said distractedly. She was gaunt, Laura thought as she sat down at the other end of the sofa, and older than the sister that Laura had seen in file photographs. Perhaps in her late thirties. She found her eyes drifting to the thin, long-fingered hands that clutched at the tissue, but could see no ring.

That was as good a place as any to start.

"We understand that you and your sister lived together, Vicky?" Laura said, hoping this statement would prompt the outpouring of an explanation.

"Yes, we've lived together for a couple of years now," Vicky said, sniffing. "Actually, we grew up here. When our parents died, we both inherited half the house, and Suzie carried on living here. I came back after my divorce."

52

Laura nodded. That explained the mismatched furniture; mental strain could obviously be attributed to the gaunt look Vicky had, like she'd had trouble keeping or putting on weight. "Did you get on well?" she asked.

Vicky gave a half-smile. It told of bitter pain, of a lifetime of love and good memories, of knowing someone so intimately you weren't afraid to recognize their flaws. "We're sisters," she said. "Sometimes yes, sometimes no. A lot better the past year, once we'd got over all the little irritations of living together again."

Nate shifted slightly, raising his voice. "What can you tell us about your sister, Vicky? What was Suzie like?"

Vicky bit her lip, smiling through tears. "She was like the sun," she said, breaking off to dab the tissue against her eyes. "She was so bright and fun and friendly. She got on well with everyone. She was always convinced she was going to be a star; I think we all were, really, but it just never quite happened for her."

"She had dreams of being a big actress?" Laura prompted.

"Oh, yes. She even moved to Hollywood, you know? To L.A. For a while, anyway. But she couldn't cut it. She was living on Mom and Dad's handouts, working as a waitress, never quite managing to get the audition. When they died, I think that was a wake-up call for her. She came back and started teaching, instead."

"How long ago was that?" Nate asked. He pulled a notebook out of his jacket pocket, making rapid notes.

"About five years, or so," Vicky said, shrugging slightly. "She took to it like a duck to water, I think. Teaching. It turned out that was her real calling. She was such a people person."

Laura glanced at Nate; he was scribbling something down, so she took the initiative of asking the next question. "Do you know if she kept a list of her students at all?"

"Oh, God," Vicky said, shaking her head. It was more of a helpless gesture than a denial. "Suzie was never into that kind of organizational stuff. She hated making people stick to schedules and promises, said it made them quit too early. But if she did have a list, I guess it would be on her laptop."

"Could we take a look at that laptop?" Laura asked, seizing onto this very real possibility of a lead.

"Yes, it's… oh, it's over there somewhere, I think," Vicky said, gesturing vaguely behind Laura.

53

Laura turned, shifting in her seat and then getting up to examine a side table. It was littered with all kinds of things – unopened mail, newspapers from a few days ago, takeout menus. But there was the silver edge of something poking out, and Laura carefully lifted everything to reveal a slim laptop covered in stickers bearing the logo of the community center.

"Was there anything notable you can think of in the last days, weeks, or even months?" Nate asked. "Anything strange? A change in Suzie's mood or behavior? Someone suspicious that she might have told you about?"

"Nothing like that," Vicky said, shaking her head as Laura sat back down beside her. She opened the lid of the laptop, and it turned on; she was glad it still had battery life. "I've been racking my brains all night, I really have. I just can't think of anything."

Laura's relief at seeing the machine turn on was thwarted by the sight of a login screen. A smiling face in the center of it – Suzanna's, she recognized – proved that it was her laptop, but the password box was ominously empty.

"Do you know the password?" Laura asked, holding the screen so that Vicky could see it. She reached out to pull it closer to her, belying her short-sightedness, and their hands brushed as she did so. Laura felt a small pulse in her temple, a jolt of pain that was hardly big enough to be registered, but it was there.

"No, sorry," Vicky said, but Laura could already feel herself fading

–

She was watching Vicky on a hillside somewhere, green scrub around her feet. She had a little more weight on her bones, her hair longer and better cut. There was color back in her cheeks. She was clutching a large vase against her chest.

Not a vase – an urn.

"Alright, sister," she said out loud, though Laura could see no one else around in the vision. "I know this place meant so much to you. I hope you'll be happy here, up in the hills. Watching it all go on below you."

She opened the lid of the urn and then turned, assessing the wind. Her hair blew gently into her face as she lined herself up in the right direction and then tipped the urn, letting ash flow out into the breeze to scatter across the hillside.

"There you go," Vicky said, her voice brittle but still bright. "I hope you appreciate this, you silly, wonderful woman. I could get

arrested if they come out here in time to catch me. I'd better get off and leave you to it."

She turned, and that was when Laura saw it spread out below her, unfamiliar from this angle but still recognizable. The tops of huge white letters propped up on metal stilts.

The Hollywood sign.

Laura blinked as the vision left her. She moved the laptop back to her own lap, a motion started before the vision took over and easily completed when it disappeared. Neither of them would have noticed anything more than perhaps a slow blink as she navigated the vision.

She looked down at the keyboard. It was old and worn, a shiny spot right in the center of the space bar where a couple of thumbs no doubt often rested. But there were other keys worn down, too. All of the vowels had a good amount of shine on them, which was normal enough. But for the 'H' key, and the 'D', and especially the 'W' – that was much more unusual.

She typed in 'Hollywood' to the password bar, and the screen cleared.

"I'm in," she said, surprising even herself.

"How did you get that?" Vicky asked, her voice holding utter astonishment and disbelief.

"It's what you just told me," Laura said quickly. "I looked at which keys showed the most wear and tear and put two and two together. Hollywood. The password was her favorite place."

She glanced up unwillingly, and saw Nate looking right at her. Frowning.

"That was a lucky guess," Vicky exclaimed.

"Very lucky," Laura agreed, bending her head back to the screen. There were a number of documents saved to the desktop, placed in what looked like a haphazard order. One of them was a spreadsheet named 'CC' and Laura tilted her head in consideration.

CC for Community Center?

"Let's take a look at this," she said, double clicking the file to open it. If it wasn't easy to find, they could bring it back to the precinct, ask the Captain to put one of his tech experts on it – if he had one – and then…

The file loaded up, and Laura blinked. It was a list of names. It looked exactly like she would expect a class roster to look.

Across the top there were lists of dates, consecutively numbered. Where each column and row intersected, some were filled with green squares and others left blank. An attendance record?

"Which days of the week did Suzanna teach?" Laura asked, scanning the headers and working out the most recent dates.

"Wednesday nights and Saturdays," Vicky said promptly.

Laura nodded. "Okay. We've got the class list. Have you got a printer here we can use?"

"Yes, of course," Vicky said. She turned to start the printout going, and Laura looked at Nate and the Captain. She didn't want to wait until they were all the way back at the station.

"Captain Mills, you have the list from Lucile?"

"Yes, I can access it remotely," he said, tapping the pocket where Laura guessed he was storing his cell phone.

"Let's get back to the station," she suggested, prompting the Captain to nod and make his way outside.

"Here," Vicky said, pointing to the printer that was whirring to life in the back of the room. "There's two pages."

"Thank you very much," Laura said, moving to grab them as the printer spat them out. "We'll be in touch with updates soon. For now, I'm afraid we have to get going."

"Of course, of course," Vicky nodded. "Don't worry about me. Please – bring my sister's killer to justice."

Laura nodded gravely back, before turning to rush out of the building with Nate close on her heels. They both piled into the back of the car again, waiting for Captain Mills to bring up the list of Lucile Maddison's students.

"Got it," he announced, turning it to show them the screen.

"This isn't in any kind of order," Laura said, scanning the rows of the printout. "Can you sort yours alphabetically?"

"Yes," Mills said, tapping on the screen a few times. "Do you want me to send this to you?"

"We'll need it later, yes, but for now I need you to check each name as I call it out," Laura said. "Do you have a Richard Loday?"

"... No," Captain Mills said, his brow furrowed as he used his index finger to scroll up and down the screen.

"Jenny Pho?" Laura asked, as Nate gathered the second page of the printout ready to join in.

"Nothing on that one," the Captain said. Laura had the uncomfortable feeling this was going to take a while.

"Caleb Rowntree," Laura read again, going back to the entry she had been marking with a finger. The only name which was the same on both.

"We need to find out who he is, and where he is right now."

"Can we give you a ride to a car rental?" Mills asked, checking his watch. "I've got another case to check in on, and I need Sergeant Thornton with me."

"Excellent idea," Laura said, as Thornton silently glanced in her mirrors and switched lanes to take them in a different direction. It would be good to get the chance to drive around on their own, without an escort. Being with the Captain all the time would get old, fast, and would mean potential clashes in their investigation style further down the line.

Right now, Laura just wanted to focus on the case. And that meant tracking down and talking to Caleb Rowntree – and hoping that he was the killer, so she could end all of this and get back home to ensure things were going smoothly with Amy.

CHAPTER THIRTEEN

Laura got behind the wheel of the car, assuming the driving detail at least for the first leg of their trip. Nate did not argue with her, but as he settled into the passenger seat, she could sense that he was unsettled. She could almost count in her head the seconds it would take for him to take a breath and ask her what was on her mind.

Three, two...

"Laura," he said, shifting in his seat uncomfortably. "About the laptop."

Laura bit her lip, concentrating on following the GPS so that she could find her way to the place they had been told they could find Caleb Rowntree. He was supposedly at home right now, and the quicker they got there, the quicker they could interrogate him. The quicker, therefore, they could get home again once they had proven he was the murderer. She said nothing, half wishing that Nate would just give up and leave the sentence dangling in the air alone, and half knowing that he would continue even if she did not reply.

"It's just," he said. "How did you know the password?"

"I told you," Laura said, using the excuse of checking her mirrors and switching lanes as a distraction. "I just got lucky. She said that Hollywood was the most important thing in her sister's life, and some unusual keys on the keyboard had worn down, so it made sense."

"You can see why I need to ask," Nate said. His tone was fair yet pleading. He wanted her to just tell him the truth. He wanted her to stop hiding away. She knew that was what he wanted, was what he had wanted for a long time. But it didn't mean that she could just give in as easily as all that. "It's just one more thing, isn't it? You always know how to do these things. Things that no one else ever thinks of."

"Well, maybe I'm just a better agent then the other people you're comparing me to," Laura said dismissively, regretting it as soon as the words had come out of her mouth. It wasn't fair. Not only did it make the people they worked with seemed like idiots, but it also reflected badly on Nate himself, who of course had had no chance of guessing the password either. And it wasn't just that she was a better agent. She really did have help. She just couldn't admit that right now.

58

"You're a good agent, Laura," Nate said, his tone just a touch reproving. "But so am I."

Laura felt herself sagging slightly over the steering wheel. He never pushed her too far, never demanded the truth. It was always gentle like this, a push from a friend. If he had screamed and shouted at her, it might have been easier. But instead, he carried on being nice, being kind, giving her chance after chance. He didn't deserve to be kept in the dark. She should tell him.

She just had to get up the nerve.

She didn't think she could get up the nerve.

He was the one person in her life she could really lean on, the one person she could trust with anything. Maybe because of that more than anything else, she couldn't bear to risk him thinking she was crazy. Or worse – being afraid of her. On top of that, being her partner meant that he could also get her fired. Laura couldn't lose her job and Nate at the same time. Especially not when those things combined would probably mean losing Lacey for good as well.

Laura opened her mouth to answer, not even sure quite what she was going to say but found herself cut off by the phone ringing in her pocket. She fished around for it with one hand, keeping the other on the steering wheel, and then thrust it out towards Nate. "Who is it?" she asked.

Nate took it and looked at the screen, but then hesitated. "It says Marcus," he said.

Laura groaned. This was the last thing she needed right now. Her ex-husband trying to... what? Complain at her over the phone? Tell her off for something else she hadn't realized she had done? Remind her yet again that she couldn't see her own daughter?

But then again, there is always the risk that he was calling about Lacey. That Lacey was in trouble, in the hospital or worse. Laura could never miss one of his calls. She pulled over quickly to the side of the road, taking advantage of an emergency breakdown lane. She knew she wasn't supposed to stay parked up there for long, but at the end of the day, they were FBI agents. If they could take advantage of getting away with things that law enforcement would fine or even charge others for, in order to help out their families, they might as well.

"Hello," Laura said answering the phone as quickly as she could before Marcus gave up and stopped trying to call.

"Hi, Mommy," the voice came down the line.

59

Laura clamped her hand over her mouth immediately, holding back a cry of surprise and joy and pain. It wasn't Marcus on the other end of the line at all.

It was Lacey.

"Hello, sweetheart," Laura said, just managing to keep her voice in check. Even so, to her own ears it sounded high pitched and strained. "Are you using Daddy's phone?"

"Yeah," Lacey said, her sweet and innocent young voice reminding Laura of Amy. Both little girls had so much in common, from their age to their looks to the fact that Laura was supposed to be there for them. But Lacey was a little bit younger, and when Laura heard her voice, it pinched in her chest that much harder. "Daddy said I could call you for a few minutes."

"Oh, well, that was nice of Daddy," Laura said trying to keep herself steady. Beside her, Nate was shifting uncomfortably, looking like he wanted to get out of the car. With traffic rushing by them at all times, it wasn't a sensible option. But Laura saw and was grateful for his attempt to respect her privacy, even if he couldn't actually carry it out.

"Mommy, why are you on vacation for so long?" Lacey asked. She sounded half-distracted. Laura pictured her little girl playing with her toys while she talked, and that mental image together with Lacey's question forced her to bite her tongue to stifle a sob.

On vacation. That must have been what Marcus had told her. That Mommy was on vacation for... for months. That's how long it had been. Months.

"You know that Mommy's job is stopping bad guys, don't you?" Laura said, keeping her voice gentle. She wouldn't go against what Marcus had said, but she wanted Lacey to know that she wasn't just ignoring her daughter to lay in the sun.

"Yeah," Lacey replied. "You stop them from doing bad stuff."

"That's right," Laura said. She wiped a hand across her eyes, fighting the urge to sniff and give herself away. "And Mommy's been stopping some bad guys all across America. There was another little girl who needed saving, too."

"Did something bad happen to her?" Lacey asked, her voice piquing in concern.

"Yes, darling, but I stopped it from happening anymore," Laura said. She didn't want to scare Lacey. At her age, the question of

60

whether another little girl was safe was also, in some ways, a question about whether she herself was safe. "Now there's no need to worry."

"Does that mean you're coming home?" Lacey asked, and her voice was so full of hope that Laura had to dig her fingernails into her palm to keep from making a noise and steady her voice.

"Soon, I hope, sweetheart," Laura said. "I just have to stop one more bad guy, okay? And I promise I'll see you soon."

Soon. It was such a vague concept. She couldn't commit to anything. Not when she didn't know what Marcus was thinking. But he was letting her have this call. Surely, that meant he was softening? Changing his mind?

"That would be nice, Mommy," Lacey said, clacking something together on the other end of the line. "And we can all have tea."

Laura's eyes brimmed with tears as she pictured Lacey playing tea party with her dolls and toys. "Yes, sweetie, we'll have a lovely tea party and invite everyone," she said, playing along.

"Alright, that's enough now." Laura heard Marcus's voice through the phone with a wrench. He was far away, but getting closer, and she could hear him perfectly. "Say goodbye to Mommy."

"Bye, Mommy," Lacey said, cheerfully enough.

"No, wait!" Laura said. "Lacey – I love you – just…"

"I'm hanging up, Laura." That was Marcus, much closer – the phone must have been against his ear now, in his hand –

"No, please, Marcus!" Laura cried out – but it was no use. He'd already hung up, the line going dead. She knew she had to play by his rules, after everything that had happened. But still…

She stared at her phone for a moment, blinking back tears of pain and anguish, coupled with the relief and joy at finally hearing her daughter's voice.

"Hey," Nate said, his voice a deep rumble. "Do you think I'd better drive?"

***

Nate settled into the driver's seat, catching his breath. He'd had to wait for a gap in traffic and then spring out of the car and run around, making sure that neither he nor Laura would be at risk of getting hit by any passing vehicles. He'd seen enough footage of RTAs in his time to know that they weren't pretty when a pedestrian went up against a car.

61

He notched the seat back to give himself more room, glancing over at Laura as he started the engine back up and got the car moving. She was subdued now, quiet and staring at her own lap. At least she didn't look like she was about to burst into tears anymore.

Nate hated it when Laura looked like that. He had no idea what to do. No way to comfort her. They had been partners long enough that seeing her upset was enough to break his own heart. But she had never quite opened up to him. Even in the depths of her despair, when he knew that she must be missing her daughter terribly, she never allowed herself to really break down.

He didn't ask about Lacey or the phone call. He had heard enough of it, not that he had wanted to. It had been awkward to just sit there in the passenger seat and listen to her try to talk to her daughter, then desperately call for her ex-husband to give her a little bit longer. He wasn't able to help with that, either.

And even if he had been able to help, he was doubtful now that Laura would want to talk about it with him. She didn't seem to want to talk about anything anymore. She was clearly hiding things, something that he thought must be pretty big, and he had thought they were past this.

He took an exit from the highway and kept an eye on the GPS, following through twists and turns into a more residential area. Years they had worked together, so many cases, and yet she still didn't seem able to trust him fully. Why was that? What had he ever done to make her think he couldn't be trusted? He'd always tried to have her back, to let her know that she was safe when he was at her side. He always listened to anything she had to tell him. All of her strange whims, her hunches that always seemed to turn out correct. He had listened and respected them. Even when they didn't seem to make sense.

Even when other people told him that she was strange, maybe even that she was crazy, that she didn't know what she was talking about. He had backed her up every time, and the fact that they had always been proven right was just the icing on the cake. He would carry on backing her up, even if she wasn't so bizarrely good at this. That was what being partners meant.

And he liked to think they were more than partners. Over the years, they had become friends. So, why was it that there was still a wall up between Laura and him, on her side and not his? Why was it that she still didn't see him as someone that she could trust, talk to, confide in?

Why did she feel the need to keep on lying to him about what was going on?

Nate resolved to himself that it wasn't over. He wasn't going to stop asking her. The sooner he got to the bottom of this, the sooner they could carry on trusting each other again. But the more she lied to him, the harder it was for him to keep supporting her. To keep backing her up without question. Even believing, as he did, that partners should always have each other's back, it was starting to feel like everything was one-sided.

Laura needed to trust him, the way he trusted her.

He considered revisiting the question about the password, trying to ask her again. But it wasn't the time. The GPS showed that they were nearly at the suspect's apartment, and they couldn't be arguing in front of someone they were about to arrest. Nate simply followed the instructions on the screen and pulled up outside the apartment without saying a thing, glancing over to check that Laura had managed to compose herself again before turning off the engine.

"Do you want me to handle this on my own?" he asked, because it was the decent thing to do, and because trust issues or not, he wanted to make sure that Laura wasn't put into a compromising situation.

"No, I can do this," Laura said. She seemed to take a deep breath and wake herself up, as if she was emerging from a dream. Even though she had been on the verge of crying not long before, now she looked completely normal, as though nothing had happened. The professional mask had come down over her face, shuttering out any emotions. "I need the distraction."

Nate nodded once, accepting this at face value. He knew how it felt to have a situation at home that made you want to bury yourself in work. He could, at least, respect that.

They both got out of the car, and Nate led the way up to the apartment building. By coincidence, someone was just leaving as they approached, so they managed to enter the building without any trouble. They were just approaching the door to the apartment numbered for Caleb Rowntree when they heard it.

Angry shouting, coming from inside the door. Coming from inside the door that they were about to knock on. Nate exchanged a glance with Laura. Whatever was going on inside there, it did not sound good.

Then, there was the unmistakable sound of a smack, flesh hitting flesh. A woman cried out in shock and pain, and all of Nate's instincts kicked in. He tried the door, and finding it locked, reared back on one leg to prepare to kick it down.

CHAPTER FOURTEEN

Laura's attention snapped back to the door at the sound of a slap, shocking and unmistakable. As a member of law enforcement, it was something that they had both heard far too often. She barely had time to react before she realized that Nate was gearing up to kick down the door, and then he launched himself towards it with a powerful kick that splintered the frame.

It didn't quite give yet. He kicked one more time, grunting with effort as he did so. This time, the door came away from the hinge, the wood giving way under the force of his strength. "FBI! Get your hands up!" he yelled, drawing his gun.

Laura did the same, grabbing her gun out of its holster and raising it in the standard hold she had been taught in the Academy so many years ago. Braced in both hands, it remained steady as both she and Nate moved one by one into the apartment and down the hall. It was not difficult to trace the source of the noise they had heard - only a few rooms branched off from the corridor, and one of them was a large open space composed of the kitchen, dining room, and living room.

Two people, one man and one woman, were standing in the center of the floor with their hands up. They both looked absolutely terrified, and notably, neither of them looked as though they had been beaten recently.

There was no red mark on either of their faces, and neither of them seemed distressed beyond the fact that they were obviously scared.

"Keep your hands up," Laura said, keeping her voice steady. "We heard sounds of a disturbance."

"Oh my God," the woman said, shaking her head rapidly. A cloud of dark hair whipped around her face as she did so. "No, no, we were just rehearsing. We're actors. We were rehearsing, I swear!"

Actors. Laura took the time to exchange a glance with Nate. After all, they were looking for an acting student. The story checked out. Both of them relaxed at the same time, lowering their guns.

"No one here is hurt?" Nate asked, making sure, doing his due diligence. While they might have assumed that the woman was the one being hit, there was no law of nature that said it couldn't be the other way around.

"No, not at all," the man said. The man, who, Laura assumed, had to be Caleb Rowntree. "Honestly, we were just running lines."

Laura exchanged a glance with Nate. Both of them had to be thinking about the broken-down door out in the hall. It might have just been a trick of the light, but for a moment Laura thought she saw an embarrassed flush on Nate's cheeks.

"Caleb Rowntree?" Laura asked, addressing him directly. He nodded, his face ashy pale under dark hair swept back from his face. He had the beginnings of a beard, designer stubble carved expertly into an attractive roughness.

"And your name?" Nate asked, addressing the woman.

"Jenny Pho," she said, her voice trembling slightly.

Laura remembered her name from the list. They had her contact details already. They didn't need to speak to her now, not when they had a suspect in their sights – but she might be a useful witness later if she had noticed Rowntree acting suspicious.

"Please leave us to speak with Mr. Rowntree," Laura instructed her. "We may need to speak to you later, so if you're planning on leaving town, you'd better check in with the local police first. Got that?"

"Yes," Jenny nodded, her face still flooded with anxiety. "I'm not leaving town."

"Alright," Laura nodded, letting her know that she was dismissed.

Jenny grabbed a light jacket and bag from a chair with a quick glance at Caleb, who had stuffed his hands in his pockets and looked utterly flustered. Then she was gone, leaving with a light gasp out in the hall at the state of the door.

"Um," Caleb said. "Did you... kick my door down?"

"Yes," Nate said, with all the impressive intimidation that a six-two man with bulging muscles could bring to bear on the average civilian.

Caleb swallowed, but he wasn't put off. "Are you going to replace it?"

Laura swept forward to take control of the situation, gesturing towards the empty armchair. "Why don't you take a seat and answer a few questions?" she asked. "We'll get the door replaced for you." They weren't going to like it at HQ, but the odd bit of property damage often came with the territory. It was much better to break down a door and ask questions later than to leave someone in danger.

Caleb seemed to have recovered, at least slightly, from the shock of their entrance. He nodded and sat down. Laura noted that he was handsome, in rakish sort of way. He would probably do well in Hollywood. If he was any good as an actor, at least. "What is this about?" he asked. "Did someone call because they heard us running through the scene? I didn't think we were being that loud."

Laura and Nate took a sofa, both of them angling their bodies towards their suspect. "Mr. Rowntree," Laura began, taking out her notebook ready to record his answers.

"Caleb, please," he said, sending her a charming smile.

Laura shifted slightly and cleared her throat. "Caleb," she said, starting again. "Can you tell me where you were last night?"

"I met up with a few friends for a drink in a bar downtown at around ten," Caleb said. He leaned over the arm of the armchair towards her, as though they were engaged in a fascinating discussion instead of a murder investigation. "It was at Mulroon's. Have you ever been there?"

"We're from out of town," Laura said, shaking her head. "How long did you stay?"

"Oh, that's a shame. You really should check it out before you go," Caleb said. "Well, let me think. We got deep into a discussion about acting techniques, so it was last call before we finally left and all went home. Probably just before two in the morning."

Laura squinted at him slightly. "You didn't have work to go to in the morning?"

Caleb spread his hands wide as if to indicate the apartment. "That was work you just saw," he said. "I'm an actor. We were rehearsing for a play we're going to be in together. Sorry, what is all this about? Did something happen at the bar last night?"

"No," Nate put in, his voice sharper than Laura's had been. He was clearly going for the bad cop angle, against her good cop. "We're here conducting a murder investigation."

Caleb's eyes went wide with shock. Either that, or he was a very good actor. But given that he looked to be in at least his mid-twenties, and was living in Seattle rather than L.A., Laura did have her doubts. "Murder? Who?"

"Suzanna Brice," Laura said, her voice soft. "We believe she was your acting coach."

A hand flew over Caleb's mouth, and tears sprang to his eyes.

Yes, Laura thought – if he was acting, then he was damn good.

"Oh, my God," he said, his voice seeming to fail him. "I... are you serious? Last night?"

"That's right," Laura said. "We believe it happened just after her acting class."

"I was in that class." Caleb shook his head wordlessly and stood up, pacing away a few steps with his hand on his forehead. "I was literally with her last night, just... just before it happened."

"Did you see anything suspicious?" Nate asked. "Anyone unusual that you haven't seen before?"

It was a perfect opportunity, Laura could see, for him to make something up. Create a new suspect for them to chase after. If he was the killer, and he wanted to get away with it, he would probably do something like that. He would probably throw them a false lead to distract them so that he could either escape or convince someone to support his alibi.

"No," Caleb said, his voice still completely raw and open. "No, I had no idea something like this was going to happen. Anything. God, she was fine when I saw her."

"Did you have any other acting coaches?" Nate asked, snapping Caleb's attention away from the wall he was leaning against.

"Yes," Caleb said. "Yeah, loads, actually. I've taken just about every acting class in Seattle. Why?"

"Where were you the night before last, Caleb?" Laura asked.

Caleb paled again and sat down in the armchair. "You're not telling me there's been another one?"

"If you could answer the question, please."

"Yes, I... the night before last, I was at my improv class. We tend to run late. Um... I don't know exactly when we finished, but you could speak to the coach. I'm sure he'll be able to tell you."

Laura nodded, noting down the details of his two alibis.

"Have there been two murders?" Caleb asked. He shifted forwards to the edge of the seat, pressing his hands together in front of him. He was the picture of worry.

"I'm afraid we're also investigating the death of Lucile Maddison."

Caleb's hand shot over his mouth again, and for a minute he looked like he might be sick. He shook his head slowly. "I've had classes with her, too," he said at last.

"We're aware of that," Nate said, with an unfriendly edge in his voice.

"God," Caleb said, shaking his head still. "What a waste. They were both so talented. Suzanna was the best, but… but I learned a lot from Lucile, too. This is just horrible. Do you have any idea who did this to them?"

"That's what we're trying to ascertain, Caleb," Laura told him, with a wry smile.

He looked at her for a moment, then blinked. "Me?" he said. "God, you think I could have done this?"

"We'll be checking your alibis," Nate informed him. "Now's the time to tell us if there's anything you think we should know."

"No, I can't think of anything," Caleb said. He was supremely confident – he didn't even blink when Nate mentioned checking the alibis. Like he had no worry at all about them finding anything untoward. "It's just such a shock. I don't know why anyone would want to hurt them – either of them. They were nice people. Then again, I guess I can't really understand why anyone would want to kill someone."

"Isn't that what you're supposed to do, as an actor?" Laura asked him. "Put yourself into someone else's shoes, understand their motivation?"

Caleb smiled at her. He had perfect, straight, white teeth. It was such a dazzling smile, she was almost expecting a 'ting' sound effect to come up over a shining star, like in old cartoons. "Yes. I guess that's why I've been to so many acting coaches and I'm still not famous."

Laura flipped her notebook closed, glancing at Nate. He nodded. They were done here. There was no point taking Caleb in for further questioning, not when he'd provided them with alibis. If they turned out to be fake, they could revisit him later. "Alright, Caleb. Thank you for your cooperation. We'll get the local police to call someone out about the door."

"Thanks," he said, springing to his feet out of what seemed like automatic polite impulse to show them to the door.

They were almost about to step over it when he spoke again.

"Um, sorry," he said. "I didn't get your name, Agent?"

"Laura Frost," she said, turning to look at him as Nate stepped over the ruins of the door. "My partner is Agent Nathaniel Lavoie."

"Right," Caleb said. "So, Laura – can I call you Laura?"

Laura inclined her head silently, waiting for him to go on. She preferred Agent, because it meant the suspect was showing respect, but she wasn't going to be a stickler about it with a man who, she was fairly convinced, was innocent.

"Great. Laura, can I get your number?" Caleb asked. "In case I think of anything or anyone that might help solve this case. I'm really sorry to hear about both of them, I really am. I'm going to be thinking hard about this, and maybe talking to a few people if I can."

Laura dug one of her official cards out of her pocket. "This has my cell," she said, handing it over. "Anything you think of, we'd be very keen to hear about it."

"Right," Caleb said, glancing over the card and then looking up to fix her with another of those dazzling smiles. "Thank you, Laura. I'll be in touch."

"Of course," she said, turning to step over the door herself and out into the hall. Nate was waiting for her, but as soon as they were together, they set off walking.

They were outside of the building before either of them spoke again, conscious that it was possible for Caleb to hear them without his door blocking the noise. "There's nothing to follow here, I don't think," Laura said. "We can ask Mills to put one of his detectives on following up the alibis, but it seems like he was being sincere."

"I agree," Nate said, shooting her an amused look that she didn't quite understand. "We should head over to Lucile Maddison's home, speak to her boyfriend."

"Agreed," Laura said. "Hey, maybe we'll get lucky. Maybe he was having an affair with both of them, and this is just a classic case of 'the partner always did it.'"

Nate chuckled. "We can dream," he said, getting behind the wheel of the car before she could protest that she was still fine to drive.

CHAPTER FIFTEEN

Laura watched Seattle flash by their window. They were driving into the more recognizable parts of the city now, the parts that were shown on television or in tourist guidebooks. Sometimes, being an agent and traveling all around the country meant losing track of where you really were. Cities could blend into one another, particularly those that were developed around the same time. All of the architecture from a particular time period looked the same, and it was only in the historic centers that things started to look different.

She was distracted from the view by a buzzing in her pocket. Grabbing the phone out just in case it was a necessary update from Captain Mills, Laura was somewhat disappointed to find that it was only a message from the man she had met in the bar back in Washington, DC. Nolan, she remembered – with a little difficulty. All of that had been pushed so far back in her mind by everything else happening.

Hey, it was great to meet you. I know you had to get going for work, but I'd really love to see you again. I didn't get a chance to show you the truth about me. – N

Laura read the message over a couple of times, trying to figure out if she believed him. It was possible that he was just a massive flirt, and trying to impress girls with stories of being psychic was his thing. It was also possible that she had been too hasty, and that he really was psychic. Just a different kind of psychic to her. She had no idea about her ability, about where it came from or why she had it, or even really how to control it. If she didn't know any of that, how could she say for sure that she knew whether or not different kinds existed?

Laura didn't reply, not right away. She turned off her phone screen and put it back in her pocket, trying to think. There was so much going on right now. She didn't even know when she was going to be back from this case, whether it was going to take a single day or several months. That was the thing about being an FBI agent. Until you solved the case, the case wasn't solved. What looked like something open and shut could turn out to be the most complex thing you had ever come up against.

Of course, Laura sincerely hoped that was not the case this time, because she needed to get back home. Lacey, Amy, all of it needed her attention. So, even if she did manage to go back home tomorrow, crossing the case off her list, this Nolan character would not be anything close to a priority.

Which did not mean that she wasn't curious.

"I think this is it," Nate said, wrenching Laura's attention back to the present. They were pulling up outside a modern-looking apartment building, clearly a more recent addition to the neighborhood.

The home where Lucile Maddison had lived, until now, was on the fourth floor. Nate spoke quietly into the intercom, introducing himself and Laura on her behalf, holding up his badge so that the camera set above the speaker could catch it. After a short pause, the door buzzed to indicate that it was unlocked, and Laura headed inside first.

They took the stairs rather than the elevator, a choice that Laura regretted after about the third floor. It wasn't as though she was unfit - being an FBI agent meant that you always had to be ready to run after a suspect at a moment's notice, and that meant plenty of gym time in her days off - but being an alcoholic for so many years had put her off-balance. It was just one of the many things that you didn't really notice building up on you while you were drinking. Now that she was sober, she was starting to realize just how much work she had to do to get back to how she used to be.

Which, of course, made her want to drink even more. That was the Catch-22 of it all.

Still, they made it to the correct door, and Nate had only managed to put his hand out to knock on it when it opened. Evidently, Lucile Maddison's boyfriend had been watching through the peephole, waiting for them to show up.

"Come in," he said, his voice ragged and raw with the grief that he had been going through for the past two days. His face was pale and drawn, and there were huge dark circles under each of his eyes. They were also red-rimmed, a clear sign that he had been crying this morning.

"We're very sorry for your loss," Laura said. "Mr. Long, is it?"

"Call me Jay," he said, turning to lead them inside. "Has something happened?"

"We don't have anything new to share at this stage," Nate said, following him down the hall to a small living room. It was decorated with cheap or old-looking furniture, the kind of things a young couple

72

might put in their first home together. Hand-me-downs and thrift store finds.

"I've already told the police everything I could think of," Jay said wearily, flopping down to sit on the sofa. There was only one other chair in the room; Laura took this, with Nate roaming around the room liked a restless panther, prowling from one thing to another.

"We understand that," Laura said, keeping her voice is sympathetic as possible. In the meantime, she was studying Jay closely. He was Asian-American, dark-haired with soft dark eyes that seemed to be full of sorrow. Laura tried to keep an open mind. There was a well-known fact that the partners of murder victims were almost always the ones to blame, but that did not necessarily mean he was guilty in this particular case. For one thing, Suzanna Brice was an anomaly. They didn't seem to have any connection. At least, nothing that the investigation had found so far. "We're just trying to conduct the most thorough investigation possible. If you could tell us again anything that might help."

"I just don't know," Jay said shrugging helplessly. "Lucy was a great person. Her students liked her, she never told me about any quarrels with any of them. We had a great bunch of friends that we spent a lot of time with. She's never had any enemies. She wasn't that kind of person."

"Okay," Laura said gently, making quick notes in her notebook. Not that there was much to write, so far. "And you didn't notice anything unusual in the days or weeks leading up to Lucy's death?"

"No, not at all," he said. Jay leaned forward over the coffee table, putting his head in his hands. "We've been planning to go on vacation at the end of the year. She was really looking forward to it. We put down the deposit a couple of weeks ago. She never said anything about anyone suspicious; she wasn't nervous or scared or angry about anything. She was happy. We both were."

Laura couldn't help but feel sympathy for him. He was acting like the grieving partner, but then again, she had seen men who were not the boyfriends of acting coaches and who managed to fool police investigations. Right up until the DNA evidence came out. This whole case was made more complex by the fact that actors were involved, but she had to remind herself that she knew what a liar looked like. She had seen enough of them in her time. People from all walks of life could be deceptive.

"Did you know a woman called Suzanna Brice, another acting coach?" Laura asked. She watched Jay closely, trying to gauge his reaction.

"No," he said shaking his head. "It doesn't ring any bells."

Nate turned from where he had been examining a few framed photographs on a shelf. All of them showed Jay with the late Lucile, happy and smiling in times gone by. "So, you didn't pay much attention to your girlfriend's professional life?" he asked, pointedly.

"What's that supposed to mean?" Jay asked, his head going up. He was on the verge of getting defensive, Laura could see. It wasn't good when the suspect was put on the defensive, unless they were the type to be pushed far enough to scream a confession. She hadn't yet figured out whether Jay was one of those or not.

"Suzanna Brice was one of her rivals," Nate said. "A fellow acting coach."

Jay shook his head. "Well, that doesn't make them rivals," he said. "Lucy always said there were enough acting coaches to go around in Seattle. Enough aspiring actors to fill up all of the classes and more. She wouldn't have thought of her as a rival at all. Just a kindred spirit."

He was making Lucile sound like a saint, which Laura had serious doubts about. But the man was hardly about to say horrible things about the girlfriend he loved who had just died. "Okay, Jay," she said moving on. "What about ex-boyfriends? Did Lucy have any?"

Jay hesitated, just for a second. "Well, of course, she's dated other people before me," he said.

"And anyone in particular that springs to mind?" Laura asked. She hadn't missed that moment of hesitation. She knew it had to mean something.

"I'm not sure it would be relevant," Jay said.

"Anything could be relevant, no matter how small," Laura said.

"Well," Jay said, scratching the back of his head nervously. "There was this one guy. He was kind of a creep. I guess he wouldn't accept that Lucy had moved on with me, wouldn't leave her alone. He even came around here once or twice after we'd moved in together. She told him to go away, and I haven't seen him for a couple of months now. No, more than that - it must have been... I don't know, six months."

"Well, that's something," Laura said. "Do you happen to remember the guy's name?"

"Yes, I can't forget it," Jay said. "His name was Scott Darnell. I think they met in one of her classes."

74

"Thank you for that information," Laura said, getting up with a significant glance at Nate. "We'll be back in touch if we have any further questions – or any updates for you."

"Thanks," Jay said vaguely, but Laura was already moving on. She nodded at him and strode out of the apartment, waiting for Nate to catch up for only a second as she grabbed her cell phone out of her pocket.

"We go and speak to Scott Darnell?" Nate said.

"We go and speak to Scott Darnell," Laura confirmed, feeling much more like they were on the right track than she had all morning.

CHAPTER SIXTEEN

Laura took the call when they were halfway to the address that the local PD had managed to dig out for Scott Darnell. Seeing that it was Captain Mills on the line, she didn't hesitate in answering it.

"Agent Frost," she said, putting the phone to her ear.

"I think you might want to see something before you speak to Scott Darnell," Captain Mills said. "We've just been analyzing some phone records that were released to us by the network provider. It's pretty interesting reading."

"He was still in touch with Lucile Maddison?" Laura asked, signaling to Nate to turn the car around with one finger in the air.

"Not Maddison," Captain Mills said. "Like I said – you're going to want to see this."

He ended the call, and Laura quickly reprogrammed the GPS to get them through the unfamiliar streets and over to the precinct.

Laura dug her phone out of her pocket, while Nate handled the driving and left her hands free. She sent a quick text off to Agent Jones: *Have you heard anything about Amy?*

She hadn't expected an instant reply, but it came before she even had time to look up at the street again: *Nothing yet. Chief R keeping it very hush-hush.*

Laura sighed to herself, staring out of the window and seeing nothing. She wanted to know that everything was alright. Being so far away and unable to help was like slow torture.

The precinct loomed out of the middle of a city street, other municipal buildings and residential apartments all around it. It towered high above them, and the front steps seemed to play host to a constant stream of cops in uniform and civilians coming in and out.

Nate pulled around the back and found a place for them to park. Laura got out of the car while he was still searching and walked ahead, up to the main lobby, where a desk sergeant sent her in the direction of the third floor. There, Laura walked into a bullpen rowdy with detectives sitting at their desks and suspects, victims, and all manner of others filling the spaces. At the back of the room, she could see an office with glass windows. Inside it, she recognized the form of Captain Mills, and headed over there immediately.

"Ah, Agent Frost," he said, looking up as she knocked sharply and then opened his door. "I've asked Sergeant Thornton to prepare the records for you upstairs in one of our offices. It's lying empty temporarily, so you won't be putting anyone out. I'll show you up there now."

Nate joined them as they passed the elevator, heading back into it and up one floor to a long hall where they found the office. It was a small room, not even as big as Captain Mills' office in the bullpen, but at least it was quiet and private.

Sergeant Thornton was pinning up a map to the wall as they arrived; Laura saw that it already had the locations of the two bodies marked in red ink. Across the table were the pages of phone records.

"Sergeant, could you take them through what you found?" Captain Mills asked, hanging back near the door to watch his employee at work.

"Yes, sir," Thornton said, tucking her dark hair behind one ear. "So, these are text message exchanges between Suzanna Brice and a number which we've only just managed to identify as Scott Darnell."

Laura took the page she was holding up, scanning over it. "The first message looks like it's already part of a conversation," she said. "Is this where it starts?"

"Yes," Thornton said smartly. "We believe that the conversation started on Tinder. Suzanna was a member of the dating app and she had been chatting with other men as well. Looking back over her call and text history, it seems like there's a pattern of starting to talk to someone, going on a date or two, and then the conversation petering out."

"Lots of frogs and no princes," Nate said. "When are these dated?"

Laura shook her head in disbelief. "Just over a week ago," she said. "Scott Darnell was in contact with both victims, and Suzanna very recently. It looks like they organized a date and place to meet up."

"That's right," Thornton nodded, lifting up another page for her to see. "They do appear to have gone on the date. Afterwards, Suzanna is quiet, then Darnell sends her a message saying it was a nice night and it was a shame she had to go home early."

"Or she said she had to go early because the date wasn't going well," Laura said, with a raised eyebrow. It wasn't hard to imagine the scenario. It was one of the oldest tricks in the book. She'd

77

practically used it herself last night, although she had been telling the truth.

"Right, and it definitely sounds that way," Thornton said. "She at first didn't respond, so Darnell sent her another message saying he wanted to meet up with her again. Suzanna said she'd rather not, and she was pretty polite about it. That must have rubbed him the wrong way, and he then said some not very nice things about her."

Laura scanned the messages. They weren't hard to predict. He'd called Suzanna a bitch, prissy, a prude, accused her of only being out for a free meal. Eventually, Suzanna had told him to leave her alone or she was calling the police, and the messages stopped.

"He gave up?" Laura asked. The date was timestamped for three days before Suzanna was killed.

"She blocked his number," Thornton said, with a gleam in her eyes.

"That's really good work, Sergeant," Laura said, smiling at her. "This is a good lead. The sister, Vicky – she didn't mention anything about this."

"Maybe Suzanna didn't tell her," Nate shrugged. "It was an unremarkable date, by all accounts."

"But this harassment…" Laura said.

Thornton shook her head. "There are a few other men who had similar reactions," she said. "I think the fact may have been that Suzanna was used to this kind of behavior from men she met on Tinder. I was compiling a list of people we might want to speak to, judging from the language they used, when I heard that you were looking for Darnell. I thought he might be the best priority."

"You're absolutely right," Laura said, then hesitated. "But we don't want to miss the other leads, either. Sergeant, can you distribute this list among yourself and some other detectives, get alibis from as many of them as you can? If we can rule them out, so much the better."

Thornton nodded, already gathering her own notes to take them back downstairs to the rest of the team.

"In the meantime, we'll head back out to speak to Scott Darnell," Laura said, grabbing a copy of the text messages. She wanted to read them out to him and see what he had to say for himself – because she couldn't imagine any way that a man could possibly justify the kinds of things he had said.

In fact, she couldn't imagine how a confirmed stalker who was obsessed with one of the women and, very clearly upset with the other, could possibly talk himself out of being their prime suspect in both of the murders.

CHAPTER SEVENTEEN

He found a spot on the opposite side of the road and parked. It was perfect. He would be able to see from here, and he wouldn't even need to get out of the car. He made sure that all of the interior lights were off, that the streetlights weren't shining in through any of the windows to illuminate him. If she looked out, she would only see a dark car. That was the best way to do it. He didn't want her to know she was being watched.

That was always the truest test. When someone was alone, when they had no idea that they were being observed, they would be their truest self. It was all well and good being the perfect muse when someone was watching you. But his muse, his perfect one – she was the same all the time.

That was what excited him the most. Knowing that he was about to see perfection at its finest, its most pure. He was going to get a glimpse of something that the rest of the world never saw, something truly special. And it was all going to be a perfect show just for him.

He hunched in the seat, eventually scooting over to the passenger side in order to get a better angle of her windows. She had left the curtains open, turned on the lights against the encroaching darkness of the evening. He couldn't see anything. He needed to get closer.

He stole out of the car into the darkness of the night, dressed all in black so that no one would see him. A quick run across the street and he was right by the side of her house; a glance through the windows to check she wasn't there, and he darted around back. There were bushes lining the side of the house, and he could creep into them, get cover, crouch down at just such a perfect angle to see right into the windows without being seen. The house was quiet, and the windows were empty.

She was at home, though, and when he saw her come into view at last, she wasn't acting as though she was being watched at all. Her hair was up in a messy bun, rather than the sleek curls she normally wore.

She had changed since getting home, too. Instead of the chic and fashionable outfit she had been wearing outside, now she was in slouchy, old clothes. Pajamas, maybe, or just something that was more comfortable for a relaxing evening. That was alright. It wasn't perfect –

80

it meant that there was a hidden side to her – but it was also fine. She was flowing with the rhythm of the day. Some moments called for stiletto heels and skinny jeans, and some moments called for soft textures and oversized fits. He understood that.

In fact, if anything, it was an indication that she was able to go with the flow of the universe better. That she didn't resist and stay rigidly the same. That made her even more worthy of his worship. It was better than those fake girls who were always trying to be perfect for social media, always filtered and manicured and never able to take the bad with the good.

No, his muse – she knew both the ups and the downs. She knew how to be. She was perfect.

He watched her settle down in front of the television, switching it on. The glow of it bathed her face in an unnatural blue light, flickering occasional through different colors. She seemed absorbed, but after a short while she picked up a fashion magazine and began to flip through the pages. After that, her phone rang, and she stopped whatever show or movie she was watching to answer it.

He couldn't hear what she was saying, but he watched her. As she spoke, she fished out a thin blanket and laid it over herself, keeping herself warm. She scratched her chest, a movement that struck him as unexpectedly lewd. He frowned.

She reached up a hand to her face and pulled off two strips of fake eyelashes, the long lashes he had admired in her when she blinked and waved them around. They were false. He swallowed, taken aback. Without them, at this distance, her eyes seemed to be so small. Like they were almost disappearing. She stuck the eyelashes onto a side table without looking, and one of them fell onto the floor. When she looked around and noticed, she left it where it was.

He began to feel a sick sensation right in his stomach. A burning in his chest. What was happening? Why was she being like this? Was this some kind of joke? What had happened to the beautiful, fairy-like goddess who seemed to light up the whole street as she floated along on the current? Who was this dirty, vulgar, fake person taking her place?

Then he knew. It was all an act. It had to be. She was just as fake as the others. She made herself seem perfect on the outside – just to fool people like him, he expected. To make them fall in love with her, with a person who did not actually exist.

She was all fake.

81

An anger was swelling up inside of him. How dare she put on this face to the world, make them think that she was something she was not? He had trusted her. He had loved her, worshipped her. He had made her his muse. And it turned out she was no muse at all – all style and no substance, completely vapid behind the façade. He gripped the leaves of the bush he was crouching in and ripped them off the branch, then tore them to shreds in his hands, his eyes still fixed on her.

She had let him down. She had lied to him. And he knew with a sudden certainty what he was going to have to do now.

CHAPTER EIGHTEEN

Laura pulled the car up outside the house, peering at it past Nate's head in the window as she did so. It was a small enough house, but with three cars parked outside and all of them looking like cheap second-hand models, it was clear enough that they were looking at a shared home. Three roommates, maybe more if someone was out right now or didn't own a car. It was late enough at night that she suspected everyone would be home from work or school, so long as they didn't work the graveyard shift.

The more people they could expect at any location, the more complicated things could get. That was unfortunate. But they had to talk to Scott Darnell – and if all went well, hopefully, they would need to arrest him.

Hopefully, because if they were right with their suspicions, then they could get a murderer off the streets faster than expected. Not only did that mean going home to sort out the two little girls who needed her, but it also meant the women of Seattle would be safe.

At least, from this particular killer.

"Are you ready for this?" Nate asked. He was looking at Laura, not at the house.

"Yeah," Laura said, trying to shake off the thoughts of all the responsibilities that waited for her back at home. "Yeah, I'm ready."

They got out of the car and walked up the short path to the door together, able to move in time after these years of working together. Nate had a way of shortening his stride to make sure that she could keep up with him, and Laura would lengthen hers to reduce the difference. Nate knocked heavily when they were close enough, and they both waited, tense with the anticipation of the confrontation.

A young man answered the door. He was in the right age range to be Scott – his late twenties or early thirties. But he wasn't Scott. Laura knew this, because the man they were looking for was Caucasian, and this man appeared to be Chinese-American.

"Hello?" he said, looking at them with a puzzled expression.

"We're looking for Scott Darnell," Laura said, her eyes flicking past the man who had answered the door and towards the hall. She was looking for any sign that would clue her in as to whether the man they were looking for was home.

"Scott?" the guy repeated, glancing behind himself almost involuntarily. "Uh… what's this about?"

Laura lifted her badge, synchronized with Nate's movement. "I'm Special Agent Laura Frost, and this is Special Agent Nate Lavoie," she said. "We need to speak with Scott about an ongoing investigation. We believe he can help us with our inquiries."

"Oh," the man said, and blinked slowly. "Um. No, I don't know Scott."

"You clearly do," Laura said, but even as she spoke, her attention was taken by something else. By the sound of movement behind him.

He must have heard her say his name, and that she was an FBI agent. Because then there was the sound of rapid footsteps and a door being wrenched open, and both she and Nate were familiar enough with those sounds to know exactly what they meant.

"I'm going around back," Nate said, darting off to the side before the words had even left his mouth.

"Let me through, if you don't want to be charged with obstruction of justice!" Laura snapped, pushing past the bewildered-looking housemate and dashing straight down the hall. The sound of the door opening – it must have been a back door to the property. In case Nate's route was cut off by a fence or something in the way, Laura shot through the house, following instinct and also the sound of the road towards the back of the property to lead her to the door.

It was swinging open, Scott Darnell clearly having raced through it without bothering to close it behind him. As Laura emerged, she saw a blank, empty yard – literally, because it was only dirt, the residents clearly not finding the time or effort for landscaping. Nate dashed around the corner, his long legs carrying him far, but Laura saw that his face was as lost as hers. They hadn't seen where he'd gone.

There was another home on the other side of a fence, an almost identical property. Perhaps Scott had jumped the fence and run that way. The problem was, where had he gone after that.

"I'm over the fence," Nate said, his words coming short and sharp to conserve breath, and then he was gone, his tall frame vaulting over the blockage with a leg-up from a locked storage box resting against the fence. Laura couldn't follow him – she couldn't jump like that. They had to split up here, go their own ways.

She turned and re-entered the house, throwing out a hand to steady herself. She landed on an item of clothing that had been discarded on the side, and a jab of sharp pain shot through her forehead –

Laura was looking at a city street from above. It was illuminated by stree lights, small pools of illumination that fought back that shadows that always swirled in her visions. She was watching as...

As a man ran into view, glancing over his shoulder. He had messy brown hair, curls bouncing with each step and in the wind of his passage. He was running full tilt, around a corner and then another, going around three sides of one big building. Laura thought she recognized it. She thought she had driven past it on the way to the house.

He stopped, slowing to a walk when he saw the car parked outside the house. The open front door. He stuck to the shadows of the building, creeping by. He flattened himself against the wall like he was in some cheesy spy film and then sidled along. At the side of the building was a small alleyway that didn't go all the way through – just ended in a brick wall.

He snuck down into the alley and behind a large, industrial bin beside a door. Glancing around one more time, he pushed the door tentatively – and it opened. He slipped inside, the darkness of the interior of the building swallowing him fully.

Laura gasped as she came back to herself mid-way through a step, still at a run. She faltered for a moment, stumbling, then charged onwards. The building on the corner. He was going to be running around the building on the corner. If she went now, maybe she could intercept him before he got inside.

No matter what, he wasn't getting away from her now.

Laura dashed through the house, almost knocking over the housemate who was still standing around in the corridor. Him, she would deal with later – possibly on an obstruction charge, since he had obviously lied to them in order to give Scott more time to get away. But for now, Scott was the priority, and she threw her body down the street and towards the corner as quickly as she could, drawing burning breaths into her lungs with each stride.

She didn't have the backup of Nate to rely on. In the vision, he hadn't even been in sight. Either he'd lost Scott as soon as he was over the fence, or he was so far behind that he would never understand where Scott had gone. That meant she was on her own, going up against an adult male who had possibly already killed two people.

But Laura didn't feel scared as she ran towards him. She didn't have time to feel scared. She only knew that she had to stop this man from killing again, and her job was to accept the risk that might come with that.

Laura reached the building at the end of the street – a modern-built church, she now saw, closed down for the evening, home to some obscure religious group that she had never heard of. There was no sign of Scott. Had she missed him?

She knew where he would be, if she had – inside. There was no point in waiting. She rushed forward, down the street towards the corner where he would turn, or had turned, she had no idea. She just had to follow the vision, to trust that she was putting herself into the right place –

She collided bodily with another person as she reached the corner, the momentum taking both of them to the ground. She was slightly winded, but with her hands up in front of her as she ran, the impact had been smaller – the other figure, a man, had been twisting around the corner and she'd hit him full in the chest and stomach. She rolled, seeing him only managing to gasp for breath and not get up.

Laura launched herself at him again, not mindful of the bruises or scrapes she might have sustained in the fall, only thinking of securing him before he could run off again. She rolled him over, getting him onto his back so that she could force his arms behind him. "Scott Darnell," she panted, catching her breath just enough to give him his caution. "We're placing you under arrest on suspicion of murder." She pulled her handcuffs off her belt, fitting them onto his wrists just as Nate was coming around the corner.

"Laura," he said, an ejaculation of surprise as well as of concern. She nodded to let him know that she was okay, despite the blow that she had taken. Now that the adrenaline was wearing off and Scott Darnell was in cuffs, she could feel it: a dull ache on her left knee and through all of her left side where she had gone down, as well as pain in her wrists and arms where she had taken most of the impact of hitting him.

But it didn't matter. Her efforts had secured the suspect, and he wasn't going to be able to kill again. Laura would take any number of blows to prevent a killer from getting away long enough to take another life.

"Let's take him in," Laura said, stepping back and allowing Nate to haul Scott to his feet. She breathed deeply, running a hand back through her blonde hair, allowing herself to recover.

The biggest pain was in her head, pounding now because of the vision. She could only hope it was the last one she was going to need today, or for the rest of the case, giving herself time to recover. But with visions being as unpredictable as they were, she had little hope that she was going to avoid another one piling on top of her headache.

Just another reason to want to drink. But, as Laura watched Nate push Scott Darnell's head down to avoid hitting it on the side of the car as he got in, she knew there were reasons to stay sober. Lacey. Amy. Keeping an eye on Nate and making sure he stayed alive. And most of all, because the drunker she was the less able she would be to wrap this case up and get home to what really mattered.

CHAPTER NINETEEN

Laura sipped at her coffee, lukewarm and about as strong as a muddy puddle, taken from the precinct's machine. She didn't know how people here could put up with it. This was Seattle, home of the coffee shop. There should have been riots about this coffee machine.

"Are you ready?" Nate asked, gesturing towards the door of the interrogation room.

Laura nodded. They had been standing outside for a good ten or fifteen minutes already, letting Scott Darnell sweat. It was better this way. Let him get nervous on his own, let him worry. He would be much more likely to make a mistake then, or just blurt out a full confession before they even had to try hard.

"Let's get this creep," Laura said. He was looking more and more likely to be the killer; he had a strong build, which meant he would have no problem at all with holding an adult woman back against himself and forcing a knife through her chest multiple times. He had the connection to both victims, and he was undoubtedly suspicious. Running when the cops came to your door was never a good sign.

They walked in together, Nate first and Laura behind, both of them deliberately keeping a dramatic and imposing presence. They sat without a word, staring at Scott, as if expecting him to say something. Laura put a large case folder down in front of her, then tilted it towards herself and started to leaf through the pages in a way that meant Scott Darnell could not see what she was looking at. It was a good tactic, a common one but easy to use over and over again. It didn't matter if they even knew it was a tactic. Humans always felt the need to fill the silence, especially when they were expecting a conversation in the first place.

Finally, Scott Darnell broke. "Look," he said. "I didn't mean anything by it. I really honestly thought that she was into it."

Laura blinked. "You thought who was into what?" she asked.

Scott looked between Nate and Laura as if searching for an answer. But neither of them was prepared to give it to him. "The girl," he said. "Marta. It was all a misunderstanding."

Lower leaned back in her chair, narrowing her eyes at him. "Why don't you tell us the whole story with Marta, and we'll make up all our minds as to whether it was a misunderstanding?" she said. She had no idea what he was talking about, but she was more than happy to give him enough rope to hang himself with.

"We went out on a date," Scott said. "I mean, a date. You can't blame me for thinking that something was going to happen. I thought she wanted it. We had a good time."

Laura had a terrible growing feeling that she was going to hear something that would make her want to punch him in the face. "What did you think she wanted, Scott?"

"Well, you know," Scott said, shrugging as if it should be obvious. "What happens at the end of the date. I thought she was just playing coy, and she really did want me to come inside."

"And then?" Nate said, his tone dangerous.

"And then I pulled her towards me and kissed her," Scott said, his body language strained and his facial expression pleading. He looked like a man who was begging to be understood, to be believed. "That was all. My hand slipped down – I didn't even mean to grab her ass. I mean – I didn't grab it. This is all a mistake!"

Laura looked at Scott evenly for a moment, and then back at Nate. Something unspoken passed between their eyes, the agreement that he had told them enough about what he thought was the problem.

"Well, I'm going to be very interested to hear what Marta thinks happened," Laura said. "But actually, Scott, we aren't here to talk about that."

"You aren't?" he said, looking between them with a frown. "But…"

"Did you hear what I arrested you for, Scott?" Laura said.

"For Marta," he said, with a certain degree of stubbornness.

"No, Scott," Laura said calmly. "I arrested you on suspicion of murder."

He stared at her.

"M-murder?" he repeated.

"Yes. So, now that you've given us something else to look into in terms of your conduct with women, I'd quite like to speak to you about what you were doing last night." Laura watched him carefully, trying to gauge whether his startled response was real or put-upon.

"Last night?" Scott said, wiping what might have been sweat from his forehead. "Um. I was at home. I got back from work around seven at night and then I had dinner and went to bed. Why?"

"And the night before?" Laura asked.

"The same thing," he said. "I'm shooting on this show at the moment as an extra, and they have us wait around from five in the morning until past five at night, so when I get home, I'm pretty tired."

"Okay," Laura said, opening the file for real this time. "So, what you've just told me – is there anyone who can verify it? That you were at home all evening?"

"No," Scott said. "No, I live alone. That's why I was on a date with Marta." He blanched slightly as the name came out of his mouth, as if realizing that he had just reminded them of his own culpability.

"Do you know who this woman is?" Laura asked, taking a photograph out of the file and laying it down in front of him. It was a photograph of Lucile Maddison, as she was when alive and well.

"Yes," Scott said quickly, then looked up in what Laura thought might be shock. Perhaps he was putting the pieces together. Realizing why they might want to talk to him about it. "She was my acting coach a while ago."

"She was more than your coach, wasn't she?" Nate asked, finally speaking up. He had a raised eyebrow, and his tone was playful, as if he was chatting with one of the boys. "A woman like that?"

"Okay, fine, we dated," Scott said. He looked harassed now. "But we haven't spoken in ages. Months. Honestly. What's... wait, is she the one who...?"

"It was more than dating, wasn't it, Scott?" Laura said. "You wouldn't leave her alone after the relationship ended. You didn't want to accept it was over. You only haven't spoken to her because she told you she would call the police if you spoke again, isn't that right?"

"But I haven't," Scott said, desperately. The idea of the threat had been a nice touch Laura had thought of; to make him admit it had gone that far when they really had no proof it had. "Spoken to her, I mean. I haven't seen her. I did what she wanted. I left her alone!"

"Is that true?" Laura asked. "Or did you see her two nights ago, Scott?"

"No, I didn't!" Scott exclaimed. "Please, you have to tell me – is she... is she alright, or...?"

"I'm afraid the woman in this photograph is dead, Scott," Laura said. She held his gaze, saw him crumble a little at the words. He was acting like he was in grief at hearing it. But then, a murderer might well be affected emotionally by hearing the police talk about the crime he had committed, because he would be worried about getting caught.

90

Without leaving Scott enough time to fully process what she had said, she slipped another photograph in front of him. "Do you recognize this woman?"

"What? Oh... yeah. I know her," Scott said, confused and put on the back foot, still reeling from the first thing.

"How do you know her?"

"We went on a date recently. Suzie. I don't think it's going anywhere."

"Do you always date acting coaches, Scott?" Laura asked.

Scott looked up with a frown. "What?"

"Suzie was an acting coach as well. Do you not date women who aren't in the acting profession in some way?"

"I didn't..." Scott shook his head, blinking. "I didn't know she was a coach. But yeah. I mostly date actresses. We hang out in the same places. People who aren't like us don't get it. The struggle, the schedule. They can't appreciate what it's like."

Laura noted that, thinking it might be something to circle back to later. The frustration, the self-pity. Maybe it could build into his motive. "You say you don't think it's going anywhere with Suzie. We have some text messages which you wrote to her, Scott, which suggest you think the date went well."

Scott blanched again, before a red patch appeared on his neck and crept up towards his ears. "I... I thought it did. But she wasn't into it. Which was fine, I've moved on."

"You didn't seem to think it was fine at the time," Laura said. She lifted out a page of the text message transcript and laid it in front of him. "'You'll pay for this, you bitch'?"

"Oh, God," Scott said, his voice muffled as he covered his face with his hands. "I was drunk when I wrote that. I didn't mean it."

"How was she going to pay for it, Scott?" Laura asked. "Was she going to pay for it with her life?"

"What?" Scott looked up, raising his head out of his hands sharply. "You don't mean... they both..." He looked back down at the images in front of him uncertainly, his eyes widening.

"Yes, Scott," Laura said. "We found Suzanna Brice's body last night. Could you tell me again what you were doing between the hours of seven and midnight?"

"I didn't..." Scott shook his head rapidly. Tears were filling up in his eyes. But it could all be an act, Laura reminded herself. It could all be part of his prepared performance. "I... she was... she can't be..."

Laura glanced at Nate, who gave her a slight nod. Scott was staring at the images in front of him, until Laura whipped them away from his reach and back into the folder. She stood up smartly, Nate following her.

"We'll be back to talk to you again later," Laura said. "In the meantime, Scott, you might want to consider what you're going to tell us. If you make a full confession, the judge may be persuaded to go easy on you. There's no death penalty in the state of Washington anymore, so you might just get the chance to live as a free man again before you die."

"Wait – I didn't have anything to do with this!" Scott shouted, calling desperately after them as they opened the door to step outside. "I swear, I didn't do it!"

Laura closed the door, shutting out the sound in both directions with the heavy construction. "Well?" she said, looking at Nate as they both began to stroll towards the elevator that would take them back to their makeshift office.

"Oh, he definitely did it," Nate said, flashing her a grin. "We can hold him overnight, see if he cracks."

"Agreed," Laura said. "I wouldn't be surprised if he lawyers up, but we can handle that."

Her phone buzzed in her pocket, distracted her. She grabbed it out, Nate turning to look for the source of the noise.

"New lead?" he asked.

"Maybe," Laura said. "I just got a message from Caleb Rowntree – the guy whose door we broke down. He wants to meet me. Maybe he has new information about the case."

"Maybe," Nate said, though Laura could have sworn he was smirking as he turned away. "You go. I'll stay here, organize the evidence we do have and start thinking about what else we need to gather. I'll go through Scott's phone records, for a start. Maybe we can find some threats against Lucile as well."

"Good idea," Laura said, turning and heading back in the direction of the exit.

Whatever Caleb Rowntree had to tell her, she hoped it was good – the kind of good that could get this case closed without having to wait for a confession, so they could get this signed off and finished before the day was up.

CHAPTER TWENTY

Gypsy Sparks was tying her shoelaces, tightening her sneakers to make sure they were secure. It was late, dark out, and all the streetlights were on. Perfect for going for a walk. She couldn't wait to get out there, to feel the stretch, to breathe fresher air now the bulk of the traffic had gone down.

Gypsy enjoyed walking at night, especially since she had moved to this neighborhood. It was good to get some air, to get away from people. If she saw anyone, it would be a neighbor wishing her a good night. Maybe walking their dog. It meant she could get out every night and clear her mind before she needed to go to sleep.

Today, she had a lot on her mind that needed clearing away. Gypsy buttoned up her jacket and opened the front door, stepping outside. It was brisker now that the sun had gone down, but still warm enough. The early Fall was a great time in Seattle. Mild weather, warmth and sunshine, not yet the bitterness of winter. It was good. She liked it a lot. She'd found it much more comfortable since moving here.

Gypsy set off down the street, pushing her hands inside her jacket pockets and moving at a good pace. She liked to start fast and then gradually slow down, getting a bit of exercise as well as clueing her body in that it was time to wind things down for bed. The air pumping into her lungs made her feel better, and if there was any ache in her legs by the time she got home, it was the satisfying feeling of exercise done well that helped her to drop off.

She noticed someone up ahead, and felt tension go through her body. As much as this was a safe neighborhood, you could never be too careful. It looked like a man from here, but he was just standing in the middle of the street, looking up. He was out of the line of the bright lights overhead, and she couldn't make out his features. Only his shape, his head tilted up. What was he looking at? Why was he studying the house?

Gypsy swallowed, her attention swept off the things she had been thinking about and focused on him. Was he a robber, casing the place for later? She hoped not. What was she supposed to do? Call the neighborhood watch? And hadn't she just heard on the last radio news bulletin on the drive home that there had been a couple of women killed in Seattle over the last couple of days?

Her keys were in her pocket. Her hand curled around them, gripping them tight. If she had to fight to fend him off, then…

"Oh, Gypsy!" he said, and she recognized his voice before she got out of the glare of the lights to see his face. "Come and take a look at this – do you think our new blinds are on straight?"

Gypsy pitched up beside the man, who had turned into her neighbor, Jerry. He was an older man in perhaps his seventies or eighties, originally from the Caribbean and now somewhat shriveled and shrunk with age. He still had so much energy, and Gypsy often saw him on her walks.

"I don't think so," she said. "Have you got a spirit level?"

"Good idea," he said, thoughtfully. He squinted at the house a little longer before turning to her with a shake of the head. "Anyway. What's going on with you?"

"Oh, just work stuff," Gypsy sighed, shaking her head. "Trying to get my head empty before bed."

"Well, come on child, pour it all into my head instead," he said. "Walk with an old man and tell him your troubles, and you'll have none when you reach home."

Gypsy laughed, taking the arm that he offered for her. Hooked together, they began a stroll around the block. She had no qualms about Jerry being able to keep up – sometimes, with his retirement and his freedom to exercise any time of the day, she though he was fitter than her. "It's just staff problems," she said. Jerry already knew all about her job at the bookstore in town, how she'd risen to be manager there a couple of years ago. "I don't know what to do with this young girl. Honestly, she's got no work ethic. She's on her last warning. But when I pulled her up about it, she started begging me not to fire her. She says she really needs the job."

"Yes, but you really need a worker," Jerry said. "Go on."

"I don't know. It's so much harder now. Being a manager, I mean," Gypsy sighed. "When I was just one of them, we used to look out for each other. I would cover for someone if they needed me to. But now…"

"Now you have the responsibility," Jerry said. "It's tough to be king."

"I wouldn't exactly call myself the king of Otto's Books," Gypsy laughed. "But you're right. It's hard to have responsibility. I think I need to fire her next time she messes up."

"If it makes you feel better, you can come and cry on me after," Jerry said. When she looked at him, his eyes were twinkling in the lights. "I'll have a shoulder saved just for you."

"Thanks, Jerry," Gypsy said, rubbing his hand. They'd turned twice already, Gypsy keeping the route short since she knew she needed to be up early for work again. She turned the third corner now, and it was only a short time before they would be back home again.

"I think I'll go to the store," Jerry said, gesturing ahead of them. At the next intersection, there was a twenty-four-hour store that sold all kinds of essentials, including a particular type of rum that Jerry always said reminded him of home. "Now, child, you call on me if you need to!"

"I will," Gypsy said, letting him go. "I hope those blinds work out for you."

"And be careful," Jerry said, throwing the last words over his shoulder. "They say there's a maniac at loose in Seattle. You've got to watch yourself!"

"I will," she promised him again, waving as she turned the corner back towards home, just in case he would turn around to see.

Gypsy took a deep breath, letting the air fill her lungs. Yes, Jerry was right, she thought, as she walked across the front of the building next to hers. She would have to take the responsibility – the girl knew the rules, and if she broke them again, there was no way Gypsy could give her a second chance. She didn't want to risk her own job, after all, and –

There was a wrench; for a moment Gypsy didn't quite understand what had happened, except that she was suddenly a lot further back in the space than she had been. Then she registered an arm across her shoulders, and for a moment, absurdly, she wondered if Jerry was trying to play a trick on her.

But this wasn't Jerry.

"Hey -" she started, but she never got the chance to make another sound. His hand shot out to cover her mouth, and the scream she tried to make was too muffled. She made to run, trying to use the grip she had on the sidewalk to push away from him and make it up to her front door, but he was too strong, holding her too tightly, her head crushed back against his shoulder.

95

A knife flashed out in the darkness in front of her and plunged into her chest, the streetlights no longer reflecting on the reddened blade as it was pulled out and struck into her again.

CHAPTER TWENTY ONE

Laura pulled up outside a small café, one of the only venues that was still open along this strip of the road. In the yellow lights of the interior, she could see Caleb Rowntree through the window, looking annoyingly good under what she was sure would not be flattering lighting for her own skin.

She got out of the car and headed inside, joining him directly. A waitress followed her from the door to pour coffee into a cup, which Laura accepted gratefully. Maybe it would be better than the swill at the precinct.

"You wanted to meet?" Laura said. It felt strangely anticlimactic. What should have been their initial greeting had been essentially stolen by the waitress, who swept in just as Laura had been about to say hello.

"I did," Caleb said. He flashed her a wide smile, as charming as it was attractive. "You must be tired. You've been at it all day?"

"Yep," Laura said, sipping her coffee. She almost rolled her eyes in pleasure. It was good coffee – strong and flavorful. Just what she needed to both combat the headache and keep her awake long enough to do what she needed to do.

Caleb laughed, obviously watching her reaction. "Good coffee?"

"Better than what they have at the precinct," Laura admitted. "So, what was it?"

"Right," Caleb said, leaning forward over the table conspiratorially. "Well, I think I might have a lead for you."

Laura raised an eyebrow. She hadn't told him that they had already arrested a suspect. It would be interesting if he could name the same man. "What is it?" she asked, leaning forward as well in spite of herself. Caleb had the kind of nature that could just draw you in, make you want to listen to him.

He was probably going to be a star, as soon as he got his foot in the door with a movie or two.

"There was a student in the class," he said. "With Suzanna, I mean. I think he could be suspicious. He only came once or twice, and I never saw him with Lucile – but if he tried one class, I'm living proof that it's possible to have tried more than one."

"What was his name?" Laura asked.

"I'm not entirely sure, but I know it was Robert something," Caleb said. He lifted the sugar shaker and poured some into his own coffee, stirring it around. He liked it sweet, apparently. "I was thinking you might be able to get his full name from the class records?"

"It's possible," Laura said. She sipped her coffee again. This clearly didn't line up with Scott Darnell, but there was no harm in listening. "Go on."

"Well, he was just kind of creepy," Caleb said. He was animated as he spoke, his face moving expressively and his hands darting through the air. Laura found she could hardly look away from him. "He had this way about him, always skulking to the back of the class and refusing to take part in things. I think Suzanna took him aside at the end of the second class and told him he had to take part if he wanted to join the group, and then we never saw him again. Or I didn't, anyway, and I haven't missed a class."

"Thanks," Laura said, taking a note of the name and the details. "And how long ago did you last see him?"

"Oh, I think it was at the start of last summer," Caleb said.

"So, about four or so months ago?"

"No, I mean last summer," Caleb said. He had the grace to look a bit sheepish. "More like a year and four months."

Laura set her pen down. "That doesn't seem as promising as we might wish," she said, choosing her words carefully. She didn't want to put him off telling her things he did know, because any lead could be a lead. "But thank you for bringing that to our attention. It's something we can keep in mind as we go forward."

"Sure," Caleb said. He glanced down into his mug of coffee, spinning it slowly between his fingers for a moment. Then he carefully looked up, as if he wasn't sure he wanted to make eye contact for the next part. "Actually, I kind of thought it might be a bit out of date. Truth is, I wanted to see you again."

Laura blinked at him. She wasn't even sure she had heard him right. "Sorry?"

Caleb broke out into a grin, which was accompanied by a very slight flush, as he looked away and out across the café. "Uh, yeah. It was a stupid idea, I guess. I just felt… drawn to you, somehow."

"Drawn?" Laura repeated, then shook her head as she realized she was probably starting to sound a bit like an idiot. "I mean… what do you mean?"

"I can't explain it," Caleb shrugged. "It was just a kind of... a flash of inspiration. Being an artist, you know, sometimes inspiration just strikes you in ways you can't explain. We have to get more in tune with our intuition, you know. Follow our guts."

"You wanted to see me again... to help with your acting?" Laura said, not sure if she was following him correctly. Inspiration from nowhere – that, though, she could identify with. Except there was a lot more to her inspiration than she usually let on.

"No, no," Caleb said, laughing self-consciously. "Sorry, I'm probably not explaining this right. I wanted to see *you*. Like, as in, maybe after this case is done, we can go out and get a drink together."

A drink?

Something in Laura wanted to accept, but there were many reasons why that would be a bad idea. First of all, he was a suspect in a murder inquiry, and even though his alibis appeared to clear him, Laura still hadn't had them checked out. And even if he did have alibis, it didn't mean that he couldn't be somehow connected to the case, perhaps as an accomplice.

Secondly, she should not be going out to get a drink with anyone. Not an alcoholic drink.

And thirdly...

"I'm not from Seattle," she said. "The FBI kind of sends us where we're needed. I actually live closer to the national headquarters." She refrained from quite saying the name of the location. Of course, it was only a Google search away from being easy to find, but you couldn't be too careful. At least this answer was vague enough that she could be from any one of the towns or cities around Washington, D.C., not just the city itself.

"Will you be going back home right away?" Caleb asked, still toying with his coffee cup. It was kind of cute. The way he'd been smooth and charming, and yet had a little bit of bashfulness when trying to ask her out. "I'd really like to see you when you're not, you know. Chasing down a murderer."

Whatever thoughts she might have been having were chased out of her head fairly easily by that. The thought that, yes, there was a murderer still to be found. And if she didn't do it, it wasn't likely that anyone would for a while, because there was too much legwork for Nate to do alone. Which meant she had to concentrate – and, yes, try to get home as soon as possible.

"I don't know," Laura hedged, sipping her coffee. "It depends on what the case demands. Whether we have to stay and help them prepare for trial after the case is solved. Sometimes we're away for weeks or even months, sometimes just days."

"Then, maybe we'll get lucky," Caleb said, smiling over the rim of his coffee cup. "I'd love to help out more if I can, too. I'll let you know if anything comes to mind. Don't hesitate to call me if there's something I can help with."

"Sure," Laura said, about to say more, but her cell phone lit up from where she'd left it on the table. It was Nate's number flashing up on the screen, and she grabbed it up to answer.

"Laura, you need to come and pick me up from the precinct," Nate said, his voice urgent and clipped. "They've found another body."

Laura ended the call immediately, leaping out of her seat before she even had time to lower it from her ear. She started to dig in her pocket for some change, but Caleb raised a hand. "I've got the coffee," he said. "If you have to go, go!"

She nodded her thanks and turned to dash through the café and back to the car, her heart thundering in her chest at the knowledge that her worst fear for this case had come true.

CHAPTER TWENTY TWO

Laura and Nate pulled up outside the house, only to find that the majority of the activity was focused on the sidewalk in front of it. There was an ambulance and several other police cars parked around, blocking their way. Laura swore under her breath and pulled up a little further down the road, managing to get parked in a position where they could quickly dash back to see what was going on.

"This isn't good, Laura," Nate said as they got out. There was a brief pause as they both closed their doors, then hurried around along the sidewalk. When he caught up with her, he continued. "If this just happened, then it means we haven't got the right guy in custody."

"You don't need to tell me that," Laura said, her steps turning into a run as they drew close to the scene. Now she was wondering if she had made the right call about Caleb's lead. Yes, it had seemed inconsequential, and so long ago. But if they didn't have the right suspect in custody, then any lead was a lead, no matter how dubious. She was beginning to doubt herself in all kinds of ways, including whether she was ever going to get another helpful vision. What did she need to touch in order to get a glimpse of the killer?

Captain Mills was waiting for them, standing with his hands crossed over his chest and watching the activity with a dour expression on his face. Several uniformed officers were erecting a tarpaulin over the body, so that it could be shielded from view while forensics worked and protected it from the elements. Laura caught just a glimpse of it before it was covered, then ducked her way over to Captain Mills to get the scoop.

"What's going on?" she asked.

"Two stab wounds to the chest, both done overhand and most likely from behind, is the initial report," Mills said. He looked tired. Laura didn't doubt that most days of work for him contained their fair share of stress, but this was an unusual case. Three deaths now with the exact same M.O. Even if stabbings were fairly common, the specificity of it left no doubt in Laura's mind. That made this a serial killer, or at the very least a spree killer, given the close timing of the attacks. It would attract serious headlines, not just in Washington but around the country.

Maybe even internationally if there were more. That meant Mills had just inherited a huge PR nightmare, and there was no end yet in sight.

"Who found her?" Laura asked – because, yes, the body she had glimpsed had been that of a woman. A woman in jogging gear, looking like she was out for a quick bit of exercise before bed.

"Her neighbor," Mills said, turning to indicate a huddled figure sitting on the steps of the building next door. An officer was sitting beside him, and it looked from here like he was wrapped in a foil blanket. "He was just coming back from a walk to the store and found her. He was the last person to see her alive, too."

Laura nodded her thanks and pointed the way ahead for Nate. She followed her partner as he approached the witness, lowering his tall frame to sit on the steps just below him and look up.

"Hello, sir," he said, his tone respectful and quiet. Laura saw that the man he was talking to was elderly, white hair contrasting against dark skin. He focused on Nate, seeming to take in what he was saying easily enough. "My colleagues tell me that you were the last person to see our victim alive."

"Gypsy," the man rasped, his voice raw. "Her name is Gypsy."

"What can you tell me about what happened to Gypsy?" Nate said. "What did you see?"

"I didn't see anything," the man said. "We were just walking and talking. She was worried about work. I just left her at the corner over there, to go to the store, and she said she was coming right home. It was only ten minutes that I was gone for. I warned her about the killer, but I never thought..."

"What's your name, sir?" Nate asked.

"It's Jerry," he said. "I didn't see anyone else in the area. I keep thinking about it. There wasn't anyone coming down the street, and the only person leaving the store was a woman. Her name is Martha, and I think she's older than me."

"Alright, Jerry," Nate said, making his tone even more gentle in response to the man's obvious distress. "Any information you can give us is really crucial. How long have you known Gypsy?"

"Oh, several years," Jerry said. "She moved in here and we got to know each other immediately. She was such a good girl. Always came to look after me if I needed it. We used to walk and talk together all the time."

He wiped a tear from his eye, and Nate reached out to pat his shoulder for a moment before continuing. "What can you tell me about Gypsy? Did she live alone?"

"Yes, she was alone," Jerry said, sniffling. "She broke up with her last boyfriend a few months ago. I think his name was Joe, or something like that."

"And what did Gypsy do for a living?" Nate asked. Laura glanced up at the building as he spoke. The homes here were small, but they weren't apartments. As much as they might have moved out of the center of Seattle, these places still wouldn't have been cheap. You had to have some degree of professional success to live here. Laura's mind moved through the possibilities: former soap actress, child star, coach at one of the more prestigious academies…

"She was the manager of a bookstore in town," Jerry said. "Otto's Books."

Nate blinked. He looked around at Laura, sharing a confused expression with her, before turning back to Jerry. "That was all she did for a living?"

"That's it," Jerry confirmed.

"No hobbies, side jobs, anything like that? Something she did as a volunteer?"

Jerry let out a laugh. "After the hours she worked at that place, poor girl had no time for a life. Gypsy worked. That's it. I kept telling her to take some time out, but she… Oh…" Jerry shook his head, tears falling down his cheek again. "Oh, she was so determined. She told me she didn't want to find love again because it was too painful. And now…"

"Okay, Jerry," Nate said, soothingly. "Thank you for your help. That's been really great. I want to ask you some more questions later, maybe, but for now you should get some rest. Do you have anyone coming to stay with you?"

Jerry wiped his face, the blanket rustling as he did so. "My wife is inside," he said. "I told her not to come out. I couldn't let her see that."

Nate took a card out of his pocket. "If you think of anything that might be useful, please give me a call," he said. "I'm Agent Nate Lavoie. Just call me Nate, alright, sir? Just call me whenever, don't worry about the time."

"Alright, son," Jerry said, nodding feebly. As Nate got up and stepped back, the officer beside him helped him to his feet, leading him away.

Laura stood by Nate to watch him go inside, then they both turned. If Nate's heart was as heavy as hers, she wouldn't be surprised. Watching a man suffer like that, an elderly man who didn't need to see this kind of thing at this point in his life – it didn't get easier just because they had been on the job for years.

"Not an acting coach," Laura said, knowing that Nate was going to feel as mystified about that as she was.

"Maybe he got it wrong," Nate suggested.

Laura couldn't help but frown. "It sounds like he knew her pretty well."

Captain Mills walked up beside them, holding a piece of paper in his hand. It appeared to be a torn page out of a notebook, and when he held it out, Laura instinctively took it. "I thought you might like to see this," he said. "We've got detectives inside checking the house. We found her unlocked phone in her pocket, and a lot of messages from months ago that look to be romantic in nature, from a contact called Joe. Now, we're not entirely certain, but there was an address book in the house which did have a listing for a Joe. One of the detectives noted this down, thinking you might want to get over there to talk to him as soon as possible."

"Thank you, Captain," Laura said, checking the address. It was in the city, and not too far away. "We'll head there right away."

"It's midnight, Laura," Nate said, checking his watch. "We don't know if this guy is going to be awake."

"Then we'll get him out of bed," Laura told him. "Nothing is more important than this. I don't want to be standing in another part of the city this time tomorrow, standing over another stabbed woman. Come on. Let's go."

They lingered by the body for a few minutes, looking it over carefully. There didn't seem to be any clue that would give them the killer, at least not at first sight. The forensics experts might give them something more, but Laura and Nate couldn't help with that. Laura turned to the car, leaving the rest of the examination of the body to the forensics team. She knew she wouldn't get anything from touching the poor woman now, anyway. There was nothing in her future.

If she was going to have a vision that led her to the killer, she needed the knife – and so far, he'd been careful enough to avoid leaving any kind of physical evidence that she could even try with, let alone something as crucial as that.

But as she started up the engine and Nate input the address into the GPS, Laura was at least heartened by one thing: a new body meant new leads. And if they could find the one person or thing that linked all three of the women, they would be closer than ever to getting this case solved.

She just had to hope this ex-boyfriend had the answers – and they weren't just running around Seattle on a wild goose chase that allowed the killer to get further and further ahead.

CHAPTER TWENTY THREE

Laura took advantage of stopping at a red light to rub her eyes. She was tired. It was getting too late for her to focus properly; after the lack of sleep and the flight this morning, she only had so much energy in the tank. The headache still throbbing behind her temples wasn't helping.

"So, what did he have to say?" Nate asked.

"What?" Laura asked, so confused for a moment that she didn't even move right away when the lights changed. Thankfully, there was no one behind her to get annoyed; the roads were much clearer than they had been during the day.

"Caleb Rowntree," Nate said. "You were meeting with him when we got the call about the new body."

"Oh," Laura said, shaking her head briefly. "Nothing, really. At least, I don't think so. He had some information about a suspicious client in the acting class, but it was over a year ago."

"Really? He didn't say anything else?" Nate asked.

"Nope."

"Not even asking you out on a date?"

Laura glanced at Nate, then refocused on the road. They weren't far from the house where Joe Barnes was listed in the address book. "He said he'd like to see me when I wasn't investigating a murder."

"Ha!" Nate crowed. "I knew it! So, what did you say?"

"I said maybe," Laura replied, focusing even harder on the road in the hopes it could somehow get her out of this conversation. "I just don't know right now, Nate."

"Going on dates could be good for you," Nate said. "Even if you don't think it will go anywhere. Get out, socialize, talk to someone who isn't in law enforcement."

"Oh, and how many dates have you been on since splitting up with Katya?" Laura asked. She immediately regretted it. It was catty, and she was better than that. Now that she was sober, anyway.

"None," Nate said, scratching the back of his head as if uncomfortable. "But it's only been six months."

"Seven," Laura corrected him. Then she was surprised at herself. How had she been counting? She hadn't realized she'd been keeping such a close eye on Nate's personal life. But then, they did spend almost every hour of every working day together – and in the FBI, working days could be very long hours indeed.

"Well, anyway," Nate said. "Me being a loner is no excuse for you not getting back into the saddle. You should move on from Marcus, find someone who makes you feel good."

Except, Laura thought to herself, that wasn't really an option. She couldn't get close to anyone again. Because whenever she did, she always had one big secret that she had to keep from them. On top of all the FBI stuff, all the confidential cases she couldn't talk about that haunted her late at night, she could never come clean about her ability. Without trust, a relationship would rupture. She had experienced that already with Marcus and had no intention of experiencing it again.

"Maybe," she said noncommittally. She didn't want to get into an argument with Nate. Not about this. He wasn't going to win, no matter what he thought.

"You deserve it," Nate said. "You deserve to be happy at home. I know this job takes its toll, and I know it can be hard for our significant others to deal with, but that's no reason not to try and find someone who can accept it." He reached out, before Laura could stop him, and patted her arm.

The wave of death rolled over her immediately, making her feel sick to her stomach. The shadow was still hanging over Nate thick and fierce, like a physical presence shrouding his entire body. It filled the air, made it hard for her to breathe. Even when he withdrew his hand after a moment, she could still feel the lingering presence of it, clouding everything. She was only lucky it hadn't been a vision, because it might have caused her to lose control of the car with how strong it was.

But she wanted it to be a vision. She wanted to know what was going to happen to Nate. Just feeling this shadow of death and not knowing what it meant - it was horrible. Almost unbearable. She didn't want to do it anymore.

She said nothing, shrugging off what he had said and pretending that she was simply feeling awkward about it. That way, he didn't have to know that it was his touch that had silenced her. He didn't have to know what she was hiding from him.

Hiding from him, like she always had to hide from everyone else. How long would it be before her relationship with Nate went sour as well?

"We're here," Laura said, as much to distract herself as to move the conversation on. She pulled up outside a house that was considerably smaller than the one they had come from, a narrow, terraced building with properties close by on either side. It was squeezed into the street, like the whole row of houses had been pushed up against each other until they rose higher and thinner.

The neighborhood was quiet, almost silent, and none of the lights were on in the house. But that didn't stop them from walking up to the door and knocking on it loudly, tilting their heads back as one to look for any sign of life. A light flickered on in the room in the top left window, and they waited patiently for the homeowner to make his way down to the front door.

He opened it wearing pajamas and a robe over them, looking bleary at them and rubbing his eyes. "Hello?" he said, clearly wanting some kind of answer as to why they had interrupted his sleep.

"Joe Barnes?" Laura said, taking him in. He was ruffled from sleep and the open robe showed he was slightly overweight, but he wasn't bad looking. Sandy-colored hair and blue eyes contrasted against tanned skin, like he spent a lot of time outdoors.

"Yeah?"

Laura flipped open her badge. "FBI Special Agent Laura Frost," she said. "This is my partner, Special Agent Nathaniel Lavoie. We'd like to ask you some questions. Can we come inside?"

Joe blinked at them, then nodded. "Um, yeah," he said, glancing up and down the street as though he was worried about them being seen. "Come in."

They entered the house as he closed the door behind them, then hurriedly turned on a light and ushered them to a living room. It was comfortably decorated in soft and modern furniture, which surprised Laura. She had been expecting some kind of bachelor pad, but this wasn't it.

"Who is it?" someone – a female someone – called from upstairs.

"Sorry, I'll just go – I'll go let her know," Joe said, casting about himself as though he didn't quite know what he was doing before turning to the stairs. "I'll get dressed, too."

Laura and Nate took a seat on the sofa while they waited for him to return. Looking around, Laura spotted a framed photograph of Joe with a woman. She pointed towards it, and Nate nodded. The reason for the comfortable furnishings was clear. He wasn't a bachelor any longer. He must have moved on fairly quickly if he was already living with someone, after breaking up with Gypsy only a few months ago.

Eventually, Joe came back down the stairs in a pair of faded jeans and a baggy sweater, slightly creased. Clearly, they were things he had just picked up from the floor and thrown on. He was still combing a hand through his hair as he reached them again and took the armchair facing them. It was the only chair left in the room, so it wasn't as though he had much choice.

"What is this about?" he asked, finally stopping fiddling with his hair and resting his hands on his knees.

"Joe, are you familiar with a woman by the name of Gypsy Sparks?" Laura asked. The full confirmed identity had come through from Captain Mills while they were on the way.

"Gypsy?" Joe said. "Yes, of course. We dated for a while. Why? What has she done?"

"You assume that she has done something?" Laura said. "You're not concerned about her?"

"No," Joe said. "I mean, yes, of course. It's just, she's always had a bit of a wild streak."

"How so?" Laura asked, pulling out her notebook ready to write down anything that might be relevant.

"Just, living on the edge, I guess," Joe said. "To be honest, she's calmed down a lot, I think. She always used to tell me about things she got in trouble for when she was younger, though. Like pretending to be someone else to get into a party, or underage drinking, or stuff like that."

"That's interesting," Laura said. "But, no, she's not in trouble. In fact, I'm afraid we have to tell you that we're here because Gypsy Sparks is dead."

She watched his face carefully. She saw shock written all over it. After a long moment, he covered his mouth as if he was going to be sick. It took him a moment to be more composed, wiping his mouth on the back of his sleeve. "I... I can't believe it," he said. "What happened?"

"That's what we're trying to ascertain," Laura said. "If you could sit down again, Joe."

"It gets worse?" he said, blanching. He did as he was told, taking his seat much more tentatively this time. "How could it be worse?"

"I'm sorry to be the one to tell you this," Nate said. "But we're investigating Gypsy's death as a murder."

"Oh, God," Joe said, covering his mouth again. This time, he didn't run off. He just closed his eyes for a moment. "Who would do something like that?"

"We were hoping you might be able to shed some light on that," Laura said. "Do you remember anyone who Gypsy had a problem with? An ex, a student, anyone like that?"

"A student?" Joe said, frowning. "What do you mean?"

"Was Gypsy an acting coach?" Laura asked. She'd hoped the casual question would have thrown the information up, but Joe was looking baffled.

"No, she worked in retail," he said. "She's a manager at a bookstore."

"Okay," Laura said, noting it down with a sinking feeling. She had been hoping – desperately – that he would come up with some link that contradicted what they had been told. "So, can you think of anyone?"

"No," Joe said, rubbing a hand back over his head. "No, there was no one. Maybe the odd difficult customer, but I wouldn't know any of their names. And I don't think a customer complaint would be grounds for murder – would it?"

"We're hoping it would be a deeper connection than that, but anything is possible," Laura said. "That's why anything you can remember, no matter how small, will really help."

"No," Joe said, at length. "No, there's nothing. I'm sorry. At most, I guess I would have pointed to myself. We broke up about five months ago. But, I mean, I had nothing to do with it."

"What time did you get home tonight?" Laura asked, just in case.

"About six," Joe said.

"And you were alone, or…?"

"With my wife," Joe said, gesturing upstairs to the woman who had called out earlier.

Laura almost winced. His wife? After just five months? There must have been some overlap there. Or worse, he had been married for years. She didn't ask. If both the husband and the wife were at home all evening, there was no way it could have been them.

Of course, both of them would have lied for the other. But even if they did, it didn't give them much of a motive to kill the other two women.

"While we're here," Nate said. "Do you know of anyone by the name Suzanna Brice?"

"No," Joe said. "Oh, wait – wasn't that the woman who was killed yesterday? Hang on – are you saying – is this the same killer?"

Laura groaned inwardly. The press had the story, and it was spreading now, gaining momentum. Before long, every single person they spoke to would have heard of all of the victims. This was going to make it even more difficult to get to the bottom of any interrogations they needed to carry out.

The press was both a blessing and a curse when it came to cases. They could warn the public, tell them how to keep safe. But they could also give out information that made their fact-finding missions even more difficult.

"We can't be sure just yet," Laura hedged. "If you think of anything that could help us out, no matter how small, please do get in touch."

"Yes, of course," Joe said. "Will you... I mean. I know Gypsy didn't have any family. Has anyone ID'd her body?"

"Yes, we've had a positive identification," Laura confirmed, at which news Joe seemed to sag with relief.

"Great," he said. "I mean, obviously, it's not. It's awful. I just... I would have done it, if you needed it."

"We understand," Laura said, giving him a brief smile. She actually did. There was no way it could be easy to have to see the dead body of a former lover, even if you'd moved on. "Thank you, Joe. We'll let you get back to bed, now. But do call us at any time."

"I will," Joe promised. He ran a hand over his head with that same distracted motion as before. Laura got the impression he probably wasn't going to get any sleep any time soon.

They walked out of the house, not speaking in the empty silence of the night until they were back inside the car. From the doorway of his home, Joe Barnes watched them for a moment, then turned to go to his wife.

"This ruins everything," Laura muttered, sitting behind the wheel but not yet starting the engine. "It shatters everything we thought we knew. She's not an acting coach. It was all just a coincidence that the first two were."

"And it's a dead end," Nate sighed. "Yet again, no enemies, no one who comes up as suspicious. Except these two, and they were clearly in bed. They wouldn't have had much time to get back here and genuinely look like they just woke up."

"We only saw Joe," Laura said thoughtfully. "Not his wife. Maybe we should keep her in mind."

"If we can find any link between her and the others, I'll put her in cuffs with pleasure," Nate said. "But right now, we have nothing. Our only leads have all panned out into nothing. We're back where we started when we got off the plane."

"Except now, there's another dead body," Laura said grimly. "And if we don't get a handle on this situation soon, there could be a fourth."

"Sleep, first," Nate said, stifling a yawn. "We're no good to anyone exhausted. In the morning, we tackle this again. Maybe we'll have some kind of divine inspiration while we sleep and figure it all out."

In normal circumstances, Laura would have argued. She would have told him that they needed to press on, to get this solved no matter how long it took. But she was tired, so tired, and he was right. Even if they worked on through the night – they had nothing.

She turned the car towards the motel they were booked into, wishing as she always did that she had the power to stay awake for days until the case was solved, remaining sharp and clear.

CHAPTER TWENTY FOUR

Laura locked the door to her motel room and turned to see Nate just emerging from his own. He nodded a greeting. "You sleep okay?"

Laura shrugged. In truth, she hadn't much. She'd tossed and turned for most of the night after they got back, and with her alarm set for the sunrise, there hadn't been a lot of hours of actual shuteye. But it had been enough to get her moving again, and she didn't want Nate to order her back for more rest, so she didn't say it. "Let's just pick up something to eat on the way," she said. "I don't want to waste time at a diner. We can eat at the same time as investigating."

"No arguments here," Nate said. He held up a hand for the car keys, and Laura tossed them to him, not wanting to argue with him either. If he wanted to drive, she had no problem with it. She slumped into the passenger seat and shut the door after herself, wishing the sun wouldn't be quite so bright.

"I've been thinking," Nate said, starting the engine. "Even if we can't find a link yet between Gypsy and the others, we still have a really strong link to the acting world. Chances are that the killer knew both of our first two victims from those circles. I don't think we should give up. When we find the missing link that connects all of them, I still think it's going to be a student or colleague."

"You could be right," Laura agreed. Despite her own restless night, she hadn't managed to get much thinking done at all, it seemed. She still had no better ideas than that. "I guess we can start with the two class lists, start going through them and looking for connections. Even if it's not a current student, one of them might know something about someone from the past, and they can help us put it together."

"Sounds good," Nate said. "I think Lucile's list had phone numbers. We can start with those, ask the detectives to find us some contact details for the others while we work through them."

"Better yet, they can help us with the calls," Laura said. "All hands on deck. Anyone that Captain Mills can spare. The quicker we get this done, the quicker we'll know if we have something or not."

"I'd like to speak with a few of our previous suspects and contacts again, too," Nate said thoughtfully. "See if they can shed any light on a connection to Gypsy."

The motel wasn't far from the precinct, and they were already pulling into the car park within a few minutes. Laura spared a moment to wish she was going to a place with better coffee before getting out of the car and heading inside, trailing in Nate's wake. He seemed far more awake than she was already. That was a good thing. Maybe he would be able to carry her a little this morning.

Talking on the phone with all the contacts they could get, though, was a great idea. Maybe they would get lucky, and Laura would happen to call the killer. If she did, she might trigger a vision, see him in action. That would give her everything she needed to start tracking him down, and all she would need to say was that he had seemed suspicious in the phone call to make everyone follow her lead.

Laura sloped into the elevator to head up to their investigation room and gather the first set of numbers to work on, while Nate went to speak with Captain Mills and beg him for some detectives to man the phones. She took a deep breath and picked up her cell phone to make the first call, knowing that it wasn't going to get any easier if she waited for him to come back. She was still going to be tired and feeling like hell.

The phone rang for what seemed like a long time, and Laura was about to give up and move on to the next number when it finally connected. "Hello?" the sleepy voice asked, clearly having been woken up by the call.

"Hello, is that Matthew?" Laura asked.

"Yeah. Who is this?"

"My name is Special Agent Laura Frost. I wanted to talk to you about a case we're currently investigating."

"Oh, man – is this about Lucile? I saw it on the news," Matthew said, suddenly sounding a lot more awake. "It's awful."

"That's right," Laura said. "We're trying to find any information that could help us to bring her killer to justice. First of all, can I ask you if anyone suspicious or any unusual events come to mind over the last few months? Something you might have witnessed in class, for example?"

"Oh, yeah," Matthew said, making Laura sit up and click her pen on. "There was this one guy. He's been losing it lately."

"Okay, can you tell me his name?" Laura asked.

"Everyone calls him Duck," Matthew said, with a slight laugh. "He's kind of pathetic. He had a breakdown recently, I think. Ended up in some kind of center."

"Can you think of what his real name is?" Laura asked. "That would be really useful."

"I'm not sure. Donald maybe?" Matthew said, and then gave a short laugh again. "Oh, I just got the joke. Yeah, his name is Donald something."

"Right," Laura said, noting this down. She wondered privately why Caleb hadn't mentioned this guy. "Anything else you can tell me?"

"I don't know," Matthew said. "Um, there was this girl as well. She dropped out a while back because she kept getting bad notes all the time. Michaela, I think? She just wasn't cut out for it. I think it made her really mad."

"Okay, Matthew, thanks for that," Laura said. "If you do think of anything else, just give us a call back and let us know, alright?"

"Yeah, I will," Matthew said. "I hope you catch them. Lucile was nice. And the best acting coach I've ever had."

Laura ended the call and scanned down the list. There was a Donald there, and a Michaela too. Laura was dialing for Donald when Nate walked in, and she gave him a tense smile. The call rang out with no response, and she swung her wheeled office chair towards the computer they had been given to work on, quickly logging in to access any records she could find on him.

"Anything yet?" Nate asked, perusing the list and picking out a number to call for himself.

"Maybe," Laura said. "Couple of leads. I'm going to chase them down, see where they get me."

***

Where they got her turned out to not be very far. Already, Laura felt like they were sifting through a haystack to look for a needle. Donald was not available because he was still recovering in a treatment center; it turned out his breakdown had been very severe, and he had been confined to his room at the center ever since. Patients required a day pass to leave, and he had never requested one. That would explain why Caleb hadn't brought him up as suspicious – he couldn't possibly be involved in any of this.

Michaela turned out to be working at a marketing firm and loving it and had moved on from acting entirely. She wasn't mad about changing careers – she was happy. By the time Laura had worked through them, Nate had another five leads from the people he'd called, all of them accusing other students from the acting classes.

All of the actors in the class, it seemed, had some kind of neurosis or issue. Some of them were transient because they couldn't make a living from acting, moving from one place to another every week but still managing to turn up to class. Some of them had had breakdowns like Donald, in varying degrees of severity. Some of them had just quit the class to focus on some other aspect of their lives or gone to a different coach and held no grudge against Lucile. There was gossip in every quarter, enough rumors to fill a whole tabloid paper, and none of it seemed to actually lead anywhere.

By mid-morning, they had a pile of reports from Mills' detectives, who were finding and calling the students from Suzanna Brice's list one by one. It was a much harder process. Suzanna hadn't kept good records: some of the students were just listed by first name or nickname, and none of them had contact details. But the story was emerging in a similar light. Lots of rumors, no real leads.

It was enough to drive Laura to a breakdown, herself.

She looked over the names they had already investigated – dozens, by now, and buried her head in her hands for a moment. She couldn't keep doing this. She needed a break, something to keep her going.

Glancing at Nate to check that he was still distracted by his own calls, Laura picked up her own phone again and called Division Chief Rondelle, hoping he wouldn't be angry at her for checking in.

"Rondelle."

"Hi, sir, it's Agent Frost," Laura said, keeping her tone as deferential as possible. "I just wanted to check in and see how things are going with Amy."

She heard Rondelle sigh, but to his credit, he didn't brush her off. He probably knew that she wouldn't concentrate, or do as she was told, until she heard some news. "She's in a temporary home and seems to be doing well, according to the latest report," he said. "I've made sure she's been settled in a place where Governor Fallow isn't going to find her easily. I don't think he's going to be able to make contact with her."

"That's good," Laura said, breathing a little more freely. "Can you give me the number of the home?"

"No, I can't," Rondelle said bluntly. "Laura, I don't think that's a good idea. Aside from the fact that we're not supposed to give out that kind of information, even to investigating agents – we're trying to keep her hidden. The fewer people who know where she is, the better."

"But," Laura began, only for Rondelle to cut her off.

"I know you want to speak to her, and I know you'll feel you have a right to because it was you who rescued her from that place," he said. "I'll try to find a way to connect you later. But not right now, Laura. She also has to begin to settle. There's a lot going on for her right now."

"I understand," Laura said. She wanted to argue that Amy would feel better settled if she could talk to someone she trusted – to Laura. She wanted to point out that the girl was with strangers and probably needed to hear a friendly voice. But she didn't. Her long, drawn-out fight to get access to Lacey had taught her that women who argued were branded trouble, or troublemakers, or too unstable. They were told they would harm the child with their attitude and made to stay away for even longer.

Laura wasn't going to make that same mistake again.

"Alright. Any progress on your Seattle case?" Rondelle asked.

"Some, and then none," Laura sighed. "We've had a couple of very good suspects, but nothing viable so far. We're just making calls to individuals from a long list of potential witnesses, and I wanted a quick break. I'll get back to it now."

"Glad to hear that," Rondelle said. "Keep working hard. I want results as soon as you can. The press are starting to catch wind of this, and we need to get it wrapped up before we have a city-wide panic on our hands. Don't let yourself get distracted."

"Yes, sir," Laura said, as if she was going to try for anything else.

She put the phone down and was about to go downstairs to find out where the other detectives had managed to get to on their list, when she realized Nate was talking with a renewed note of interest in his voice. He made several affirmative noises and then thanked who he was talking to, putting the phone down and giving her a triumphant look.

"What did you get?" Laura asked.

"Maybe something, maybe not," Nate told her. "I just got off the phone with a photographer – one of the students from the list referred me to him. Apparently, Lucile Maddison used to refer her students to him for a slight discount on their headshots – and she wasn't the only one. He reckons he covers at least half of the aspiring actors in the city because of his connections."

"Which include other acting coaches?" Laura asked, her eyebrow raised in hope.

"Oh, yes," Nate said with a grin. "Such as Suzanna Brice. I said we'd go over there now to talk to him."

"Thank God," Laura said, getting up from her chair. "Maybe he'll actually be able to tell us something. If I have to listen to one more melodramatic actor tell me that someone in their class was suspicious because they were also melodramatic, I might just have to scream."

Nate chuckled. "Lots of bad leads for me, too. But I have high hopes for this one. He spoke about Suzanna and Lucile like friends, not just people he'd made a deal with. He might know more about them than the students do."

Laura nodded, leading the way out of the precinct. "Let's hope he can point us in the direction of the killer – and help us figure out how Gypsy Sparks fits into the whole picture."

Because, if he didn't, Laura knew, time was getting on. Soon, it would be mid-day. Mid-day would lead into the afternoon, and then swiftly on into the evening. And if all they still had to go on by then was a confusing web of cross-accusations and missed calls from drama students, then they were not going to be in any position to stop the killer from taking his fourth victim in four nights.

And that, Laura was determined, was never going to happen on her watch.

CHAPTER TWENTY FIVE

Laura and Nate got out of the car outside a photographic studio, made obvious by the full-length portraits displayed in the floor to ceiling windows of the ground floor. They were actually a little bit terrifying, blown up larger than life as they were. Each of them depicted different men and women holding emotive expressions - a frown, a laugh, a cocky eyebrow raised.

If they had had any doubt that they were in the right place, all of the coding here clearly screamed that this was a place for actors to come and get their headshots.

A bell above the door jingled gently as they pushed it open, and within seconds a gray-haired man with a sprightly build emerged from behind a door. He was more youthful around the eyes than his hair suggested, and he looked at them with obvious inquisitiveness.

"Are you the agents I spoke with on the phone?" he asked.

"Yes," Nate said, showing his badge and then holding out a hand for the man to shake. "I'm Agent Nate Lavoie, we spoke on the phone. This is my partner, agent Laura Frost."

"Great to meet you," the photographer said. "Guy Andrews. I was really glad when I got your call. It's terrible, what happened to Suzie and Lucy. I can't believe it. If there's anything I can do to help, I'm only too glad."

"Well, anything you can think of might be useful," Laura said. "We're really looking for any lead we can trace down that might point us to someone who had a reason to kill these women. Even if it doesn't seem like a logical reason to us. As they were both acting coaches, we were thinking that their students may hold the answer – and I gather you may have known many of them?"

"Oh, yes, certainly," Guy said. He held out a hand towards the door he had come through and then began to lead them through it. "If you'll come this way, I can take you through my archives. I'm much better with pictures than words."

"Of course," Nate said, leading Laura behind Guy through to a much bigger, more open space. Here they could see the hallmarks of a studio: white backdrops, large lighting rigs, monitors and cameras sat on tables. One of them was obviously a permanent desk, with a large computer setup including several monitors. Guy led them here, quickly turning on the screen in the middle and beginning to click rapidly through folders.

"Actually, there was one person who came to mind right away. I don't know if you've heard about anything about him yet," Guy said, seemingly satisfied when he clicked up another folder and then sat back in his chair to look at them. "He was referred to me by Lucy, but I gather he never actually ended up going to any of her classes. They knew each other from another walk of life, some other work she had done, I think. I think he had a small part in an advertisement campaign, it went to his head. He thought he was the be all and end all, but of course he wasn't. They never are. Anyway, as I understand it, he ended up going to classes with Suzie instead."

"That's very interesting," Laura said. "Do you know what his name was?" Internally, she was praying that it was not the same named they had heard before - Caleb Rowntree. Given that they had already cleared him from the investigation, this could easily be one more dead end. But if Guy had stopped at pictures of a Black man with a buzzcut and a noticeable scar to the left side of his face for any reason, Laura hoped it was because they were looking at a new suspect.

"It should be in the file," Guy said, clicking around again. "Yes, here we are. His name was Spike Greendale. Stage name, I think. Bit of an odd one."

"And was there anything about his behavior in particular that made you think he might be suspicious?" Nate asked. "Other than being a bit big-headed?"

"Oh yes," Guy said. "So, as I said, it was Lucy who referred him to me for the headshots. Gave him a nice discount, too. Anyway, we come to take the shots, and everything seems fine. But when I do the review with him one week later, showing him all the edited files to choose from, he throws a fit. Decides that they all make him look fat, or they haven't captured his best side. I mean, it was all just rubbish. You can see for yourself; the shots weren't that bad. He looks exactly the same in person. I can't control how a person looks. Anyway, he wasn't happy. He threw an angry fit with me. If I hadn't told him to get out of the studio, I think he might have ended up hitting me."

"Have you witnessed or heard of any other violent behavior from this man?" Laura asked, quickly scribbling down the name in her notebook.

This was starting to sound more promising by the second.

"No, nothing else. I just know that if he was able to leave his rag that way with me, I'm sure he could do it with someone else. Someone who told him he didn't really have the talent, maybe," Guy said. He shook his head sadly. "He was exactly the kind of man that you could imagine hearing about on the news a few years later as being a serial killer or something. I just wasn't expecting to hear it quite this soon."

"Thanks very much for that information," Laura said. She was about to nod to Nate to see if he was ready to go, when it came to her mind again. "Oh, by the way. We wondered if you might know about somebody else - a woman by the name of Gypsy Sparks?"

"Oh, sure," Guy said, leaning back in his chair. "I know Gypsy. Why, is she wrapped up in all of this too?"

"Sorry," Laura said, gaping at him. "You do know her? In what context?"

"Well, the same as all the others," Guy said. "I did her headshots, years ago. And then she went into coaching, and I used to get referrals from her as well. That was years ago though. I heard she got out of the business."

"She certainly did," Laura said. In her mind, the comment was a rather dark one, but of course Guy couldn't know the hidden meaning behind what she was saying. He didn't yet know that she was dead. "So, how long ago was this exactly?"

Guy thought for a moment. "Oh, probably... eight years ago? I'd have to look back in my records to remember the last time I had a referral from her. I didn't exactly get a lot, because she was only doing the one-to-one work. I get a lot better business from the coaches that do the big classes, because they can refer tons of people at once. Anyway, on the other hand, the people who can afford the one-on-one coaches usually tend to spend more on their upgrade packages, so I don't mind. How is she wrapped up in all of this, then?"

Laura bit her lip for a moment. She was going to have to tell him, she could see. "I'm sorry," she said. "Gypsy actually died last night. We are investigating her death in conjunction with the other two."

Guy stared at her for a second as if she had grown an extra head. Then he turned his face slowly towards the monitor, as if seeking solace in the images. "Christ," was all he said, his voice shaky and quiet.

"Is there any way you can think of that Gypsy might have been linked to Suzie and Lucy?" Laura asked. "Obviously, the three of them all working in the same industry is a big one, but we're really looking for perhaps a person who would have worked with all three of them, a job they all did, something like that."

"I don't know," Guy said. "But one thing that might help you is if you have both of her names to search with."

"Both of her names?" Laura said. "What do you mean?"

"Well, because she changed her name legally," Guy said. "Gypsy Sparks. That's not her real name. Or at least, not the one she was born with. It was a stage name."

Laura turned and looked at Nate, seeing his shocked expression mirroring her own. This all made sense, in a strange way. If it was eight years ago that Gypsy had given up working in the acting industry, then those who had only met her in the time since might not know all the details about it. Her ex-boyfriend, who was probably more interested in his wife than in Gypsy. Her neighbor, who was there for a friendly chat about the day's work but nothing more in-depth than that. None of them would have known about her name change or the acting career, which explained why it hadn't come up yet.

And it meant the M.O. of the killer still fit. All acting coaches. All three of them.

"What was her name before this?" Laura asked, thinking they needed to take it down just in case it was useful.

"I'm not sure," Guy shrugged. "Georgina, I think. I don't know about her last name."

"This has been extremely useful, Guy," Laura said, making a mental note to ask for a check-up on her previous identity. "Thank you. I don't suppose you have the contact details of Spike Greendale?"

"I do," Guy said, double clicking something on his screen. Beside him, a small printer whirred to life. "It wasn't too long ago I did the shots, either, so this should still be accurate, with any luck."

With any luck, Laura thought. With any luck, they had the killer's address in their hands.

"Thanks again," Laura said. "We'd better go."

She nodded at Guy and turned to leave, heading right for the car. There was no way she was going to risk a delay now, when they could go and arrest the man who had been doing all of this and get him off the streets.

One by one, all the other suspects had fallen away. So many leads, all come to nothing.

This had to be the one.

CHAPTER TWENTY SIX

When they knocked on the door that Guy had given them, Laura found herself standing slightly behind Nate, as if to hide behind him. It hadn't been her choice. He had instinctively stepped forward, acting as a human shield.

A flash of fear ran through her. What if this was what killed him? What if this man really was the killer, and he was going to come out with a knife in his hand, a gun in his hand, something they couldn't react to quickly enough? What if this was what she had been seeing in that shadow of death all along?

She found herself pushing forward, squeezing her shoulder in beside Nate's on the narrow step, almost knocking him down in her haste to get in front of him.

He looked at her and opened his mouth as if he was about to say something, probably to ask her what the hell she was doing. But before he could make a single sound, the door in front of them opened, and both of them were on alert in a different direction.

"Hello?" the man at the door said. He was Spike Greendale, that much was clear. Laura recognized him exactly from the headshots that Guy had shown them. And Guy was right - he really did look exactly like the pictures.

"Spike Greendale?" Laura said. She held up her badge, tensing herself for the possibility that he was about to run as soon as he saw it. "Special Agent Laura Frost. We'd like to have a word with you, if we can."

"FBI?" Spike said, tension immediately strumming through his body as well. The atmosphere had changed markedly, all three parties now on edge. Laura felt the muscles in her arm tensing with the instinctual urge to reach for her gun. "Why do you need to talk to me?"

"Have you been watching the news lately, Spike?" Laura asked.

"Not really, Spike said, scratching his own chest. Laura took him in, the adrenaline of fear starting to go away just a little bit when he didn't immediately make a break for it. He was dressed in loose pants and a plain white shirt, almost as if he was still in his sleeping gear. It was lunchtime. Had he been asleep when they knocked? "I've been, well, kind of out of it for a few days. Why?"

"Perhaps we'd better discuss this inside," Laura said. "I think you're going to prefer it if your neighbors don't hear about this."

Not that they were in a neighborhood where the neighbors were particularly close. In fact, Spike Greendale had a very nice home indeed. What Laura couldn't quite workout yet was how a man who apparently had done just one advertising campaign and wasn't particularly great at acting could live somewhere like this. That was one of the questions he was going to have to ask answer.

"Um," Greendale said, hesitating. "Do I have to talk to you?"

"You don't have to," Nate said. "If you don't, we can go away and then come back with an arrest warrant and take you in to the local precinct. Or, on the other hand, you can talk to us now and we can save all of that trouble. What do you think?"

Greendale paused for a moment, looking down at the ground as if thinking. Then he looked up, meeting both Nate's and Laura's eyes in succession, as if he needed to test something in them. Finally, he nodded. "Okay," he said. "Come in."

They followed after him into a well-decorated and large living area, mostly decked out with dark woods and the kind of furnishings that would be described as masculine in a catalog. It looked as though he had asked a set designer to create a bachelor pad. Still, it looked lived in. They were framed photographs here and there, of Spike with different people. Some of himself as a younger child, with what had to have been his family. Some of him just on his own.

Laura and Nate both took a seat on a brown leather couch that squeaked unnervingly when they sat. Spike flung himself down opposite them, sprawling his arms out across the top of the cushions of a matching sofa and leaning back.

"What did you want to ask me, then?" he asked.

"First of all, we need to know what you were doing for the last few days in the evening," Nate said, taking the lead on the questioning. Laura sat back and let him, thinking that it would be both easier for Spike to identify with him and easier for Nate to drive the knife home if he needed to follow a more aggressive line of questioning.

"Not much," Spike said. "I've been working on setting up my new business, so I haven't been going out. Just registering domain names, setting up websites, all of that sort of thing. There's a lot that goes into it that you don't realize before you start."

"And what is this new business?" Nate asked.

Spike grinned, leaning forward slightly on the couch. "I'm glad you asked. I'm actually starting up my own coaching business. I coach actors, you see."

"You coach actors?" Laura asked, her eyebrow raised. Now her mind was working overtime. Was he bumping off the competition so that he would be able to get a larger share of the market? She had heard of more outlandish reasons to murder someone, even if it did seem disproportionately violent.

"Well, I'm going to," Spike said. "The truth is, I've been trying to make it as an actor myself for quite a while now. But I have to face facts. I'm not going to make it in that sense. The thing is, I've had a lot of really great coaching. Actually, it was my coach, Suzie, who made me think about going into this line of work. I think I'm going to be really good at it. And the great thing is I can always ask her for help if I need to, because we're not even going to compete. I'm going to be looking for high end one-on-one clients, while she does community classes. So, between us we'll be able to cover most of the city."

"That's quite ambitious," Nate said.

Spike grinned. "One thing I've never been short of is ambition," he said.

"So, let me just understand this," Nate said. "You have the acting talent and skills, and you have the ambition. Why haven't you made it in Hollywood yet?"

Spike shrugged. "You must know what it's like," he said. "Look at the color of my skin. I'm too dark for them. That's all it is."

Laura was beginning to doubt exactly how truthful he was being with them. Playing the racist card was easy. There was every possibility that it was true, but then again, from what she had heard, this guy had other problems.

He was so calm and cool, so accommodating. He didn't seem nervous at all. But if he was a talented actor, then that was to be expected. Maybe he was just playing a role right now. It was time to turn things up a notch, try and put the heat on him.

And for that, Laura knew exactly which direction to head in. Nate had established himself as the lead in the conversation, spoken to Spike about something that he was passionate about in order to draw him in. Now, Laura could play the bad cop, push his buttons until he said something he regretted. Or did something, if the description of his angry and violent behavior from Guy was anything to go by.

126

"You had some headshots done recently with a photographer called Guy Andrews, is that right?" Laura said, making Spike snap his attention to her.

"If you can call them that," Spike said, making a face. It was more of a casual, laughing face than Laura had expected, however. He wasn't getting red in the face or clenching his fists. "They weren't very good. I ended up not being able to use them."

"Really?" Laura asked, deliberately trying to push him. "That's funny. I've seen them, and I think they look quite accurate to life. In fact, I'd say they're exactly realistic to how you look in front of me now."

A darkness flickered over Spike's face and then away. "I think he made me look a bit heavier than I really am," he said.

Laura let her eyes flick over him, up and then down. "No," she said. "I think they were accurate."

She saw his jaw clench. Now she was making some progress. "Well, anyway. Why are you asking me about the headshots?"

"Because you weren't very pleasant to Guy Andrews, the way he tells it," Laura said. Nate was quiet, letting her nettle him and try to trigger a reaction. "In fact, he said he thinks you could be a serial killer."

"A serial killer?" Spike exploded, frowning heavily. "What is this? Just another white guy who sees a Black face and thinks we must all be violent thugs, is that it?"

"Well, aren't you?" Laura said.

It wasn't something that would ever normally have left her mouth. She had no tolerance for racists. In fact, she'd seen enough of death and violence to have no time for any kind of prejudice. Gender, race, religion – none of it mattered in the end. You would still bleed the same color when they stabbed you.

Much like the killer had stabbed three women so far. If it took underhanded tactics to prevent there from being a fourth, Laura wouldn't hesitate to use them.

Spike's upper lip curled, and now she saw that his hands were fists, tightly held and ready. Strain stood out in the muscles of his arms and neck, and he bared his teeth in a snarl. "Get out of my face, fed," he said, his voice dangerously low. "Before I make you get out."

Nate laughed, his tone scornful. "You can't make her do anything. People who look like us? You wouldn't last a minute in front of the judge, and she can get you put away for whatever she wants."

Spike leapt to his feet with a shout, but in the same moment Nate was also standing, one broad hand planted firmly on Spike's chest to hold him in place. For a long second, they faced off against one another, Spike brimming with anger and pushing back against that hand, ready to spring on Laura. But Nate carried on looking at him with dead calm, almost boredom, and finally Spike stopped trying to fight him.

"Take a seat, Mr. Greendale," Laura said, her voice completely different to how it had been a moment ago: no more needling, no more false arrogance, back to her professional and blank voice that she usually used for suspects. "We heard that you have anger problems, and you've just confirmed that for us."

Spike stared at her, then dropped down into his seat. He seemed to be shrinking now that he realized what he had done. "That doesn't mean anything," he protested. "A lot of people get angry. I haven't done anything!"

"Is there any way you can prove what you've told us? That you were at home, working, alone for the past three evenings?"

"No," Spike said, spreading his hands to either side, turned up as if to measure his innocence. "I was on my own. What am I supposed to do to prove that?"

"That's what we're asking you," Nate said, remaining calm and steady. "If you can't prove it, then I'm afraid we're going to have to take these allegations seriously – because right now, we can link you to at least two out of three murders that have taken place in the last few days."

Spike's jaw fell open. He stared between the two of them, as if to check that Nate was being serious. "Linked how?" he managed, at last.

"We have strong reason to believe that you knew both Lucile Maddison and Suzanna Brice," Laura said.

"Yes, I know them both," Spike said. "But they're not... dead...?"

"I'm afraid they are," Nate said.

They all went silent, allowing this news to sink in. Spike's eyes drifted to the floor, his hand covering his mouth. A flash of anger lit up his eyes as he glanced around, as if seeking the person responsible for this turn of events. Then it died out again, and Laura only saw sadness.

As real as it seemed, it only lasted a short time. Then, he shifted, sniffing and rubbing his face quickly before gesturing to a laptop on the coffee table. "Can I show you something?" he asked.

Laura nodded and gestured for him to go ahead. Her body tensed. Was he about to show them something innocent? Or something that would explain why he had killed them?

But when he opened the laptop, tapped a few keys, and then spun it around to show him the screen, it was only a website builder that was open – open to a log of recent changes.

"Look," he said. "The work log. It has all the times I've made changes to any page on the website. Even small changes like adding a word or moving a block. It's all there."

Nate shifted closer on his seat, peering at the screen. "These timestamps cover a large range of last evening, and the evening before."

"Exactly," Spike said. "Even if it doesn't prove I was here, it proves I was working on this. I couldn't kill someone and then go back and change something on my website a moment later. I've been adding all kinds of things. And filming videos, too – they'll have timestamps on, and they'll show I was right here. There's no way I would have time to do anything else in-between. I've barely had time to eat."

Nate leaned back, glancing at Laura with a nod. "It does appear to back up what he's saying." He glanced back at Spike. "If I was you, I would take screenshots of all of that data in case it disappears from the site. That's your alibi right now."

Spike nodded, reaching for the keys. Laura felt a headache growing in her temples, and not the kind that signaled a vision.

It was the kind that told her she'd been doing this for too long and wasn't getting anywhere. That there was a killer on the loose and yet again, their one lead had panned out to nothing.

"Thank you for your time," Laura said, standing up. "It looks like we can clear you from our investigation. We may need to talk to you again, but for now at least, that's all we needed to know."

She left Nate giving him more of a proper debrief and walked out of the building. She needed some fresh air, but it was stiflingly hot outside with the sun at its peak. When were they going to catch the break that would allow them to solve this case – and get a killer off the streets at last?

CHAPTER TWENTY SEVEN

Laura slumped inside the car and hit the A/C, covering her head with her hands for a moment until it kicked in. With the refreshing cool blasting over her face, she finally relaxed as much as she could. She pulled her cell phone out of her pocket to check her messages, anxious not to miss the chance to talk to Amy.

There were no messages from Chief Rondelle, or calls from unknown numbers, or anything else that might be a sign she was being given the go-ahead to check up on her. It was frustrating, having to just wait to be given permission. She wanted nothing more than to call every foster home in the state until she found Amy and could hear that she was alright. That would have been stupid, though, and she knew it.

She couldn't even risk chasing Chief Rondelle again. He would end up branding her a troublemaker. She couldn't talk to Marcus and beg him to let her talk to Lacey, because there was no way he would let her again so soon. And if she did start bothering him, he would think that allowing her to talk to her daughter in the first place had been a mistake.

Getting any kind of custody or visitation agreement in place was so far off that Laura could barely even imagine it. But hearing her daughter's voice had almost wrenched Laura loose from the world, knocked her out of her carefully held-together calm and back into the chaos that had forced her to drink in the first place. She couldn't go back to that, now. Not when Marcus had finally given her one tiny sliver of trust.

And with the case going badly as well, Laura couldn't help but feel the walls closing in on her again. She felt like she was running as fast as she could but getting nowhere, like in those awful dreams you sometimes had. She couldn't even talk to Nate, and he was getting more distant by the day.

The man who'd claimed to be a psychic, Nolan Perry, had left her another message asking her to meet him. She ignored it. Even if she wanted to, she had no way of knowing when she'd be able to get back into town. Or how long it would be before she had to leave again. She wasn't going to try to schedule something, not now.

"Alright?" Nate asked, getting into the driver's seat beside her. Glancing up, Laura saw the figure of Spike Greendale for just a moment as he closed his door behind him.

"I don't know," Laura said.

"If this is all getting a bit too much for you," Nate said, leaning across to try to look into her face properly.

"I'm fine," Laura said. The last thing she wanted was him getting suspicious that she was about to fall off the wagon. She wasn't. She didn't want that. "How far are we from the precinct?"

"About a ten-minute drive," Nate said, checking the GPS. "We have to pass through a bit of work on the road, otherwise it would be quicker."

"So, not far as the crow flies?" Laura asked.

"No, not far at all."

She nodded and reached for the passenger-side door. "I'm going to walk back," she said. "Get some air, clear my head. If I stick to the left side of the road, I should be protected from the worst of the sun by the shade of the buildings. I'll see you back there."

"In fifteen or so minutes?" Nate said, his tone clearly concerned, though he tried to hide it in a casual manner.

"Yes," Laura said. She turned to give him a direct look. "I'm not going to a bar on the way, Nate. I'll be fine."

She got out and started to walk before he could argue back, and a moment later she heard the engine start up. He drove past her, at first slowly, before speeding away and out of sight around a corner.

Laura breathed deeply, setting her sights on the turn she also needed to make. She just needed to spend some time on her own, to get past all of this. To get out of the funk that her brain seemed to be in. If she could figure all of this out, find out what she had missed somewhere along the line, they could get this finished and go home. Saving a life would be the cherry on top because she had no doubt that the killer was going to strike again tonight.

She just wished she had some way to magically find all of the answers, so that she could get this done. Somehow, her usual method just didn't seem to be working.

Passing into the shade of a large apartment block, Laura adjusted the front of her suit jacket, unbuttoning it to allow some air to flow around her body and prevent her from getting too hot. She reached, instinctively, to check that her gun was still in position in the hip holster she wore. As she did so, she felt a throb of pain in the temple on her right side, much sharper than before. The cold of the metal of the gun had not left her fingers before she felt the darkness starting to take her and knew that she was finally managing to trigger some sort of vision.

She barely had enough time to be afraid that the vision she would see would be of Nate's death, somehow at her own hands with this gun, before it was on her.

She was in some kind of wide, open room. It was full of light, and the surfaces everywhere she could see seemed to be polished wood or marble. The floor stretched out far ahead, and there were seats around her, all pointing towards a large open area of the floor.

Some kind of stage, she realized. An auditorium, maybe. There was a sign on the wall that said 'Carnegie'. She wasn't an expert on the Seattle entertainment scene, and she did not recognize it immediately, but she knew what the purpose of the space must be. There was a woman in front of her, a woman with long dark hair who stood with her back to Laura, looking at something in her own hands.

She was quite far away, and Laura could not make out the woman's identity in any way. She was trying to figure out some way to control the vision, to take her own sight somewhere else so that she could look around the woman and see what she needed to, but nothing seemed to budge. The edges of the vision faded to gray and then black, telling her nothing beyond what she could see right in front of her.

Right in front of someone, she realized. Because she was not floating above the scene this time. It felt as though she was actually seeing it from someone else's eyes.

The eyes of the killer, or her own eyes? Was this a vision of what would happen to herself in the future? Would she be standing in an auditorium somewhere, seeing this woman?

But then the woman moved, walking across the stage, heels clicking impressively as the sound was picked up and carried. She walked straight backstage, without looking behind her, as if she was familiar with this place and knew exactly where she needed to go. Laura's vision began to move as well, drawing her closer over the stage, following exactly where the woman had walked.

Exactly the same place - this felt significant. It felt like she was following the woman, like she was maybe stalking her. Exactly the kind of behavior that she might expect from a serial killer who was following his next victim, waiting to get her on her own. But then, why had he not struck yet? Why had he not taken her life while she was standing in the middle of the auditorium, all alone?

Laura's eyes looked down, and she saw a male body below herself. Hands that were larger than her own, a wristwatch in a masculine style, light-colored hair on her arms. Yes. She was him. She was the killer. She was seeing what he could see.

The vision turned up again, the killer hurrying towards the spot where the woman had vanished. He slipped inside, and Laura knew. He was looking for her. He was going to kill her.

Laura came back to herself on the street, her hand coming away from her gun and her stride only hitching for a moment as she carried on walking. Her mind was running overtime, trying to analyze what she had just seen. It had to be the killer. It had to be. Why else would she see that vision?

Why else would it trigger when she touched the handle of her gun?

She was getting closer to him, even if it didn't feel like it. She and Nate both were. Wherever he had gone, someone was in danger, and if Laura could find out where it was and get there at the same time, then she would be able to stop him. She would be able to pull that very gun and point it at him.

But finding out where it was would be half the battle. The pain in her head was strong, meaning that the vision must relate to something that was going to happen soon. The strength of the vision was very clear, showing her a lot of detail. In turn, she understood that this meant the killer's intent was strong and focused, allowing her to see things so much more clearly. He had a plan, and he was not going to be deterred from it by any little thing. He was going to kill tonight, that much was clear.

But how could she figure out where it was? She needed to get back to the precinct as quickly as possible, start looking through the computer for auditoriums, for any kind of venue that could be used as a stage. Then she would have to somehow convince Nate to come and look at it with her, though she wasn't sure how. Could she fake an anonymous tip? Could she risk doing that kind of thing, in case it would jeopardize a future court case?

Laura quickened her steps, racing back towards the precinct as quickly as she could. Although the time out had clearly given her the clarity she needed to have the vision in the first place, she now almost regretted getting out of the car. There was hardly any time to lose. She had to find this place and get there before the evening came on, and there was so much to do before then.

If she missed it, she might never find him again. This was it. Her chance. She wasn't going to let him kill another woman.

CHAPTER TWENTY EIGHT

He was standing in line at the coffee shop when he saw her. Of all the places to meet your muse, it had to be the most cliché and also the least obvious. He had never imagined that inspiration would strike in such a banal and mundane place as this.

But that was what inspiration was like. You never knew when it would strike. You never knew what form it would take, until it was right in front of you.

The truth was, this had been right in front of his face for a very long time. He should have seen it so much earlier. He should have recognized in her the inner beauty and grace that he had been searching for, for so long. He should have known that the thing he was seeking would be under his nose all along. It was like a movie, like a perfect script. And of course, that was exactly how it should be.

So, when he saw her in the coffee shop, he did not reach out or greet her. He let her pass by without noticing him, like they all tended to do. He knew he would be able to talk to her later, whenever he liked. But for now, he wanted to simply watch her, to bask in the pleasure of her perfection. He wanted to watch her, like he watched all of the others, learning from her and worshipping everything she did.

So, he had left the coffee shop without his hot beverage, or anything iced to keep him cool on this hot day.

He had walked after her, down the street at a respectable distance, tugging his cap down over his head whenever she thought of turning slightly or looking behind herself. He ducked into doorways and pretended to study window displays, always staying just far enough away that she would not be able to pick him out from the other pedestrians on the street so easily.

Ah, it had taken him so long to find her. It felt so sweet to follow her now, to watch her walk down the street towards her yoga class. He would wait outside, while she unfolded the mat she held under her arm, while she chatted with all the other people in the class, while she stretched and posed. And when she emerged, he would be able to follow her again.

He should have seen it earlier, if he had been thinking properly. There had been so many distractions along this journey. So many times that he had been taken in by someone who appeared to be perfect, but was really just a fake. A fraud. He had always thought that he had found the right woman, so many times.

He had always been wrong. And now he understood why. He had been wrong because the real muse, the right person for him, had been going overlooked. All of these times he had seen her, and he had never even thought to question himself as to whether she could be the one. It had only been the chance way that the light had fallen over her hair through the windows of the cafe that had clued him in at last.

And talk about divine intervention! Now that he had finally seen her, he knew he was seeing clearly. He felt like everything was falling into place at last. Like everything was starting to make sense. She went inside, into the building that housed not just the yoga classes but several other self-help groups and fitness and well-being classes, and he sought out a bench. Not right outside the building, because that would be too obvious. He didn't want to creep her out. No, he sat opposite on the other side of the street, taking out his cell phone and pretending to read something on it.

He was happy to sit there and wait for her. He would wait for her anywhere, for any length of time. Now that he knew she was the one, he would pay her all the respect she deserved, and that meant following her timetable instead of his own.

He passed the time by flicking through her social media profiles, examining the photographs and seeing how real they were. Seeing how genuine she was at all times, even posting pictures of herself without makeup, fresh-faced and glowing. He investigated her friends and read all about them, the ones he didn't yet know. And when, finally, she emerged, the mat tucked under her arm once more, he even knew the name of the woman she stopped to talk to in the doorway before waving goodbye and continuing her walk down the road.

He got up to follow her, watching her so closely that he forgot to check on his own steps. He almost walked right into a woman walking a dog, which could have been disastrous. If he had caused a scene, she might have looked up and seen him, and then the jig would be up. But it wasn't the end of the world. He only had to pull back quickly and tug his cap further down on his head, as if he was shy.

"S-sorry," he said, and darted around the dog and away, keeping time on the other side of the street as she led him to their next destination.

CHAPTER TWENTY NINE

By the time she had got back to the precinct, Laura had figured it out. The perfect way to not only find out where the vision had shown her, but also to create a lead that would be easy to explain.

She was only glad he had insisted on exchanging numbers, even if she hadn't realized why at the time.

"Hello, Laura?" he said, answering her call as she stood just outside the doors of the precinct. Nate would already be in there, she knew. She could see their rental car parked in what was becoming their habitual spot.

"Yes, it's me," Laura said. "Listen, Caleb. I was wondering if you could help me with something. It's for the case, and I think it might be within your area of expertise."

"Yes, of course," he said. "I'm not doing anything right now. Did you want to meet?"

"That won't be necessary," Laura said. "It will be quicker if I just talk to you now. I'm looking for a certain place. An auditorium, or a stage, or something like that."

"Actually, this is kind of awkward," Caleb said. "But, um… you're standing in front of the precinct, aren't you?"

"What?" Laura looked up and around in alarm. "Yes. How did you know that?"

"Well, you know that café I met you at before?" Caleb said. Laura's eyes shot over the other side of the road and then down until she found it. The windows were visible from here. At one of the tables right by them, a male figure lifted a hand and waved in her direction.

"Oh," Laura said. "You're here already."

"Yeah… I wasn't being creepy, I promise. I just really like the coffee here," Caleb said. "And last time, after you left, I had this amazing grilled cheese. It's like nothing I've ever eaten. Anyway, my point is, I might as well come over there and talk."

"Alright," Laura nodded, ending the call. She would have preferred for him to hurry up and tell her what she needed to know, but maybe it would be easier to explain in person. Besides, there was a small part of

138

her – a very small, infinitesimal part – that wanted to see him again, anyway.

She watched as he threw back the last of whatever was in a cup in front of him and then got up, grabbing a satchel bag from the back of a chair and rushing out to the street. He crossed to her without incident, and then she stood awkwardly in front of him, suddenly realizing it would have made so much more sense for her to go and sit with him than for them both to stand in the street.

"So, what did you need?" Caleb asked. He was healthier looking than the first time she had seen him, with shock making him pale and drawn. He had the kind of energy that can only come from actually having had enough sleep, and she envied him that as he swept his dark hair back away from his forehead.

"I'm looking for a place," she said. "It's a very specific place that a witness described to us, but they had no idea where it actually was – just that it was in Seattle. It sounds like it might be the kind of place where performances happen, which is why I was thinking you might know."

"Sure," Caleb said. "What information did they give you?"

"Well, it's a big open space," Laura said. "A wooden stage area with marble surfaces around it. Oh, and there was some kind of sign with the word 'Carnegie' on the inside, near the chairs."

"Carnegie," Caleb said thoughtfully, then snapped his fingers. "Okay. That's the Divisionary Town Hall, over in Fremont."

"You're sure?" Laura asked. Her heart was starting to race. Could this be the break she needed?

"Yeah, they label all the different entrances with the names of other big theatres and entertainment centers around the country," he said. "Despite the name, it's used as a theatre almost exclusively now. I've performed there a few times, you know, local productions and auditions."

"How far is it from here?" Laura asked, tapping open the map on her cell phone. She had intended to search for it on her GPS, but Caleb made a loose shrugging gesture towards her car.

"It's not far. I can take you there now, if you'd like?"

Laura bit her lip, thinking. Nate was expecting her back, but it would be much easier to explain this lead if he wasn't present during the exploration. And if the killer really was going to be at this theatre today, then Nate was better off safe in the precinct, where the shadow of death couldn't be a threat.

And she didn't allow herself to think about it, but yes: it was a chance to spend a little more time with Caleb.

"Yes, alright," she said, taking him to the car. It was lucky she'd thought to pick up another set of keys from the rental place, to avoid situations in which one of them couldn't drive because the other had gone off with them in their pocket. She fired off a text to Nate telling him she was following a new tip as she walked, hoping he would be busy enough taking reports from the detectives who had been finishing up calls to the last of Suzanna's list to want to follow her.

Laura got into the car and started the engine, and it was only as Caleb reached over to buckle his seatbelt that she registered the fact that they were now sitting very close together. Closer than they had in the diner. There was a strange kind of intimacy to being in the front seat of a car with someone, unable to ignore the way they breathed or every shift in position they made.

"Take a left out of the precinct," Caleb said easily, seemingly not feeling awkward at all.

"When we get there," Laura said, following his direction. "You're going to have to wait outside."

"What? Why?" Caleb asked, sounding put out. "Take the next right."

"Because you're a civilian," Laura said. "I can't let you put yourself into danger. And we don't know who the killer is, or if he'll be there. You need to stay outside while I check it out – go home, even."

"Turn left up ahead, then straight through the next two intersections," Caleb said. "Look, that doesn't bother me. The danger thing. I can handle myself."

"I'm sure you can," Laura said, amused. "That's not the point."

"Well, how are you going to get in without me?" Caleb asked.

"I'll show them my badge," Laura said, but the moment the words left her mouth, she knew it wasn't right. If she did that, the killer might get a chance at knowing there was an FBI agent in the building. That could send them to ground – or even force them to do something drastic. She couldn't risk that. She sighed. "Or I can just tell them I'm an actress, or something."

"But just being an actress wouldn't be a reason to go in," Caleb pointed out. "You take the left turn after this intersection. I've worked there – the staff on the door will know me. I can tell them I need to go pick something up from backstage and they'll believe me."

Laura sighed.

"It's up ahead after the next right," Caleb said.

"Fine," Laura said. "You can come in. But the second there's any hint of danger, you stay behind and stay out of the way."

"Got it," Caleb said, and she didn't need to look at him to hear the grin in his voice.

A large building loomed up in front of them. It was decorated out front with huge posters advertising upcoming productions – a musical, a new stage production of a classic play, a charity concert night. Laura didn't even need to be told that this was where they were headed for. The Divisionary Town Hall stood out, a pale stone against the more modern buildings around it, clearly designated now for the purpose of entertainment despite the strict and utilitarian style of the exterior.

Laura pulled up in the parking lot and killed the engine, sitting in thought for a moment. Should she go in? Maybe she would recognize the woman, be able to get her to safety. But she was alone without backup, and Caleb was a civilian.

But Caleb was also her way in, if she wanted to get in without alerting every person in the building that there was an FBI agent on site.

"Let's go take a look," she said, turning to find him watching her expectantly. "I want to check out the exact auditorium we're looking for. Can you take me there?"

"Sure, if they'll let us inside," Caleb said. "But that shouldn't be a problem for you, right? Being an agent?"

"Let's keep that between us, for now," Laura said. "I don't want to put any potential suspects on alert. We're just two actors, right?"

"Got it," Caleb said, unbuckling his belt to get out of the car. He flashed her a grin. "I'll introduce you as my leading lady."

Laura felt her cheeks momentarily heating and was glad he wouldn't see because he was already getting out of the passenger door. She mentally shook her head, trying to stay focused. Flattery, or flirting, was nice, but it wouldn't get a killer caught.

They approached the entrance together, but Caleb quickly pointed out a white piece of paper attached to the door. It read: "LEFTSIDE PRODUCTIONS – AUDITIONS INSIDE".

The perfect hunting ground for a killer who liked acting coaches.

CHAPTER THIRTY

Laura took an unsteady breath, looking at the sign with apprehension. She had never been inside an audition space before, had no idea what to expect. Would they even let her inside unless she was trying out? She didn't want to blow her cover before she'd had a chance to find the killer, and while showing a badge might get her in, it would also make her obvious.

"This is good news," he assured her. "I'll just say we're here for the auditions. You can just follow my lead. If anyone asks, we can say that you're here as my moral support, not to audition yourself."

Laura nodded. "I'll let you lead the way," she said, with some relief. The last thing she wanted was some comedy of errors where she somehow ended up having to accidentally fake her way through an audition in order to avoid alerting the killer that she had found him.

They threaded their way through a marble entrance hall, past a bored-looking receptionist who simply waved them through. On the other side of a set of double doors was some kind of clerk with a clipboard, taking names with the same level of enthusiasm.

While Caleb offered up his details, Laura looked past him and into the auditorium. The space was exactly as she remembered it, and this was the view she had seen. There were people sitting in the rows further back, loosely grouped; Laura gathered these must be actors waiting for their turn or others who had come to watch. Caleb turned to tell her he was done and beckon her forward, and they quickly joined the ranks of those sitting to watch.

The stage was currently occupied by two actors, a man and woman. They appeared to be playing a scene together, holding scripts in their hands. In the front row, there was a director, or so Laura assumed, sitting on his own. He had a stack of files beside him on a chair, and he was watching the actors with interest, occasionally calling out directions to them. She had not noticed him in the vision, but then she had only been able to see so much. The killer had been so focused on the woman he was targeting that he had not turned from side to side. She had no way of knowing if the director had really been there in her vision, or whether she needed to wait for him to leave before it was time for things to happen.

And then again, it was also possible for things in her visions to change before becoming reality. The very act of her coming here had could have changed the order of things. For all she knew, it was Caleb who was the killer, and having Laura at his side meant that he would not strike at all. A shiver ran down her spine at the thought, and Caleb glanced at her with concern.

"Are you cold in here?" he asked.

"No, no," Laura assured him. "Just someone walking over my grave."

The phrase was an unfortunate one, particularly since once she had said it, she could not take it back. The image echoed in her mind, adding to the general feeling of suspense and apprehension that she felt. The killer could be here, even right now, and she needed to identify him before he took the chance to strike again.

Laura focused on the actors playing their roles. The director called out to send the woman off stage, letting the man continue alone.

"Do you know this play?" Laura whispered. She could hardly follow the lines. She had too many other things to think about.

"No, it must be something new," Caleb whispered back. "I'll see if I can spot a script lying around."

"Alright!" the director called out. "Thank you."

The male actor nodded and turned, obviously dismissed, and the assistant near the door called out two more names to send them onto the stage.

Rather than coming out from the chairs in the audience, the two new actors appeared from a partition that was not immediately obvious at the back of the stage. They had clearly been preparing behind there, both of them ready with their scripts in their hands. The man who had been running his lines passed them and went through the same gap they had appeared from, moving out of sight.

"I need to get backstage," Laura said, leaning over to murmur it in Caleb's ear. She was sure this was what she had seen. The killer and the woman would both walk off the stage together, him coming from further back in the rows of chairs and her perhaps leaving the stage after her audition. That partition was where they would go. But from this side, Laura could do nothing. She couldn't just get up and run after them – not if she wanted to actually catch the killer doing something incriminating which would stand up in court.

No, she needed to be on the other side of the partition, so she could see what happened.

"I'll get you there," Caleb said. He stood up with a grin, gesturing for her to follow him again. He slipped out to the wings, following the direction of another piece of printed paper bearing an arrow, and then through to a door which was once again guarded by a clipboard-wielding assistant. This time it was a man, or rather a boy, who looked about seventeen years old. Laura guessed he probably worked in the theatre part-time alongside his schoolwork.

"Audition number?" he said, staring at them both with dull and uninterested eyes. Laura guessed from the way all the staff seemed to be bored out of their minds that it must have been a long and repetitive day of auditions.

"I'm seventy-three," Caleb said. "And then seventy-four."

Laura tried not to tense up. What would happen when the kid looked at his list and realized he hadn't been given a seventy-four yet? Or that he had, and the person who had walked in after Laura and Caleb had been a man?

"Okay," the kid said, jotting down the numbers on his clipboard. He didn't ask any further questions, but simply waved them through. "You'll be about forty minutes, at least."

Laura tried not to look too wide-eyed as she followed Caleb inside. That was far too easy. At no point had either of them been asked for identification, and the log of who was actually here was laughable. All of which meant that if the killer was here and he managed to escape, identifying him would be more difficult than Laura had hoped.

But so long as she didn't let him escape, it wouldn't be a problem.

They emerged into a small space behind the stage, with a small number of others scattered around, reading scripts. Caleb grabbed one which had been abandoned and started to read it, effortlessly blending in. Laura, meanwhile, studied the partition which led from the stage, checking the view.

Yes, this was definitely the spot she had seen him walking towards in her vision. She felt her body tensing and wiped her palms on the side of her pants. Sweaty palms could be deadly right now if she needed to draw her gun.

There was a woman standing nearby, a woman with long brown hair reading lines from the script. Her mouth was moving silently as she practiced, concentrating fully on the words, her expression

144

contorting and changing as she emoted through them. Was that her? Was it the woman Laura had seen?

She couldn't be sure. This woman was wearing a light jacket, and the one in her vision hadn't. Maybe she was planning to take it off before going onto the stage. Laura watched as another couple of actors came through the partition and then left the backstage area entirely, talking nervously together, and another two were called on. It was just her, Caleb, and the woman now. Was this it? The backstage area had been empty in the vision, Laura thought. But she had brought Caleb here, changed the path of the future.

She had to know for sure, and the only way was to see this woman from behind, to see if she matched the right description. Laura began to move, walking around the edge of the room so that she could approach the other woman from the other side, to see how the back of her head lined up against her vision.

But before she could complete her semi-circle and get behind her, Laura saw a man lurking in the back of the room, just emerging from a door that led in the opposite direction to where they had come. He had dark, dark eyes trained right on the woman, and he had a hulking kind of figure, tall and lanky and hunched downwards. He moved one of his hands strangely, and Laura looked down to see a flash of light against metal.

He was holding a knife.

Laura didn't waste any time. She didn't want to give him the chance to strike, to stab her and get away. She sprang towards him instinctively, putting her body between him and the woman. "Freeze!" she yelled as she barreled towards him, using the element of surprise to stop him in his tracks as well as incoming force of her body. "FBI!"

She hit him full-on, knocking him backwards. A well-placed blow to his wrist sent the knife clattering to the floor, and within moments Laura had spun him around and grabbed his wrists in both of her hands to restrain him.

"You're under arrest," she said, trying hard to catch her breath as she took the handcuffs from her belt to snap onto him. He didn't resist. Either he was still in shock about the whole thing, or he knew he had been caught dead to rights and that there was no point in struggling now. "For murder."

Laura pushed the killer against the wall, glancing around to see the woman watching her in shock and Caleb staying far out of trouble on the other side of the room. He was grinning at her. She reached into her pocket to get her cell phone and call Nate.

She'd done it. Finally, one of her visions had come good and shown her what she needed to see.

It was over.

CHAPTER THIRTY ONE

Laura looked up as the door opened, allowing Nate inside the small dressing room she had found to hold the killer. He had barely said a word since she'd cuffed him, except to protest that he had no idea what was going on.

Which, of course, was exactly what the killer would say to try and get away from her. Laura wasn't buying it for a second. Not when she had actually seen the target through his own eyes.

"Special Agent Nathaniel Lavoie," Nate introduced himself, taking a seat next to Laura. She had dragged the room into a new configuration – the killer sitting against the back wall, her and now Nate on chairs facing towards him, blocking the route to the door. He was cornered. If he tried to run, it wouldn't work.

"Nate, this is Abel Clarkson," Laura said, by way of explanation, keeping her words formal to avoid any later accusations of misconduct. "I've arrested him on suspicion of the murders of Lucile Maddison, Suzanna Brice, and Gypsy Sparks, and he's been fully cautioned of his rights."

Nate nodded. "Alright, Abel," he said. "Can you tell me about what you were doing for the last three evenings?"

"I was at home, rehearsing," Abel said. "I've got a few scripts I'm working on at the moment." There was a surly kind of twist to his mouth, as though he didn't appreciate being asked the questions. He could sulk all he liked, Laura thought. It wasn't going to get him out of this.

"Can anyone confirm that this was the case?" Nate said.

Abel shifted, looking at them sideways through lowered eyes. "I was at home," he said again. "I live alone."

"So, that's a no," Nate said. He glanced at Laura with a slightly raised eyebrow, an indication that this was good news. "Can you tell me how you knew the victims?"

"I didn't, really," he protested. "I'm an actor. Or, I'm trying to be an actor. I just heard of them in passing. I did one of Suzanna's classes a while ago, but I couldn't afford to keep going. I'm just trying to keep

147

my head down, work on getting roles. I haven't got anything to do with this!"

"We'll need to verify everything you say," Nate said, a subtle warning that the truth would out. "It's better if you confess what you've done as soon as possible. Judges prefer that. If you're ready, we can go down to the precinct and get everything down on paper, get it wrapped up nice and easy. There won't even be a trial if you plead guilty."

"I didn't do anything!" Abel insisted. "I was just coming backstage to wait for my turn to audition, and this crazy lady jumped on me!"

Laura took affront at being described as a 'crazy lady.' "You were stalking your next victim with a knife in your hand," she said. The knife itself was sitting on her lap, wrapped up safely in an evidence bag. It was one of the reasons she hadn't moved to take Abel Clarkson to the precinct immediately: she had shut down the theater instead, sent everyone out and had a caretaker lock the doors to only admit members of law enforcement, to give them time to examine as much physical evidence as they could. "That's pretty conclusive, Abel. You're fighting a losing battle here."

He burst out a laugh, forced and loud.

"You're crazy!" he said again. "Come on, man. She's crazy! I couldn't kill anyone with that knife!"

"Why did you bring it to an audition, Abel?" Nate asked calmly. "To peel apples?"

"No, to act with," Abel said. "Read the goddamn script. It calls for a death scene! I thought it would be more effective if I had a prop with me, instead of just pretending to stab someone with my hand like a loser!"

"So, you were planning to stab someone live on stage instead," Nate said, raising an eyebrow.

"With a *prop knife*," Abel insisted. "Test it! Go on! The blade slides into the handle!"

For the first time, Laura felt a flash of doubt, of fear that she had somehow managed to get the wrong guy. None of his protest had rung true in her ears so far, but this was different.

Could it really, possibly be that she was wrong?

She took the knife and tested the point gingerly through the bag. It was sharp, even without pressing directly against her skin. She applied a small amount of pressure, as much as she dared, and then stopped. Nothing had happened. The knife was staying stable.

"Not like that," Abel said, tossing his head impatiently. His hair was dark and long enough to cover his eyes, and he had to keep flicking it back out of them. "Let me show you. It slides sideways."

Laura looked up at him long enough for him to feel her scorn at the idea that she would just hand him a knife and tested pushing the blade sideways. It was sharper on one side than the other, and when she pushed from the blunt side, it slid across and down until it fitted back into the handle.

"That's not a prop knife," Laura said incredulously. "It's a switchblade!"

"Yeah, well, it was what I had at home," Abel shrugged. "I was just going to flip the blade shut right before the stabbing action, so it would look real. He has to wave it around a bunch before – the character, I mean."

"You're expecting us to believe you brought a real knife to an audition at a time when people associated with the acting world are being murdered, and you were just going to use it like a fake knife," Nate said, his tone clearly allowing his skepticism to be known.

"Yes!" Abel exclaimed. "I don't earn a lot. I don't get a lot of jobs. That's why I'm here. My last prop knife got stolen at another audition and I don't have enough in the bank to buy another that looks good, so I thought this would have to do!"

"And you were just walking up behind a woman, wielding a knife, stalking her, by coincidence?" Laura said. "Or was that all part of the character as well?"

"I wasn't stalking her," he said, his tone going surly again. "I... I like her. I was thinking about asking her out and I didn't know how to do it. I was trying to get up the nerve to go and talk to her."

"I don't think asking her out with a knife in your hand would have made the best impression," Nate said.

"I..." Abel hesitated, his shoulders sagging. "I'm not good at that kind of stuff. I get all nervous and I say the wrong thing and it all comes out wrong. I guess I shouldn't have been holding a knife. I was just so nervous, and I wasn't thinking straight."

Nate stared at him for a long time, longer than Laura thought could really be necessary. She wondered what he was doing, but she didn't ask. There was a level of trust you had to have in one another when you were facing a suspect. You couldn't show any doubt in one another's work or methods. You had to be a team. Any sign of doubt between you, and the suspect could burrow into that hole and widen it until nothing would get him to talk anymore.

"Abel, stand up," Nate said, doing the same. The killer stood up, hunching his shoulders as he had been doing before. He was taller than Nate by a good few inches, maybe six-four or five. He had the physique of a man who spends all his time bending down to listen to others, to get onto their same level. His back was probably permanently curved as a result.

But he was very tall, Laura saw that. Nate beckoned to her, asking Abel to wait there, and they left the room.

"I came with Sergeant Thornton," he said. "Let me just go get her. She can take him in and continue the interrogation."

"Wait," Laura said, reaching out. She wanted to catch him by the sleeve and pull him back, but at the last minute, she dropped her hand. She didn't want to trigger that shadow of death, not right now. Not when the case was solved, and everything felt good. She wanted to enjoy that for just a bit longer. "Why don't we take him in? Why Thornton?"

"Just hold on a moment," Nate said, turning and walking away. Laura lingered outside the door. If Abel Clarkson tried to make a run for it, she wanted to be on the scene. To be able to stop him. To foil any attempt that he made to get away. She waited with a variety of doubts surging up inside her. What was Nate playing at? Was this all because he felt he could no longer trust her? Was this the beginning of the end for them as partners? Was it finally happening?

Thornton and Nate came back together, the pretty young officer laughing at something he was saying. Laura felt a surge of jealousy. Would she and Nate ever be close like that again, or had she ruined everything?

Nate waited, avoiding her eyes and ignoring her attempts to talk to him, until Thornton had led the killer away and pushed him into a squad car, taking him back to be processed. Then, and only then, when they were alone in the deserted theater, did he finally turn to her to speak.

"Laura, I don't think it's him," he said. "I didn't want to say it earlier when he was right behind the door and would be able to hear us, just in case. But I think it's too tenuous."

"Tenuous?" Laura repeated incredulously. "He was literally stalking a woman with a knife! That's the exact M.O .we're looking for!"

150

"But his explanation, however stupid, actually works," Nate reasoned. "And there are lots of things that don't fit."

"Like what?" Laura demanded, shaking her head.

"The woman was just a fellow actress, not a coach. That's what you said in your message, right?"

"Right, I just got a chance to speak to her while I was waiting for you," Laura said. "But that doesn't mean anything. Maybe he's run out of coaches and moved on."

"Which would make sense if he'd even been coached by Gypsy or Lucile, but he's saying he wasn't," Nate said. "And, I know, he could be lying. That's why I wanted him to stay under arrest and continue interrogation. But his height, Laura. You can't ignore that."

"His height?" Laura said, frowning.

"He's too tall for the angle of the knife to make sense." Nate hunched his shoulders forward, making a stabbing motion with one of his hands. "See, for the height difference he has with Lucile Maddison and Gypsy Sparks, he should have found it much more difficult to get that straight stabbing angle with the knife. It would have twisted his wrist. Someone shorter than him, shorter than me, would have been able to do it much easier."

Laura watched his demonstration, shaking her head again. "You think my explanation is tenuous?" she said, gesturing at his hands. "You're telling me you think he's innocent because a killer wouldn't bother to turn his wrist?"

Nate sighed. "I just think we should continue investigating until we get some proof that this is definitely our guy," he said. "I don't want to miss another opportunity to stop all of this because we made a mistake. Why were you here, anyway? You didn't tell me what lead brought you here."

But Laura had proof. She had seen it. She had seen that very woman being stalked by a killer with hair on his arms and a knife in his hand, and she knew he was going to do it. Maybe he had chosen a different entrance, not struck immediately, because she had changed the future herself by inserting Caleb into it. But it didn't matter. She'd seen it.

She just couldn't tell Nate that.

"It was something Caleb thought of. It's him, okay? Abel is our killer. You have to trust me," she said, turning away from him heavily. She adjusted her jacket as she did so, her hands straying over the empty spot on her belt where her handcuffs had been, over her gun...

151

A flash of pain hit her in the temple, so hard she almost cried out, and Laura knew the vision was going to be a tough one.

CHAPTER THIRTY TWO

She was in the auditorium of the Divisionary Town Hall. The floor stretched out far ahead, and there were seats around her, all pointing towards a large open area of the floor.

There was a woman in front of her, a woman with long dark hair who stood with her back to Laura, looking at something in her own hands.

The edges of the vision faded to gray and then black, telling her nothing beyond what she could see right in front of her. The woman moved, walking across the stage, heels clicking impressively as the sound was picked up and carried. She walked straight backstage, without looking behind her, as if she was familiar with this place and exactly where she needed to go. Laura's vision began to move as well, drawing her closer over the stage, following exactly where the woman had walked.

Laura's eyes looked down, and she saw a male body below herself. Hands that were larger than her own, a wristwatch in a masculine style, light-colored hair on her arms. Yes. She was him. She was the killer. She was seeing what he could see.

The vision turned up again, the killer hurrying towards the spot where the woman had vanished. He slipped inside, after her, into the backstage area, and raised his hand...

Laura surfaced from the vision into a reality that seemed far worse. She covered her mouth, trying not to make any kind of audible reaction. She'd been wrong. The vision was still the same. Nothing she had done had changed it, which meant it was still going to happen – and by the throbbing in her head, she knew it was going to happen soon.

She remembered chasing Scott Darnell around his neighborhood, seeing him dashing down an alleyway and trying to get there to stop him. She remembered the feeling of confusion when he wasn't there. The way she had been too early, had tried to intervene too soon. That had turned out right in the end, but it easily might not have done.

153

The location was right. She knew that. She was more familiar with this place now, knew exactly what it looked like and could recognize it easily.

But the timing was wrong.

She'd moved too soon. The killer was still out there, and now she had not only to convince Nate that she had changed her mind about the suspect, but also find a reason to hang around and investigate the same place for what could be hours before the killer returned. A place that was locked to the public, no less.

"Okay, Nate," she said, trying to think on her feet. "Maybe you're right."

"I am?" Nate said. She turned to see him looking utterly confused. He folded his arms across his chest. "You're giving up? Just like that?"

"I was asking you to trust me," she said, and sighed. "But I have to trust you, too. If your gut tells you that he's not the guy, then I guess he isn't." She was skirting close to the truth. She did trust Nate. She would always trust him, so long as what he said didn't directly contradict a vision. It was just hard to figure out what to do when that was the case. And this time, he'd turned out to be right.

She just had to convince him she'd had a change of heart for that reason, and not for any other.

"No, I'm not buying this," Nate said, narrowing his eyes at her. Laura wanted to scream. Why did he have to know her so well? "You don't just give up like that. Not in these situations. Something just changed. What is it?"

"Okay, fine," Laura said, throwing her arms up in the air. "Let's go back to being on opposite sides, then. You carry on doing your investigation, and I'll carry on doing mine. I'll stay around here and look for more evidence of his intent, or of who he really is. Maybe he dropped something incriminating."

It wasn't much, but it was, at least, an excuse to stay here. A search like that wouldn't take her hours, but it was a starting point. She could invent something better later.

"Laura, your behavior is starting to worry me," Nate said. His arms were still crossed, and he was shaking his head, looking at her closely. "Are you drinking again?"

"Am I - ?!" Laura began incredulously, almost wanting to hit him for even suggesting that. But she tried to rein herself in. Of course, to Nate, it would look as though she was behaving in a completely irrational way. Of course, to him, it would seem like she was blowing hot and cold, running through mood swings by the second. And what would cause that but falling off the wagon?

He hadn't known her when she was sober. It had been before they were assigned as partners. But he'd seen her try time and time again to get right, to get off the drink. And he'd seen her fall back on it. Sometimes disastrously.

Could she really blame him for thinking it was happening again – even if the accusation felt like a hot knife sliding into her heart?

"Are you?" Nate pressed.

"No," Laura said heavily, blinking back tears that threatened to spill down her face. "No, I'm not. I'm going to talk to the witnesses we asked to wait outside first, and then look around. It might take me a while. You do what you have to do."

Nate looked at her for a long second, opening his mouth as though he wanted to say something. Then he closed it and shook his head and stalked away.

He was angry with her. Laura could see that much without the help of a vision. He wanted her to come clean, to tell him what was really going on. It was the one thing she couldn't do, and it was breaking them apart. It wouldn't be long before he refused to work with her anymore, asked Rondelle to assign him to someone else. It wouldn't be long before there was one less person in Laura's life that she could count on, and then how was she going to drag herself out of the pit the next time the bottle came calling?

She buried her head in her hands for a moment, trying to compose herself. Maybe this was for the best. Maybe if she pushed him away, she could somehow stop that death that awaited him from coming to pass. She still had no idea what form it would take. Maybe if he wasn't around her, he would be in less danger. Maybe she could save his life.

Laura gathered herself and headed outside, trying to steel herself only to what mattered now. She had to stop the killer. If she didn't, then alienating Nate would have been for nothing. She had to see this through and make sure that no other women died as a result of this stalker, whoever he was.

Caleb was still out there with the others, who were milling around loosely in an area outside the theater. There were a few uniformed officers, no doubt left by Thornton to keep the peace and stop anyone from leaving, who were watching everything with bored expressions.

"You got him," Caleb said, grinning at her. "I knew you would solve this."

"Is it true?" a young woman nearby asked, stepping closer. Laura thought she must have been one of the actors on the stage when it happened. "Did you catch the guy who's been killing actresses?"

She was very young, Laura realized. Maybe twenty at most. She looked scared.

Laura gave her a polite smile. "We can't comment just yet. All I would say is, don't let down your guard. Even if we do have the killer in custody, the truth is that there's more than one creep out there. Stay alert and don't take any risks."

The girl nodded and moved back away, allowing Laura to focus on Caleb again. "I need you to come inside and give a witness statement," she said. "Can you wait by the door?"

At his agreement, Laura moved on to a spot where she could be easily seen and heard.

"Alright," she called out, getting the attention of the crowd and the police officers holding them here. "I need the following people to come inside and wait in the lobby. The director, any actors who were in the backstage area prior to the incident or saw anything, the assistants who were on the main stage door and the backstage door, and the receptionist. Everyone else, please give your contact details to the officers here and then go home."

Laura turned back towards the theater, letting the police officers deal with the swell of conversation and movement that followed her words. She needed to get this done.

Caleb was first, because he was a familiar face and she felt she could deal with that easier. He had a kind of calming influence with his laidback and charming manner, and Laura thought that after talking to him, she could keep her professional mask in place with the others.

"Can you tell me what you saw?" Laura said, getting right to the point. She had her notebook in hand, ready to take down everything he said so that she could record it in her paperwork later.

"Yes, we went backstage, and I saw there were just a few people inside. Two of them went on stage, and the two that came off stage went out into the hall, which just left you, me, and the one woman," Caleb said. "Then the man came in, and I saw a knife in his hand. Next thing I knew, you were tackling and arresting him, and the knife was on the floor."

"That's good," Laura said, nodding. "I'm glad you caught it all. If we need you to testify, would you be willing to swear to all of that in a court of law?"

156

"Yes, of course," Caleb said, and grinned. "It was awesome, by the way. How you just threw yourself in the line of danger to protect someone you didn't even know. He didn't stand a chance."

"It's my job," Laura said, an automatic response. She didn't often think of herself as particularly brave or that she had done anything special. She had chosen the career of law enforcement, and this kind of thing went with the territory.

"Trust me," Caleb said. "You were awesome." He smiled at her in a way that made her think maybe she was awesome after all, before she shook her head and gestured towards the door with her notebook.

"That's helpful," she said, instead of telling him the truth: that she hadn't tackled anyone important at all, just an idiot who thought bringing a real knife to an audition was smart. "I'd better question the others. I already have your number, so you're free to go."

"Sure," Caleb said, throwing a wink over his shoulder as he went. "Make sure you call me on that number."

She froze for a moment at his words. Would she? Could she? As much as she liked him so far, he had been a suspect. Maybe he was still.

Laura was alone with her thoughts again when the door closed behind him. She stood for a moment, thinking. She didn't know why she hadn't told him the truth, that she was still looking for a murderer. The words had frozen on her tongue. Was it because she didn't want to disappoint him, after the praise he had given her?

Or was it because, given how everything had been going wrong so far, she wasn't sure she could trust her gut – the same gut that had told her he was innocent in the first place?

Laura rubbed the back of her neck, trying to get back into the game. She had work to do. Now she thought about the vision again, with the benefit of seeing it twice, she realized there had been no knife in the vision at all. She'd put one there in her own head because it was what she knew the killer used. But in reality, all she had seen was him stalking a woman – not killing one. With that in mind, she really had no idea when he was going to strike at all.

It could be right after the vision she had seen. It could be later that night. It might not even be the same day.

The only way she could find out would be to wait, to find him, and to follow him herself. Preferably, to catch him before he did anything. But now she had to figure out how to do that, and the only way she could think to do it would be to carry on with the old-fashioned

157

detective work she was doing now: speaking to witnesses, examining the scene, understanding the people in it.

Laura stepped back into the reception. Before she could call up anyone in particular, the director leapt out of his seat and walked towards her.

"I need to go next," he said. "This is taking far too long. I've got another audition session tonight, and I need to prepare!"

"Another session?" Laura asked. "Where?"

"Well, here," the director said, then gave her a horrified look. "Unless you're telling me you're not going to allow us back in?"

"I don't know," Laura said thoughtfully, a plan beginning to form in her head. "Come through and tell me all about it. We'll see what we can do."

CHAPTER THIRTY THREE

Laura looked down at her phone, at the text from Nate that had popped up on the screen. He was still going through potential suspects, he said; the detectives under Captain Mills had found a new list of students that Suzanna Brice had apparently discarded a few months ago, giving them more names of people who had attended the class in the past.

They could be there for days just calling people and untangling all the rumors and suspicion. And in the meantime, the killer could strike again.

Laura looked up again, across the room. She was seated in the auditorium, among what was now a growing crowd of others. This audition, the director had told her, was for a much bigger part than the previous ones. It turned out that he was a casting director – not the director of a specific play – and he had been commissioned to fill a role for an upcoming feature film as well as the upcoming stage performance.

The audition tonight was an open call, which meant that there was no way to know ahead of time who would turn up. People could come from anywhere in the country, he'd said, though Laura thought anywhere in the state was probably a more realistic guess. There was a buzz in the air, much more than there had been earlier. Actors were coming and going in their droves, sitting in front of the director on the stage and performing to a single camera, saying the same lines each time.

It had become boring very quickly. Laura decided the time for observation was over. She was studying the crowd, and she'd seen that there were a few instances of people who appeared to be more in charge than others. People who were coaching the actors, it seemed, straightening collars and smoothing flyaway hairs, gripping them by the shoulders to give them confidence. She drifted over to the nearest one and got her attention.

"Hi," she said. "Are you an acting coach?"

"No, I'm a manager," the woman said. She looked Laura up and down sharply. "Are you looking for representation?"

"No, no," Laura said, holding up her hands with a polite smile. "I was looking for a coach. Do you know if there are any here?"

The manager looked around, her gaze skimming over the assembled people filling the chairs. "Not that I recognize. You'd be better off searching online, dear. Coaches don't tend to come for auditions, unless they're still working actors themselves."

Laura nodded. "Thanks," she said, trying not to sound disappointed.

She repeated her questions a few more times, all with women who turned out to be agents or managers, or – in one instance – an overly pushy mother. Then she turned to speaking to some of the better-connected actors, judging by the way people would come up and talk to them. None of them could recognize any coaches around them, although a few gave her cards to recommend their own coach.

Those were leads, maybe. But it wasn't as though there was no other way to find an acting coach in Seattle than to ask an actor. If they had to investigate and protect every single one in the city, they would run out of police officers before they covered them all.

There were dozens of people in the auditorium at any one time, all of them waiting their turn to get on the stage and then disappearing afterwards. Hundreds, perhaps, overall. And there were so many women here with long, brown hair. Frustratingly so. Laura thought that she had seen the woman from her vision everywhere she turned, the details beginning to slip out of her hands as she was distracted by so many similar, but not quite right, options.

Laura looked down at her watch and realized it had been a couple of hours already. People were still going up on stage, saying their lines, disappearing. There were fewer of them left in the seats, now. She realized that the doors must have been closed, that the people who were here were the only ones left to take their turn. And still, she hadn't seen her. Hadn't seen anyone go behind the partition, even. Not from the walkway leading to the stage, which was where she knew the killer would go.

The window of time seemed to be disappearing in front of her eyes. Where was the killer? Where was his victim? Had she missed them already, somehow? Had the disruption earlier in the day changed his plan, changed her route, made him follow her somewhere else?

Laura spun in the back of the aisles, looking around. What if she'd got it completely wrong, altered events so greatly that she was never going to track him down? What if he was out there now killing his

160

victim, now that the sun had finally started to go down and he knew he wouldn't be so easily seen?

How had she managed to mess this up so badly? She should have known that the killer would never be so obvious to strike in a crowded place like this!

Laura paced the back of the chairs anxiously, trying to think. What could she do now? How could she turn this around? She passed by a young man in a long-sleeved overshirt who was standing in one of the back rows, by himself, muttering under his breath. As she drew closer, she was able to make out what he was saying, some kind of repetitive exercise.

"Kiss her quick, kiss her quicker, kiss her q-q-quickest. Kiss her quick, k-kiss her... Damnit. Kiss her quick, kiss her quicker, kiss her quickest..."

Laura stared at him, her mind racing. He was doing a speech exercise to prepare for his audition, that much she could see. But the stutter had made her realize something.

That there were different kinds of coaches that an actor might need.

How many times had she heard stories about vocal coaches? About actors learning to do a new accent or speak a new language convincingly enough for a big film role, or even learning to stutter or convincingly play a real person? And, of course, there would be actors who needed coaching to get over their own speech impediment.

Yes, that had to be it! If she was striking out on acting coaches, then it had to be another kind of coach she was looking for – and here she was, being presented with the perfect person to ask!

"Hi," Laura said, keeping her voice low to avoid disturbing the action on the stage or attracting attention. "Can I ask, do you have a speech therapist or coach?"

"Yes, I do," he said, glancing up at her in some surprise. He was in his early twenties, Laura thought, with sandy, messy hair and pale blue eyes. Such a shame for someone his age to still be struggling with a speech impediment, one that would probably impact his confidence and possibly even prevent him from going for roles that he would be great at. "Why? Do you need one?"

"Maybe," Laura said, with a put-on nervous smile. "I have this thing – it seems like it only comes out when I audition. Could you let me know the name of your coach? I'd like to see about booking a session with them."

"Yes, it's Genevieve P-Piper," he said. "Actually, she's here somewhere. She was just doing some last-minute coaching with me."

"Oh, really?" Laura said, glancing around. "Do you know where she is?"

"I don't know," he said, following her gaze and scanning the crowed. "You might have just missed her. I saw her a few minutes ago, b-but then she went to audition herself, so I didn't see her after she went on the stage. She's an actress, too."

Laura turned away, thinking. Maybe this Genevieve Piper had gone backstage after her turn. Maybe the killer had been watching her, had followed after her while Laura was distracted talking to someone else or thinking she was a failure. Or maybe Laura's presence here and the changed schedule of the day had disrupted the vision, and he hadn't followed her yet, but was instead waiting outside.

Anything could be the case. But she didn't have a moment to lose.

"Thank you," she said. "I'll try and find her."

Then she turned and walked rapidly away, leaving the auditorium – trying to ignore the voice in the back of her head which was afraid she would miss the pivotal moment if she didn't stay put – and heading towards the backstage area.

This time, the assistant on the door recognized her and let her through without a word. Laura headed into the same space she had seen before, finding it much more full this time. Actors were milling around by the stage itself, waiting next to a new woman with a clipboard and headset who was telling them when to go on. They were also gathered in a loose group around a water cooler that had been set up more recently. Laura recognized one of them from being on the stage earlier. They must be relaxing and debriefing after their attempts.

"Hi," she said, summoning her bubbliest possible self and approaching the group. "I wondered if one of you might know – I was looking for Genevieve Piper. Someone recommended her to me as a coach, but I can't seem to track her down?"

She was hoping that one of them would be Genevieve herself, but all of the people in the group shook their heads. One of them, an older man with grey hair who must have been trying out for a different role entirely, gestured towards the door with his plastic cup. "You just missed her," he said. "She left pretty soon after her audition, said she had to get home."

"Right," Laura said, and then dashed out of the room, hoping she could get out of the theater before Geneveive had gone too far out of her reach.

CHAPTER THIRTY FOUR

He watched the woman, who was so obviously a cop, walk towards the backstage entrance and smirked, heading outside himself instead. She couldn't have known that he had sent her in the wrong direction. In fact, Genevieve had come out after her turn on the stage to wish him luck and then left from the front entrance.

He'd only been doing his speech exercises as a way to pass the time, to give her enough of a lead that he wouldn't be too visible under the bright lights outside the theater before she got started on her journey home. He didn't want her to turn around and see him before he was ready. Didn't want her to strike up a conversation. It was better that he watch from a distance and follow her, like always.

Ah, Genevieve. Perfect angel. She had been under his nose for so long, and he had ignored her. It was his own fault, really. He slipped out of the back of the room and out of the theater, deliberately not greeting the receptionist so that she wouldn't remember him passing by. Out in the parking lot in front of the entrance, he could see no one, which was also good.

He knew where Genny was going, of course. He'd followed her so many times now. She had been one of the earliest women he identified as a potential muse, after he signed up for her services and saw how patient and gentle she was. A woman like that, he had thought, was worthy of anything. Certainly his worship.

He walked under the streetlights with his hands in his pockets, quickening his pace in the spaces of darkness between them. There was a shortcut he had figured out: turn left while Genny went straight on, and he would be out ahead of her on the next turn. She probably didn't want to take the shortcut because it took him through dark alleyways. Places that were full of danger. Or maybe Genny just went with the flow, and the flow told her to stay in the light where others could always see and admire her.

Back then, he had tried too hard to get rid of his stutter. Nothing had worked. Genny had tried everything, but he had been angry and impulsive. He hadn't been able to master himself. He'd had to put up with these humiliating roadblocks, these interruptions to the proper flow that he couldn't control. He could see how it should be. How others did it, so effortlessly. But for him, it wouldn't happen.

So, he had dismissed the possibility that Genny could be anyone's muse. She hadn't been good enough. It was only later, after he found the right way to vent his anger, that he realized the problem had never been her coaching.

It had been inside him, all along.

And if the problem had been inside him, he realized, then nothing was wrong with Genny. In fact, she was just as perfect as she had seemed. That was why, when his latest muse had failed him, he had gone back to his coaching sessions and looked at Genny in a new light.

And her coaching was working, this time. It was. Which was why he knew that he was right about her. She was the one. The muse he had been waiting for all of this time. Oh, it was dreamy to think about.

He emerged from his dark alleyway and stepped out cautiously, looking down the road. Yes – there she was! She was walking with her bag on her shoulder, her long dark hair swaying from side to side behind her with every step. It was hypnotic, that hair. Like the ticking of a clock pendulum. He could watch it all day.

He had, come to think of it.

He followed her with a sense of lightness in his heart, watching her every step with rapt attention. She was perfect. She was everything. She was his muse, and he knew in his heart that at long last, he had found the woman who would never let him down.

***

Genevieve was going over the audition in her head, trying to think about how well she had done. The casting director hadn't said anything about her performance; he was famously tight-lipped. Most of them wouldn't know if they had any chance of getting the part until they were called back for the next round. That was how it went, unfortunately.

She was thinking about the way she'd said the last line, with a tilt of her head. Had that been the right note to hit? She wasn't sure if she'd done it right. She tilted her head to the left a few times, then the right, repeating the line in her head. Maybe she shouldn't have tilted at all. Maybe the character would say the line and stare the other character down, no movement.

God, it was all so difficult. So many years of auditioning and trying, and Genny still didn't really know whether she'd got it right or not. There were so many variables. Sometimes it came down not to whether you were any good, but whether there had been another actress who looked just like you who was a fraction better and therefore got the callback instead. Or sometimes the casting director would decide to go in another direction than advertised and cast someone who looked totally different.

She'd done all she could. It was up to someone else now. That thought was actually comforting, in a way. It allowed her to stop dwelling on all of this and move on – and start thinking about the next audition, or the next client she was going to be working with. She pulled her phone out of her pocket, calling a familiar number.

"Hey, honey," she said as the line connected. "You off work soon?"

"Hey, babe," her boyfriend answered. "Yeah, I'm heading home now. How was your audition?"

"I think it went well," Genny replied. "I had to do some coaching with that client right before. It put me off a little."

"Yeah? That's a shame."

"Yeah, he's so needy," Genny said, shaking her head. "I mean, I would never say it to him, but he's obviously never going to be an actor. We've been working together for all this time, and he hasn't landed a single audition. I just don't think he knows when to give up."

"My train's just pulling up," her boyfriend replied. "Sorry, I'll have to go. Tell me all about it later tonight?"

"I will," she said. "Love you."

"Love you too, Gen," he said, and hung up.

Genny sighed a breath of the fresh night air. She'd be home before he called again, and she could get some tidying up done. Tomorrow, she had to -

Genny pulled up short, letting out a short cry of alarm as someone sprang out in front of her. One minute there was no one ahead of her and she was alone on the road – she had been sure of it – and the next minute, she was only a fraction of a second away from bumping right into him. She braced herself and tried to step back, but instead of doing the same, the man moved towards her, grabbing her.

The initial impact knocked the wind out of her lungs. Genny had no idea what was going on or who this was – she barely had time even to think – but something inside her knew that she had to get away. She had to get away right now. She pushed at him and tried to run in the other direction, but he grappled at her, holding her back.

Genny screamed as she felt his arms pulling her in towards him, stopping her from getting away. She had no purchase, her thin ballet flats scraping against the ground instead of pushing her away. He began to twist her around, his arms holding her in place like a bear hug, throwing her in the opposite direction. She had no idea what he wanted with her, but she had absolute certainty that it would not be good. His hold was awkward, loose, like he had something in one of his hands and couldn't grab her properly with it...

As she twisted, trying to fight, trying to get her arms up so that she could scratch at his face or something, anything, she saw him. The light in a nearby window went on, a homeowner clearly alerted by her scream, and it illuminated his face just enough for her to see him. She had not been expecting to see someone that she knew right now, let alone a client, but it was him. There was no mistaking him. Not when she'd just seen him at the audition.

"Ed," she said. "Ed, stop!"

He froze. Maybe he had not been expecting her to say his name. Maybe he thought that she would not recognize him. But she knew it was him. His arms stopped moving for just a moment and she pushed away just a little, not enough to escape him, but enough to get a little bit of distance, to give her purchase, to allow her to drive her elbow back against him, to push forward...

To look up at the sound of a shout, as another woman came into view, yelling a warning at Ed to stop what he was doing.

CHAPTER THIRTY FIVE

Laura drew her gun, pointing it at the two of them. She wasn't completely confident that she could get a good shot here, but she could try. And sometimes, the threat was enough.

At the very least, they had a Mexican standoff. Him with his knife pulled up at the woman's throat, her with her gun pointed at him. Neither of them could make a move unless the other acted first. It was mutually assured destruction, even if it wasn't Laura's own life at stake. He knew she wanted him to let the woman go.

"Drop the knife," she yelled. "Put it down right now!"

The killer hesitated, his face white and his eyes wide over the shoulder of his victim as he tried to hide behind her. But he was taller than her, just by enough that he could not quite get himself all the way behind her without compromising the angle of the knife at her throat. Laura aimed her gun carefully, trying to take a deep breath to steady her aim, focusing on the top of his head. She could blow the top of it off from here. It wasn't without risk, but if he was going to make a move to cut the woman's throat anyway, she would do it. She felt a kind of darkness settling down over her, a shroud. A feeling of...

Of death.

Someone was going to die.

"I'm with the FBI," Laura shouted. "You're not going to get away. Just drop the knife and put your hands up in the air!"

There was a flash of light reflecting off the blade of the knife as it moved, not down but across, and Laura squeezed the trigger. She knew he was making the cut. The shot seemed to echo in the otherwise silent residential street, the recoil throwing her arm back, just enough that she would have to aim again to fire a second time. It took her a moment to recover from the loud bang, the flash of the gun, the shock of having to fire at all. Then she saw that the woman she had followed was staggering to one side, and the man, the killer, was running away.

"Are you hurt?" Laura demanded urgently, rushing towards the woman. The shadow of death was getting heavier. Had she hit the woman? She did not put her gun away. She had no intention of letting him escape right now, not if she could go after him, not if the woman didn't need help.

"No," the woman said, gasping. Her hands were going all over her neck, her head, her shoulder, as if to verify that there had been no damage. The shot must have passed right over her shoulder, the knife missing her skin as the killer recoiled. But from the way he was running, from the lack of blood splattered on the floor under the faint light coming from the next house, Laura could not be confident that she had hit him. He might be getting away uninjured, unimpeded, not leaving any trail to show where he had gone.

The victim was fine. But Laura could still feel it. The shroud settling on her shoulders.

Was it for her, or the killer?

"Stay here," Laura said, breaking off into a dead run after the suspect.

She could not let him get away. If he did, she had no guarantee that she would be able to identify him. She had only seen part of his face, and the woman looked like she was in too much shock to be any help. Even if she could identify the man, there was no guarantee that he would not simply go to ground, make it impossible for them to find him.

She raced after him, trying to keep up. It was dark, and the streets were unfamiliar to her. The small patches of light afforded by streetlights, or house lights here and there, were not enough. They only blinded her for the interval of time that she was within their sphere, making it even harder to see where he was in the dark. Laura raced through a patch of light at the end of the road, then stumbled, unsure of herself. She couldn't see him. Where had he gone?

There were two directions to go. Straight ahead, or to the left. The stop-sign at the junction stood vigil above her as she stared down both directions, trying to figure it out. Which way would he have gone? Which way made the most sense?

She had no idea where she was, but she remembered looking at the GPS to help her find her way towards Genevieve Piper's house. She remembered that the road ahead led into a more commercial district, but she was sure that the area to the left was more residential. If she was trying to run, that was where she would go. She would go into the houses, into the darkness, where it would be even harder to track her down.

She took a gamble, racing to the left. If she was wrong, there was nothing to tell her it. No visions came, despite the tight grasp she still had on her gun. The vision of the auditorium made sense now - it had been his stalking the woman through that space that led to her pulling her gun on him in the first place and firing at him - but no help was coming now. There was no way for her to tell if she was on the right track.

She kept her eyes trained ahead, straining them, trying to see if there was a figure moving anywhere in the shadows. It was quickly beginning to feel hopeless, even though the feeling of death was getting stronger, starting to make her feel sick to her stomach. What if he was ducking inside one of the properties? What if he had leapt over a fence into a backyard? What if he had simply ducked behind a car, waited for her to go past, and then run back in the other direction?

Back towards his intended victim?

Laura's head whipped around in panic, looking back where she had come. That was the only reason she had any time at all to react. It was a split second only, but when he pounced out of the shadows beside a properties garage, she had that split second of warning before they collided.

She at first expected the horrible feeling of a tear somewhere in her abdomen or her chest, a knife slicing across her. But it didn't come, even as they both tumbled to the ground, the air being knocked out of her lungs as she fell on her back. He fell beside her, faring only just better, and then he scrambled on top of her to hold her in place. His hands were empty – the knife must have fallen somewhere along the way. Laura tried to bring her gun around but realized her grip on it was not strong enough, the weapon skittering away across the sidewalk as she tried to move her hand. Laura ignored it. It was gone. There was no use trying to go back for it now. It would only alert him to the fact that he could reach for it and try to get it first.

Laura instead tried to use his momentum against him, using the grappling techniques she had learned in classes at the Academy. She swung sideways, so that he tumbled forward and to the side along with her. But he was good, quick enough to roll her over again, his hands going for her throat. She pushed them aside, managing to break the lock of his elbows, but she did not have enough purchase or enough strength now to knock him off herself again. The only choice that she had was to try and find some advantage, some way to prevent him from

170

getting his hands around her throat permanently. She needed something that would make her stronger. She needed an advantage.

She needed the gun.

Laura couldn't reach. She cast her eyes to the side, but it was above her head now, out of her way, too far to be able to grab it. Not if she also wanted to fight him off, stop him from strangling her. He got his hands on her neck again and she managed to slam her fists into his elbows to knock them aside, making him fall on her, but it wasn't enough. He was still stronger.

He was going to win.

The shadow of death – it was hers.

Laura thought desperately about help, about Nate coming around the corner in a squad car with the blue lights flashing, about the woman she had saved catching them up and saving her in return. But it was useless. Nate knew where Laura had been heading, but not the exact point on the road between the theater and the victim's apartment where he had struck. The woman had been shell-shocked, stunned.

Laura was an FBI agent. People didn't come and rescue her. She rescued them.

She wrenched herself to the side, pretending she was trying to get away from the killer but really just trying to get herself closer to the gun. "Why are you doing this?" she demanded, yelling it into his face. "Why are you killing all these women?"

"I b-b-b-b…"

The killer stopped moving so frantically, slowing down, concentrating on his words and not on trying to strangle her. The combination of the stutter and the fact that he had stopped moving allowed Laura to finally get a good look at his face, and it nearly froze her in shock.

It was him. The actor she had asked for directions in the theater. The one who'd told her his coach was backstage, only for Laura to find out that she'd left the whole building already. He had been trying to delay her.

He hadn't delayed her enough. Laura had jogged all the way down the street until she caught up with them. Geneveive Piper couldn't have known she was being followed: she would have walked at a gentle pace.

He had tried to fool her, to throw her off, and it hadn't worked.

"What?" Laura said again, seeing the strain on his face, the way he fought over the 'B' sound. He couldn't get it out, not with the agitation of the fight throwing off any tactics he would normally use to overcome his stutter. She wanted to push him, to distract him more. Anything she could find, any little weakness, she wasn't going to hesitate to use it against him and save her own life. "I can't understand you. What are you saying?"

He started again, his face contorting in fury. "You b-b-b-b-! I b- I b- I *had to stop these b-b-b-b-!*"

Laura felt him shift just a little, his weight coming off her left shoulder as he tried to get the words out. As he gave in to a blind fury that was consuming him, that threatened to make him even more violent, to put her in more danger –

As he lifted his weight, she reached. She didn't hesitate. She felt her fingers close on the gun and swung it around, twisting her fingers until it was held in the correct grip, pointing it at him. She took only a single second to aim and then she squeezed the trigger, just as –

Just as, out of nowhere, Nate tackled the killer and pushed him off Laura, to the ground, both of them rolling away from her and over the sidewalk into the road.

Laura couldn't breathe. She couldn't see. She couldn't hear anything over the high-pitched ringing in her ears from discharging her weapon twice in a short timeframe, close to her own head. She couldn't think. She couldn't dare to.

She'd hit him. She'd hit him, she knew. This was it. This was the shadow of death that she had been waiting for, and it had been her fault all along. She'd fired just as Nate had jumped, and she had been the one to kill him.

She'd killed him.

Nate was dead.

CHAPTER THIRTY SIX

Laura lay on the road with her eyes closed, no longer wanting to get up. She had killed her partner. What point was there in moving, in trying to defend herself? She'd failed him, in the worst possible way. Everyone she touched ended up worse off, and now Nate...

"You're under arrest for murder, and for assault on an FBI agent," Nate said, and Laura found the strength to move her head and open her eyes. To look. To see him, kneeling in the road, his knee on the back of the killer to pin him down. He was pulling handcuffs off his belt, putting them on the wrists of the man who was crying out wordlessly below him.

He was kneeling. Breathing. Talking. He was alive.

Nate was alive!

Laura sat up rapidly, then stopped, her head spinning. She couldn't believe what she was seeing. She wasn't even sure if it was real. Was this a guilt hallucination, or the real thing?

"Laura?" Nate said, looking at her in concern. In the near-dark, he was like a phantom, Black man in a black suit kneeling on black tarmac. Or maybe it was the fear that had wrecked her vision. "Are you injured?"

"No," she said at last. Something in her head clicked into place. Nate was real. He was alive. He was right there in front of her. They had the killer in handcuffs.

They'd done it.

"You sure?" Nate said. He was grabbing a phone out of his pocket, ready to call for backup.

"Just winded," Laura said. She stood up slowly and dusted herself down, glancing back along the road. "I'm going to go find his intended victim. You'll be alright?"

"He's not going anywhere," Nate said, nodding. "You hit him in the shoulder."

"I hit him in the shoulder," Laura repeated to herself.

Nate was alive, and her vision had led her right to where the killer would be, and she'd saved a woman's life.

173

Laura allowed herself to smile as she set off walking, limping slightly, heading around the corner to see if Genevieve Piper had waited for help or run away – keeping her eyes open for a dropped knife that would be the final nail in the coffin for the killer's defense.

**

Laura lifted up her notebook, giving Geneveive Piper a reassuring smile. Under the sickly hospital lights, she looked washed-out and shaken. But they were under the hospital lights, which meant they were safe, and she seemed to be rallying.

"So, you knew Edwin Love before tonight?" Laura asked. It was more of a conversation starter than a real question. She knew that they were acquainted, had managed to make out at least that much before being dragged away for examination at Nate's insistence.

"Yes, I've been his speaking coach for years, on and off," Genevieve said. She was wearing an oversized hoodie that a boyfriend had brought around to the hospital, where Geneveive herself had also needed checking out. All in all, they'd been very lucky: the only one with any real injuries, enough to need treatment, was Edwin himself. She toyed with the sleeves as she spoke, wrapping up her whole hand as if for comfort. "He always wanted to be an actor, but he had that awful speech impediment. He couldn't even make it through a line without stuttering when we first met."

"When you say on and off, what do you mean?" Laura asked. It felt strangely quiet, talking to the woman alone. Normally she always knew Nate was backing her up, even if he didn't speak. But he'd taken over interviewing Edwin Love, and had insisted that Laura go nowhere near him again – not just because he was being protective of his partner, but also because Laura had shot him. The last thing they needed was to be accused of bullying him into a false confession – not that they didn't have enough evidence already.

"He was very frustrated," Geneveive said. She spoke softly, frowning and hesitating, seeming to pick her words carefully. "It was like he couldn't get over the speech impediment on his own, but he thought that a therapist could cure it for him instantly. When it didn't work, he would get mad. Really mad. Then he would stutter even worse, until it was this vicious cycle that he couldn't seem to get out of."

Laura nodded. "Did you ever witness violent behavior before now?"

"No, not towards others." Geneveive hesitated again. "Towards himself, maybe. He would get very frustrated, end up hitting a desk or something like that, hurting his hand. But he was just a teenager when we started working together. I put it down to that, you know? All those hormones, on top of everything else. It can't have been easy to deal with."

Laura noted that down, then looked up at Genevieve again. "So, that was the on. Tell me about the off."

"He would just stop coming to sessions for months at a time. Then I'd hear from someone else in the industry that he'd tried another therapist and got just as frustrated with them, and walked out. I think he kept coming back to me because I was his first. Like it was comforting, maybe. I tried to get him to work through his anger issues, but he couldn't see they were linked. Not back then."

"And more recently?"

"Well, he came back to me a few months ago," Genevieve said. "And, you know what? It was really strange. He was calm all of a sudden. Like he'd figured out how to control himself. He didn't lose patience or get angry or violent. I tried to ask him about it, but he just said he'd taken up acting classes and he was going to get into the industry because of this great coach he had. But I never heard from anyone I knew that they'd been teaching him."

Laura nodded. She didn't need to share it with Geneveive, but she had the explanation for that already. The first search of Edwin Love's home, carried out by Captain Mills and his detectives, had uncovered a number of false IDs in different names. After cross-checking them with the list, it had turned out that Edwin had attended classes with all of the victims, starting when he was just a teen with Gypsy Sparks. He had known them all – but they hadn't known him under his real name. He had made himself into someone else right from the beginning, almost as if he'd known that he needed to hide his identity.

Or perhaps, being an aspiring actor, that was the point. Maybe Edwin Love was trying to make himself into a different person each time, a new character, as if that would leave all of his old troubles behind him.

Either way, it had made it conveniently difficult to trace him when he had started to kill. Laura could see how it had happened, how his own strange psychosis had driven him along. From admiring actors to becoming infatuated with his acting coaches, who were able to talk so smoothly, to memorize and deliver monologues and speeches.

How that infatuation had developed into anger when things still didn't work out, even when he tried to follow their lead. How he'd continued to blame outside influences, and not himself, for the fact that he couldn't get roles. The only reason he'd felt in control of his anger was because he was using it to first mentally attack, and later really attack, the women who he felt had wronged him. He was a troubled young man, and though it wasn't an excuse for what he had done, Laura had the feeling that some psychologist was going to have a field day explaining it in court.

"Thank you, Geneveive," Laura said. She smiled, a reassuring gesture that she hoped would help the other woman to calm down. "One of my colleagues, or someone from the prosecutor's office, will be in touch if we need to go to trial. In the meantime, is there someone you can stay with?"

"My boyfriend's going to let me stay at his place for a while," Genevieve said.

Laura nodded. "That's probably for the best. Just remember, you're safe now. We have him under lock and key. He's not going to be able to attack any more women."

Laura would have liked to have said that he wasn't going to hurt anyone else, but she couldn't guarantee it. He really was a young man, and if he went to prison – which he almost certainly would – there would be plenty more opportunities for him to do harm within the penal system. Even if he was sentenced to a life in therapeutic care instead, he would be able to harm himself.

Laura wanted to feel good about solving this case, but she wasn't sure she could. The killer was a disturbed individual who might have been prevented from doing all of this if he'd had the proper mental health care earlier on. As for the problems that were waiting for her at home, they were still waiting. She was still unsure that Amy was truly safe. She still couldn't see her own daughter. The bottle was still beckoning, and Laura knew she still had to fight it with any shred of willpower she had.

In the end, solving the case didn't mean as much as she had hoped it would.

Laura let Genevieve leave first, and then followed her out after a few minutes. She headed to the waiting area; she didn't want to go on a trek through the halls of the hospital to try and find Nate, only to end up missing him and needing to head back to the waiting area anyway. She had her mind set on slumping down in one of the chairs, maybe getting a coffee from one of the machines, and letting the world pass by without her for a short while until he was ready to go home.

But she never made it to the chairs. Standing in the middle of the waiting area and studying the board covered in directions to various departments was a very familiar face: Caleb Rowntree.

"Here to visit an old acting coach?" Laura asked. Habit, and the knowledge that privacy needed to be protected, stopped her short of using Genevieve Piper's name.

"No, actually," Caleb said, grinning when he looked up in surprise and recognized her. "I was here to see you. I saw on the news that the killer had been apprehended and an FBI agent was taken to hospital. I didn't know whether it was you or your partner, so I thought I'd come visit just in case."

"It was me," Laura said, shrugging. "But I'm fine. It was just a precaution. The only care I need is a good night's sleep."

Caleb smiled at that. He tilted his head towards the wall, and they moved together, out of the general flow of traffic and away to the side. "I'm glad you're alright," he said. "I was a little worried there."

"I thought you would be disappointed," Laura teased. "Being well means I'm heading home."

Caleb looked at the ground bashfully and then up. "I am disappointed," he said, with a smile that twisted up one side of his mouth in the most appealing way. "Just not about you being well."

Laura nodded. All of a sudden, she couldn't quite work out what to do with her hands. "I guess the universe doesn't want me to stay," she said, even though it was the most new-age, wishy-washy crap she'd ever heard, and she would never normally have said it. It was her nerves, that was all.

"It just wasn't meant to be," Caleb agreed, which made her feel better about sounding like an idiot. "This time, anyway."

"What do you mean, this time?" Laura asked.

Caleb shrugged. "I'm a great believer in things happening if they're meant to happen," he said. "Like me breaking into Hollywood. Everyone always tells me I have the talent, that I should be making it big already, but I'm not. And I'm not stressed out about it. I just think if I keep putting myself in the way of opportunities, it will happen when it's meant to."

177

Laura caught on to the drift of what he was saying. "Are you planning to put yourself in my way again sometime soon?"

Caleb chuckled lightly, running his hand back over his hair. It flopped back into perfect place. "I don't know. But if I'm ever in your neck of the woods, I might just use that number I have stored in my phone."

"I guess I can say I'll do the same," Laura said. It was true that she never knew where she was going to be sent next. Sometimes she would find herself visiting the same states, even the same cities. Murders didn't happen in nice, evenly distributed geographical locations. Lightning could, in this sense, strike twice. Maybe she would find herself in Seattle again.

"Laura!"

She turned to see Nate greeting her from across the other side of the waiting room, raising a hand as he moved towards her, dodging an old woman on a walker who seemed oblivious of where she was going.

"I guess that's my cue," Caleb said, smiling that smile of his again. The one that made Laura almost wish she had really been injured, so she could get to know it better. But only almost, because she had far more important things to think about. "I'll see you around. Take care of yourself, Special Agent Laura Frost."

"You too, Caleb Rowntree," Laura said, watching as he raised a hand in farewell and then turned to slip back into the stream of people moving towards the door.

"You ready to go?" Nate asked, pitching up beside her. He looked tired, too. They both needed rest. They could get it on the plane; Laura would rather get home tonight than have to wake up in the morning in the unfamiliar motel room and have to drag herself to the airport.

"Yeah," she said, not needing to take a last look around at the hospital or the case they had prepared well enough to leave in the hands of Captain Mills. "Let's go home."

CHAPTER THIRTY SEVEN

Laura was almost lulled into a false sense of security. Nate was safe. The case was over. She could relax, at least, until the plane landed, and she could get back to dealing with everything else.

"Laura," Nate said, as they walked out of the hospital and towards their waiting car, and Laura knew from the tone of his voice that she wasn't getting away from this one scot-free.

"I'm tired, Nate," Laura said, hoping that would be enough.

She should have known it wouldn't have been enough.

"Just wait," Nate said, reaching out a hand to stop her. He pulled her towards him in the parking lot – and like the sky crashing down around her, there it was. The shadow of death, emanating from his touch, surrounding him so tightly she could hardly see him anymore. The darkness threatening to swallow him whole, making her sick to her stomach.

No.

This couldn't be.

The encounter with the killer – it hadn't been the moment Laura had been waiting for. The moment when Nate should have died. Whatever it was that threatened to end him still lingered, still surrounded him like a cloud. It was still part of his future.

Laura shook off his hand after a single second, but it felt like hours. She blinked back tears from her eyes.

He was still going to die, and she still had no idea how to stop it.

"Laura, how did you know that something was going to happen at the theater?" Nate asked.

"I didn't," Laura lied. She turned away from him so that he couldn't see her face, but when she saw his hand reach out in the corner of her eye again, she panicked. She couldn't let him touch her again. She took a step away and turned around, facing him as if she had only been shuffling her position. His hand dropped back to his side. "Caleb thought the audition might be a good place to find a lot of local actors and maybe ask about their coaches, and when the director told me they had an even bigger audition later, I thought I'd stick around."

"So you're telling me that by coincidence, you just happened to show up in the one place we could catch the killer? Again?" Nate said. "Alright, here's one. How did you know that the Genevieve Piper would be the victim?"

"I didn't," Laura insisted. "It was just luck."

"Just luck?" Nate said, shaking his head at her. "You thought that the audition was interesting enough to check out, and yet you randomly left it to follow one coach home just in case that was also interesting? And you happened to be right?"

"I couldn't find any other coaches," Laura said.

"Bullshit," Nate told her. "You could have gathered information from every single actor there, got the names of a dozen coaches. A hundred. You already told me you didn't know the killer was going to strike there, so why did you have to follow the one coach you found? You would have had no idea she was in danger."

"Exactly," Laura said. "I had no idea. I just followed my gut."

"That gut again!" Nate exploded. Laura glanced around. A couple heading to their car a few rows away were looking at them in alarm. "How is it you have this magical gut feeling that always leads you to make decisions you can't explain, and yet you always get to the right place at the right time?"

"Isn't that what gut instinct is?" Laura sighed. "Not rational, just a feeling? I can't explain how I know these things."

Except, she could. Of course, she could. She just couldn't bring herself to. Not now. Not while she was still reeling from the thought that Nate was going to die.

She couldn't lose him twice.

"You have to tell me what's going on, Laura," Nate said, reaching for her again. She stepped back out of his reach.

"Don't," she said, fear of that feeling of death forcing it out of her mouth.

"Are you..." Nate's tone dropped. "Are you afraid of me, right now?"

"Nate, don't," Laura said, using the moment and the fact that he was weakening to turn away and start walking again towards the car. "Not right now. I'm so tired."

"Then, when?"

"When we're back," Laura said, steeling herself. She didn't know if it was a promise she would keep. But she knew that she couldn't say anything else to put him off. He wouldn't accept an outright refusal. If

180

she could just keep putting him off indefinitely... "We'll talk when we're home, after we've had a day or two to rest."

"I'm holding you to that, Laura," Nate said, his tone dangerous. "Don't think I'm not. I'm only giving you this because you're my partner, and I care about you. But I swear to God, if you don't tell me everything..."

Laura opened the car door and got in, blocking out his voice for just a moment before he opened the other door and sat beside her.

"Laura," he said, and she knew he wanted her to confirm that she'd heard him. That she knew what was at stake.

Their partnership. Their friendship. Everything they had, unless she told him the truth.

"Okay," she said, and Nate started the engine, leaving her only to stare out of the window in search of the airport, trying not to think about how the hell she was going to get out of that promise.

EPILOGUE

Laura answered her phone in the taxi on the way home from the airport in Washington, D.C., familiar sights finally flashing past the windows of a cool and dull morning. Marcus' name flashing up on the screen made her grab it fast, afraid that he was going to tell her something had happened to Lacey.

Or hopeful, even though the hope was painful when it was snatched away, that it might be Lacey herself on the other end of the line.

"Laura, you're awake," Marcus said, by way of greeting.

"Of course, I'm awake," Laura said, trying not to let too much irritation creep into her voice. It was like he forgot she had a professional job, sometimes. Yes, she might end up sleeping in late with a hangover when she was off-duty, and back when she was drinking. But not on a workday, and not at all now that she was sober.

"Look, are you available today?" Marcus asked.

"What for?" Laura asked, instantly on the alert. Marcus was snappy, irritated, and that put her on edge. Had something bad happened? Had she messed up in some way again, without even realizing it, and Marcus was about to take it out on her in person?

"I want to see you," he said. Then Laura heard a short, sharp sigh down the line. "I want you to see Lacey."

"What?" Laura said, almost exploding up off her seat. If she hadn't been in a taxi already, she would have grabbed her bags and started walking in the direction of the house where Marcus and Lacey lived, even if it would have taken her hours to get there. "Really?"

"Yes, really. I..." Marcus paused, and then his tone indicated that he was giving her the truth. "My lawyer says it's better if I show a little flexibility, for the benefit of the judge. So that's what I'm doing. I'm letting you see her, just for a couple of hours."

"Wait, the judge?" Laura said, feeling as though her head was spinning.

"I knew it," Marcus said. "You're drinking again, aren't you? You don't even know what's going on with your own -"

182

"No, I'm not," Laura cut him off. "I've been out of town for a couple of days on a case. I'm just getting in now. I haven't heard anything about any judge."

"Your custody hearing that you want so desperately," Marcus said. There was more than a hint of animosity in his voice. He clearly resented being taken to court – not that he'd ever given her any choice. "It's been scheduled for a couple of weeks from now."

Laura's mind raced through the possibilities. A custody hearing. She would be up for partial custody if she could prove to the judge that she was a fit mother. Maybe even joint custody, especially if there was any speck at all on Marcus' reputation. She had never doubted his ability as a father, except in one area: the fact that he had stopped her from seeing her daughter.

"Um, so," Laura said, trying to fight her way through the chaos in her mind and stay present. "When do you want me to come over?"

"You can come as soon as you like," Marcus said. "Only for a couple of hours, Laura. I mean it. After what you did, you're lucky I'm even giving you this much. If you don't bring her back…"

"I know, I know," Laura said, guilt boiling like poison in her stomach. "I really have changed, Marcus. I mean it. This is the right thing to do. I'm not going to let Lacey down this time."

"We'll see," Marcus said. "Just get yourself over here. I'm getting Lacey ready to go out."

He ended the call, and Laura leaned forward in her seat, her eyes analyzing the GPS. She saw where they were, how far from Marcus and Lacey. There wasn't any time to lose, and she wasn't going to waste it on going home and getting changed. She was suddenly more grateful than she might ever have expected for being able to sleep on the plane.

"Excuse me," she called out. "There's been a change of plans. I need you to take me to a different address – as quickly as you can."

The driver glanced at her in the rearview mirror, and even in that quick glance she saw that he had been eavesdropping on her side of the conversation. That he understood, in some small way at least, what was at stake. "Yes, ma'am," he said, changing lanes at her direction. "We'll get you there as fast as possible."

***

Laura blinked back the tears, trying to hold herself together as tightly as possible. She couldn't let Lacey see how she felt to be saying goodbye after so short a time.

"Alright, darling," she said, crouching down beside the car. "Will you give your mom a hug?"

Lacey sprang forward into her arms, burying her tiny head against Laura's chest. Her arms barely managed to go around Laura's sides. Laura wrapped her own arms around Lacey as tightly as she could, squeezing and kissing the top of her head.

"Can we have a tea party next time?" Lacey asked, her voice muffled.

"Yes, of course," Laura told her. "But you liked the park, didn't you? And the swings?"

"Yeah, Mom. I liked it when you pushed me."

Laura squeezed her eyes shut. She wanted so badly to never let go. She could have picked Lacey back up and put her in the car. Right now, Marcus didn't have full custody. They were technically still both her parents in all the rights of the law. That was why she'd had to call the hearing – because he wasn't letting her see her daughter, and he disputed that she should be allowed to, and it was all such a mess.

But for right now, at least, Laura could hold her daughter tightly and try to remember this moment, to make it tide her over until the next time. She wouldn't take her and run, even if no one could have legally stopped her. Marcus was watching them from the doorway, and as much as Laura felt a deep and physical pain to have to part from Lacey again, she wanted to do this right. She needed to prove to Marcus that she had changed. That she was a worthy co-parent. That she wasn't going to let Lacey down, or do stupid, rash, reckless things because of the drink.

She had to show that she was willing to be the mature and sensible adult, until the court told her she had the right to see her daughter a certain number of times a week.

When they gave her that, they would be giving her everything.

"Alright," Laura said. She kissed Lacey on top of the head one more time and stood up, turning her and pushing her small body towards her father, because she needed the end part to be over now. "I love you so much, Lacey."

"Love you, Mom!" Lacey called over her shoulder as she raced up the short path to the front door, barreling inside past her waiting dad.

Marcus Amargo was still just as handsome as he had been the day he and Laura first met. His curly, dark hair was worn in a mess on top of his head, a little overdue for a cut, but his facial hair was as finely chiseled into designer stubble as ever. Eyes that seemed to shift blue to brown depending on the light contrasted against his tanned skin and the pale blue shirt he was wearing, open at the collar and with the sleeves rolled up, like he'd come from work and not bothered to change.

"You had a good time?" he said. Not to Lacey, but to Laura.

"Yes," she said. "Marcus, thank you. I..."

"Don't," he said, roughly. He pushed himself off from leaning on the door frame, reaching to step inside and close it. "I'll call you."

He left Laura standing on the pavement alone, until all she could do was get back in her car and try to process the day. She was about to start the engine and drive off when her phone rang, and seeing Chief Rondelle's name on the screen, she stopped to answer it.

"Agent Frost."

"Laura, I wanted you to hear it from me," Rondelle said, and the tension in his voice made her pause, her heart starting to race. "I know this isn't the outcome you wanted, but please do me the favor of staying calm and not doing anything we can't cover you for."

"What?" Laura asked sharply, every fiber of her body on high alert.

"It's Amy Fallow." Rondelle paused, leaving her just enough time for a flare of fear to bite into her. "I don't know how it happened, but apparently he had some favors to call in. Or threats, I don't know. She's back with her father."

Laura had to clamp her hand over her mouth to stop herself from being sick.

"I know this is terrible news, but..."

"Terrible news?" Laura said acidly. "She's... you've let her go right back into danger. She's six years old."

"I haven't let her go anywhere," Rondelle said hotly. "I feel just as strongly about this as you do. I'm doing everything I can do -"

"No," Laura said, cutting him off. She'd never been rude to her superiors, never shown Rondelle any disrespect. But he had never earned it before. "No, you don't."

She ended the call, turning on her engine and speeding down the road just for something to do, just for a distraction. She couldn't take this. She needed to get home, get somewhere she could be alone and think. Marcus could be watching her through the window, judging her, wondering if she was having a breakdown.

Hoping, probably.

The drive passed in a blur, Laura's hands and feet taking her on autopilot towards her home as her mind stayed elsewhere. She tried to think of something she could do. She imagined walking into the Governor's home and taking Amy again, but she knew there was no way it would be that easy. He would likely have extra security now, and even if she did manage it, she'd be on the run. No one would let her take that child again.

And anything she did that got her into trouble – anything at all – could land the custody hearing in jeopardy.

Laura's mouth dried up as she realized that even now, Governor Fallow could speak behind closed doors with a judge. Tell him to make a judgement in Marcus' favor. He had the power to do it, and Laura had no doubt he would have been looking into her, looking for any weakness he could exploit.

She was backed into a corner. There was nothing she could do. Not if she wanted to get access to her daughter again, on any kind of a regular basis.

But could she really abandon one little girl just to have the chance to be with another?

Laura parked outside her apartment and traveled up in the elevator, barely seeing anything around herself. She unlocked her front door and threw her keys down on the counter in the kitchen, dumping her bags on a stool. She didn't know what to do. She couldn't see the way through this. She couldn't...

She stopped, freezing halfway between steps, her foot hovering in the air for a long moment before she set it down. She stared, barely able to process what she was seeing.

On the wall above her battered, second-hand couch, someone had taken a paintbrush and smeared black paint into tall letters, sharp and angry in their execution. Letters that left a message, one that was so obvious Laura didn't need any kind of clarification.

Forget the girl.

Beside it, pinned to the wall viciously in a way that left the plaster crumbling, there were two photographs. One, of Laura herself, slumped over a table. Drunk in a bar. Laura didn't recognize the event, but she knew it must have been herself. She'd seen it before. Marcus had

186

shown it to her, after he hired the private investigator to follow her. Whoever got this shot must have had access to his files.

The other photograph was Marcus standing with Lacey, helping her put her coat on outside the school gates.

Someone had broken into her place while she was away. Someone who worked for Governor Fallow. They had left her this message as a warning and a threat: stay away from the Governor, back off and stay out of his business, or they would come for her. They already knew where she lived. They probably knew everything about her.

Forget the girl.

As if there was any way she could do that.

Laura took out her phone and snapped a photograph of the words, furious determination taking over from her initial shock. Who did Governor Fallow think she was? Some mild, meek little woman who would shut up and go away when he asked her to?

No.

Laura was not just any woman. She was an FBI agent, and she knew she was one of the best. She had taken down bigger criminals, more terrifying criminals, than him. She had faced serial killers head on and won.

She wasn't going to be threatened by a bully into leaving a child to survive on her own. No matter what fears leapt into her throat when she saw that they knew who her daughter was, she couldn't back down. Protecting Lacey by abandoning Amy – what kind of person would that make her?

Not one that was worthy of being a mother.

She was going to get Amy out of there, for good this time. She was going to do it no matter what she had to do to make it happen. Even if it meant toppling the Governor himself first, showing the world who he really was, she would do it.

And there was no way in hell she was going to let any of this jeopardize her chance to see her daughter.

Governor Fallow thought he could scare her away, threaten her into toeing the line. Instead, he'd lit a fire inside of her that was never going to die down.

Not until she had finished him off – and made sure his daughter would never have to be afraid of him again.

NOW AVAILABLE!

ALREADY TRAPPED
(A Laura Frost FBI Suspense Thriller—Book 3)

"A MASTERPIECE OF THRILLER AND MYSTERY. Blake Pierce did a magnificent job developing characters with a psychological side so well described that we feel inside their minds, follow their fears and cheer for their success. Full of twists, this book will keep you awake until the turn of the last page."
--Books and Movie Reviews, Roberto Mattos (re Once Gone)

ALREADY TRAPPED (A Laura Frost FBI Suspense Thriller) is book #3 in a long-anticipated new series by #1 bestseller and USA Today bestselling author Blake Pierce, whose bestseller Once Gone (a free download) has received over 1,000 five star reviews. The series begins with ALREADY GONE (Book #1).

FBI Special Agent and single mom Laura Frost, 35, is haunted by her talent: a psychic ability which she refuses to face and which she keeps secret from her colleagues. While Laura gets obscured glimpses of what the killer may do next, she must decide whether to trust her confusing gift or her investigative work.

25 year-old female twins turn up murdered, on the same day, in different parts of Minnesota. Could it be a coincidence?

Or could it be the work of a diabolical serial killer?

FBI Special Agent Laura Frost is summoned to solve the case—yet her psychic power floods her with an array of confusing—and urgent messages. She may have just one chance to save the next victim. But is what she is seeing accurate?

A page-turning and harrowing crime thriller featuring a brilliant and tortured FBI agent, the LAURA FROST series is a startlingly fresh mystery, rife with suspense, twists and turns, shocking revelations, and driven by a breakneck pace that will keep you flipping pages late into the night.

Book #4 in the series—ALREADY MISSING—is now also available!

Blake Pierce

Blake Pierce is the USA Today bestselling author of the RILEY PAGE mystery series, which includes seventeen books. Blake Pierce is also the author of the MACKENZIE WHITE mystery series, comprising fourteen books; of the AVERY BLACK mystery series, comprising six books; of the KERI LOCKE mystery series, comprising five books; of the MAKING OF RILEY PAIGE mystery series, comprising six books; of the KATE WISE mystery series, comprising seven books; of the CHLOE FINE psychological suspense mystery, comprising six books; of the JESSIE HUNT psychological suspense thriller series, comprising nineteen books; of the AU PAIR psychological suspense thriller series, comprising three books; of the ZOE PRIME mystery series, comprising six books; of the ADELE SHARP mystery series, comprising thirteen books; of the EUROPEAN VOYAGE cozy mystery series, comprising six books (and counting); of the new LAURA FROST FBI suspense thriller, comprising four books (and counting); of the new ELLA DARK FBI suspense thriller, comprising six books (and counting); of the A YEAR IN EUROPE cozy mystery series, comprising nine books (and counting); of the AVA GOLD mystery series, comprising three books (and counting); and of the RACHEL GIFT mystery series, comprising three books (and counting).

An avid reader and lifelong fan of the mystery and thriller genres, Blake loves to hear from you, so please feel free to visit www.blakepierceauthor.com to learn more and stay in touch.

BOOKS BY BLAKE PIERCE

RACHEL GIFT MYSTERY SERIES
HER LAST WISH (Book #1)
HER LAST CHANCE (Book #2)
HER LAST HOPE (Book #3)

AVA GOLD MYSTERY SERIES
CITY OF PREY (Book #1)
CITY OF FEAR (Book #2)
CITY OF BONES (Book #3)

A YEAR IN EUROPE
A MURDER IN PARIS (Book #1)
DEATH IN FLORENCE (Book #2)
VENGEANCE IN VIENNA (Book #3)
A FATALITY IN SPAIN (Book #4)
SCANDAL IN LONDON (Book #5)
AN IMPOSTOR IN DUBLIN (Book #6)
SEDUCTION IN BORDEAUX (Book #7)
JEALOUSY IN SWITZERLAND (Book #8)
A DEBACLE IN PRAGUE (Book #9)

ELLA DARK FBI SUSPENSE THRILLER
GIRL, ALONE (Book #1)
GIRL, TAKEN (Book #2)
GIRL, HUNTED (Book #3)
GIRL, SILENCED (Book #4)
GIRL, VANISHED (Book 5)
GIRL ERASED (Book #6)

LAURA FROST FBI SUSPENSE THRILLER
ALREADY GONE (Book #1)
ALREADY SEEN (Book #2)
ALREADY TRAPPED (Book #3)
ALREADY MISSING (Book #4)

EUROPEAN VOYAGE COZY MYSTERY SERIES
MURDER (AND BAKLAVA) (Book #1)
DEATH (AND APPLE STRUDEL) (Book #2)

CRIME (AND LAGER) (Book #3)
MISFORTUNE (AND GOUDA) (Book #4)
CALAMITY (AND A DANISH) (Book #5)
MAYHEM (AND HERRING) (Book #6)

ADELE SHARP MYSTERY SERIES
LEFT TO DIE (Book #1)
LEFT TO RUN (Book #2)
LEFT TO HIDE (Book #3)
LEFT TO KILL (Book #4)
LEFT TO MURDER (Book #5)
LEFT TO ENVY (Book #6)
LEFT TO LAPSE (Book #7)
LEFT TO VANISH (Book #8)
LEFT TO HUNT (Book #9)
LEFT TO FEAR (Book #10)
LEFT TO PREY (Book #11)
LEFT TO LURE (Book #12)
LEFT TO CRAVE (Book #13)

THE AU PAIR SERIES
ALMOST GONE (Book#1)
ALMOST LOST (Book #2)
ALMOST DEAD (Book #3)

ZOE PRIME MYSTERY SERIES
FACE OF DEATH (Book#1)
FACE OF MURDER (Book #2)
FACE OF FEAR (Book #3)
FACE OF MADNESS (Book #4)
FACE OF FURY (Book #5)
FACE OF DARKNESS (Book #6)

A JESSIE HUNT PSYCHOLOGICAL SUSPENSE SERIES
THE PERFECT WIFE (Book #1)
THE PERFECT BLOCK (Book #2)
THE PERFECT HOUSE (Book #3)
THE PERFECT SMILE (Book #4)
THE PERFECT LIE (Book #5)
THE PERFECT LOOK (Book #6)

THE PERFECT AFFAIR (Book #7)
THE PERFECT ALIBI (Book #8)
THE PERFECT NEIGHBOR (Book #9)
THE PERFECT DISGUISE (Book #10)
THE PERFECT SECRET (Book #11)
THE PERFECT FAÇADE (Book #12)
THE PERFECT IMPRESSION (Book #13)
THE PERFECT DECEIT (Book #14)
THE PERFECT MISTRESS (Book #15)
THE PERFECT IMAGE (Book #16)
THE PERFECT VEIL (Book #17)
THE PERFECT INDISCRETION (Book #18)
THE PERFECT RUMOR (Book #19)

CHLOE FINE PSYCHOLOGICAL SUSPENSE SERIES
NEXT DOOR (Book #1)
A NEIGHBOR'S LIE (Book #2)
CUL DE SAC (Book #3)
SILENT NEIGHBOR (Book #4)
HOMECOMING (Book #5)
TINTED WINDOWS (Book #6)

KATE WISE MYSTERY SERIES
IF SHE KNEW (Book #1)
IF SHE SAW (Book #2)
IF SHE RAN (Book #3)
IF SHE HID (Book #4)
IF SHE FLED (Book #5)
IF SHE FEARED (Book #6)
IF SHE HEARD (Book #7)

THE MAKING OF RILEY PAIGE SERIES
WATCHING (Book #1)
WAITING (Book #2)
LURING (Book #3)
TAKING (Book #4)
STALKING (Book #5)
KILLING (Book #6)

RILEY PAIGE MYSTERY SERIES

ONCE GONE (Book #1)
ONCE TAKEN (Book #2)
ONCE CRAVED (Book #3)
ONCE LURED (Book #4)
ONCE HUNTED (Book #5)
ONCE PINED (Book #6)
ONCE FORSAKEN (Book #7)
ONCE COLD (Book #8)
ONCE STALKED (Book #9)
ONCE LOST (Book #10)
ONCE BURIED (Book #11)
ONCE BOUND (Book #12)
ONCE TRAPPED (Book #13)
ONCE DORMANT (Book #14)
ONCE SHUNNED (Book #15)
ONCE MISSED (Book #16)
ONCE CHOSEN (Book #17)

MACKENZIE WHITE MYSTERY SERIES
BEFORE HE KILLS (Book #1)
BEFORE HE SEES (Book #2)
BEFORE HE COVETS (Book #3)
BEFORE HE TAKES (Book #4)
BEFORE HE NEEDS (Book #5)
BEFORE HE FEELS (Book #6)
BEFORE HE SINS (Book #7)
BEFORE HE HUNTS (Book #8)
BEFORE HE PREYS (Book #9)
BEFORE HE LONGS (Book #10)
BEFORE HE LAPSES (Book #11)
BEFORE HE ENVIES (Book #12)
BEFORE HE STALKS (Book #13)
BEFORE HE HARMS (Book #14)

AVERY BLACK MYSTERY SERIES
CAUSE TO KILL (Book #1)
CAUSE TO RUN (Book #2)
CAUSE TO HIDE (Book #3)
CAUSE TO FEAR (Book #4)
CAUSE TO SAVE (Book #5)

CAUSE TO DREAD (Book #6)

KERI LOCKE MYSTERY SERIES
A TRACE OF DEATH (Book #1)
A TRACE OF MUDER (Book #2)
A TRACE OF VICE (Book #3)
A TRACE OF CRIME (Book #4)
A TRACE OF HOPE (Book #5)

Printed in the USA
CPSIA information can be obtained
at www.ICGtesting.com
LVHW042241201123
764500LV00002B/5

9 781094 392226